THE RADIO MAN

Lester Earnshaw

HAZARD PRESS
publishers

ISBN 1-877161-20-9

Published by Hazard Press
P.O. Box 2151, Christchurch, New Zealand
Production and design by Orca Publishing Services Ltd

Printed in Malaysia

Larry La Salle peered through the smoke. Nearly all the people in the bar were Maori. They laughed and whooped with shrill voices oiled by the bartender's brew – not a McKenzie among them. The remaining drinkers milled in groups, each group boisterously busy within itself. Which left the morose old fellow in the corner.

Larry elbowed his way through the drinkers.

'Pardon me, are you Mr McKenzie?'

The man wiped froth from his mouth with the back of his hand.

'Aye,' he acknowledged, 'I am McKenzie.'

'I'm Larry La Salle, the radio operator. Mr Mudgway told me I'd find you here.'

'Aye.' The foreman emptied his glass, studied its inside bottom, perhaps seeking words of welcome in it, but no words came.

Larry said, 'May I get you a drink, Mr McKenzie?'

Mac looked up. 'Aye. Speights – out of the tap.'

Larry fought his way to and from the bar. He handed Mac a glass, hoisted his own. 'Cheers,' he said.

'Aye.' Mac emptied his glass in a few long swigs, wiped his mouth, belched, and said, 'Mudgway said you were in the war?'

'The air force. North Africa and Italy.'

'You lads did a grand job.' And that appeared to be the extent of Mac's small talk, except for 'Thanks, laddie' when Larry bought further rounds. Mostly Mac stood in reflective silence. Mudgway had said, 'Get him oiled and you can't stop him talking.' Larry wondered if he had enough cash to reach that point. But then, as if he'd suddenly remembered something that needed immediate attention, Mac drained his glass and said, 'Okay, let's get back to camp.'

Mac drove his war surplus 4x4 like a bulldozer. Pedestrians

and motorists yielded along the way. Not until they were well into the country did Larry relax. He studied the driver.

The foreman of the Hydroelectric Department's Karapiro to Hamilton transmission line project was named Alexander Mac-Allister McKenzie. Though he made it known that his position entitled him to be addressed as Mr McKenzie, his men addressed him, variously, as Mac, Old Mac and, just as often, the old bastard.

Mac had grown a ragged Pancho Villa moustache that hung a good two inches below his mouth. One side was brownish-red streaked with grey, the other brown-black. Somewhere, in the brown-black side, there usually nestled the half-chewed remains of a roll-your-own cigarette that sometimes he lit. He had a pale blue eye, possibly two – the one above the cigarette was permanently shuttered to keep out the smoke. A massive, purple-veined nose dominated his lean, usually unshaven face, and a sweat-stained hat minus the band shaded his forehead.

This evening he wore a ragged and food-encrusted vest that had once belonged to a three-piece suit, denim trousers, string bow-yangs to hitch the trouser legs above the mud level, and hobnailed boots.

They arrived at where a transmission line crossed the road, and a second, larger and taller row of towers ran parallel, the cables not yet hung. A mishmash of ropes and tackles dangled from the larger towers.

Mac pulled the 4x4 into the grass verge. He pointed to the smaller line.

'That's the original 100,000 volt line. Built sometime in the twenties, I've been told.'

He inched the 4x4 along the grass to the base of a taller tower.

'And this is the line we're working on – 220,000 volts. First in the country.'

Next he explained that they were laying cable that they would haul up to the insulators with blocks and tackles. The tractor would pull the cables through the blocks to precalculated sags, called catenaries. Mr Mudgway, the engineer, by sighting along the line with a theodolite would determine the correct sag by comparing the readings to a chart.

'You understand me, laddie?' Mac asked suddenly.

Larry nodded. This was not the earlier, drinking Mac. Obviously Mac enjoyed his work. He continued the description.

The cable crew relayed up-down signals through flagmen, sitting high up the towers, to the tractor crew which could be miles away. When the sags were set the riggers clamped the cables to the insulators and removed the blocks.

'But Mudgway wants to replace the flagmen with wirelesses,' he growled, plainly not enamoured of the plan. 'His reason, he says, is that we don't have men to put up the towers. Personally I think he's talking a lot of bloody rot. There's plenty of men coming back from the war. These newfangled contraptions will be more trouble than they're worth. You mark my words.'

When Mac saw the radios in operation surely he must come around, Larry mused. But if Mac convinced Mudgway that the radios were useless – and they could well be – it would be back to his pre-war job in the post office for Larry La Salle. For what choice did he have? Wherever he had inquired he had been given the same response: 'I'm sorry, now that the war's over our contracts have been cancelled.'

Only one company had had an opening. According to the name-block on his desk the interviewer was Julius Jenkins. Jenkins had small, red-rimmed, close-set eyes, thin, thin lips, and half a dozen chins. He reminded Larry of an antennae-less garden slug. Would he exude slimy foam if you sprinkled salt on him? Jenkins aired his opinion about returned men: undisciplined, disruptive, the war had spoiled them.

Though his gorge rose, Larry answered that he would not be guilty of such behaviour. He just wanted to learn the radio trade. He didn't add that if this creature were to be his tutor he'd return to his old job in the post office.

'I've heard that before, of course,' the slug answered.

Larry's gorge climbed further. He told Jenkins to cram the job up his fat arse, and terminated the interview by leaving abruptly.

Larry needed this job with the Hydroelectric Department. He swore to himself then and there that he'd bite his tongue off before he'd row with Mac. Anyhow, so far, Mac had seemed to be not such a bad old coot. Probably it was only a matter of getting him used to the radios.

The Bruntwood camp consisted of a double line of surplus army huts, placed so that their doors faced each other. A shed-like building at one end of the row housed the cookhouse. At the opposite end a smaller shed contained a cold-water shower. And twenty feet or so beyond the shower shed stood the dunny – christened the Bruntwood long drop – its seat made from rough-cut planks over a deep pit. Swarms of wasps circling above and below the seat discouraged daylight use.

Arriving at the camp Mac called to the cook – who doubled as the camp supply officer – to take care of the new man.

'Give him a mattress and blankets and show him where the dunny is,' he ordered.

Later it crossed Larry's mind that Mac might have speculated that Larry might refuse the job when he saw the dunny. But after five – or six? – pints of Speights, the dunny could have stood in a swamp full of circling crocodiles for all he minded.

GRUNTER, A MAORI, CAME from Taupo. Born with inward-pointing feet, he walked with a rotary movement, one foot over the other. At speed, his footwork simulated a Mississippi sternwheeler. But when it came to moving a reel of cable, and he dug those feet in and pushed, only the Caterpillar tractor beat Grunter.

Grunter's had been a traditional communal family. It was said that the first one up in the mornings got to wear the best pair of pants. The tradition carried over into the Hydroelectric Department's Bruntwood Camp, No. 3, where unguarded clothes, plates, spoons, or firewood migrated to the hut Grunter shared with the dog Kuri.

The dog Kuri came from nowhere. One day he was there. Recognising a kindred spirit, he moved on to the spare cot in Grunter's hut.

During the evenings Grunter celebrated the day's events with quantities of Waitemata, or whatever he could get hold of. At Christmas he celebrated in extra ways. Besides getting drunker than usual, he bought a pair each of boots and pants, both of which, because of his deformity, tended to wear out early. Then he bathed and shaved and had his hair cut. A once-in-a-while basin of water to face and hands sufficed for the rest of the year, unless there was a female prospect in the offing.

Next to booze, before women, Grunter loved pirau, traditionally made by placing corn in a flax basket and immersing the basket in swamp water until the corn rotted. Grunter said that when the handle rotted off the basket the delicacy was at its tastiest.

When the pirau was on the table, the dog Kuri, no paragon of nasal delight himself, would forsake the comfort of the lodge and sit on the firewood at the side of the hut, and howl a keening, drawn-out lamentation, until a shoe or stick of firewood sent him scurrying.

Grunter was Mac's assistant because he had always been there. The men with normal feet had gone to war. Only a few recently returned men had sought their old jobs back.

Early on the morning after Larry's arrival at the camp, Grunter stuck his head through the doorway of the newest man's hut.

'Wakey wakey!' he shouted.

Larry lifted his head.

'G'day,' he tested tentatively.

'Rise and shine, mate, if you want to get some tucker into you before we leave.'

Larry turned his watch to catch the light.

'Jeeze! It's the middle of the bloody night!'

'We push off at seven. Takes an hour to get to the job.' Grunter turned to leave, then turned back. 'If you don't get to the shower pretty soon, there won't be no hot water left.'

No queue stood at the shower. Nor was there hot water. There never had been hot water, Larry discovered. Later, on the dunny, Larry convinced himself that the rest of them had skins of alligator hide; the hole in the seat felt as if it had been cut with a chain saw.

The kai was enormous: two lamb chops, three eggs, six rashers of bacon, toast, apples, tea. Larry had a sudden urge to revisit the dunny but the memory of its serrated seat dissuaded him. He'd go in the tea-tree out on the job.

At the truck, Grunter said, 'How was the shower?'

Larry said, 'I owe you.'

The dog Kuri inspected the new man.

'Kuri! Over here, you bastard,' Grunter called. 'He'll piss on your trousers,' he explained.

They boarded the truck. Mac, Grunter said, would come later in his 4x4. He had things to do in Hamilton.

At the tractor site they heated water in an old tin billy hung over a tea-tree fire. A stick of tea-tree laid across the open billy stopped the smoke from tainting the water – an old bushman's trick.

Larry had forgotten the sweet smell of burning tea-tree. It reminded him of the smell of heather after rain, and Scotland, and of Moira, the girl he had known in Dundee during the war. He had not written to Moira; she must have wondered what had happened to him.

The water boiled. Grunter called, 'Smoko! Come and get it!'

Around the fire Grunter explained the reason for the small crew. Most had taken advantage of a cable shortage and had gone to Hamilton. They'd be back when they ran out of money, he predicted. In the meantime, the men who had stayed would hang blocks to the tower cross-arms, ready to haul the cable up when it came.

A crew 'processed' firewood, knocking over stumps with the bulldozer then blasting them into lengths to fit the huts' fireplaces. Until the second radio man came, Larry was to join the processors.

Smoko took an hour. No hurry, Grunter further explained, the wharfies were on strike, the cable was on a ship in Auckland harbour.

Lunch consisted of thick slices of roast beef held between doorstep-thick slabs of bread. The cutter's hands were not proto-types of hygiene, the table a wooden cable spool on which birds had left payment for yesterday's leftovers. Nevertheless, eating his lunch, Larry pictured the slug Julius Jenkins in his office and wished him an 'up your arse!'

Lunch had started on the tick of twelve and was still going at two. No hurry, Grunter explained again, the wharfies wouldn't return to work for months yet. They'd gone on strike during the war, hadn't they? When the Yanks and our own men needed the food up in the Pacific.

Rangi Wetini had fought against Rommel. He wondered aloud why the government hadn't shot the wharfies, and Larry, who well remembered the meagre North African food rations, voiced a firm agreement.

Mac drove up. The men held their positions.

'Stone the bloody crows! It's two-o'-bloody-clock in the bloody afternoon and you're all sittin' on your friggin' chumps! Mudgway's gonna be here in a minute, for crissake!'

Larry stood.

Rangi said, 'Don't rush it, sport. Never let the boss think you're scared.'

Mudgway pulled in. He called Mac and the men around the

ashes of the tea-billy fire.

'The only way we'll get that cable is to shoot the wharfies and unload it ourselves. But there's cable at the Karapiro end. So finish up what you're doing here. Monday morning we'll work back from Karapiro. And something else…'

He kicked at the dog Kuri.

'Grunter! How many more times do I have to tell you to get rid of that friggin' mongrel? If he pisses on me again I'll kill him, so help me God. Git! You bastard!'

The dog Kuri shrank into the tea-tree.

'What was I saying?' Mudgway asked wearily.

'You were saying that we could knock off work; that you're buying,' Rangi suggested.

'I wasn't saying anything of the sort! What was I talking about, Mac?'

Mac rolled the wet butt to the less stained side of his whiskered mouth, and back again. 'Actually, there's not much to do until we get cable,' he said.

Mudgway lifted his hat and scratched while he pretended deep concentration.

'All right then, but I'm not buying. They don't pay me enough to buy what these jokers drink.'

THE CAMP EMPTIED ON the weekends. Most of its inmates migrated to Gladys's boarding house in Hamilton. Late Friday afternoon, at the end of Larry's first week, the Hydroelectric Department's truck pulled into the kerb at her front gate. Grunter sternwheeled to the side door. Gladys's hound jumped from the veranda and smelled his trousers.

Grunter opened the door and called out, 'Glad! It's us!'

Gladys came bustling from the kitchen, wiping her hands on a flower-patterned apron.

'Well… you're all early today.'

She saw the new man among them.

'And who's the young lad? I don't remember him before.'

Grunter said, 'Glad, this is Larry. Just back from dropping bombs on Berlin.'

Larry said, 'No, I was in North Africa, and Italy.'

'Well, there now… it doesn't really matter where you were, does it? You were in the war and you came home and that's the main thing. Many of them young men didn't. All those poor mothers what lost sons… And what made you join up with this motley lot?'

'I have to work like everybody else.'

'Yes, well, we all have to do that I suppose, whether we like it or not.' She took him by the arm, walked him to the bottom of the stairs.

'I'll put you in number three, it's up there on the right.'

She turned to Grunter. 'Now you make sure you wash those filthy hands properly before you use me clean towels!'

Grunter put his arm around her shoulders, told her that she was his wahine tonight. She fought him off.

'Don't you get them filthy clothes against me clean dress,' she admonished, not too severely.

Gladys Higgs had a large bosom, but if you walked her toward a wall, it would be a toss-up which touched first, nose or belly. Grunter speculated that it would be her nose. Be that as it may, when she entered a room she commanded respect – a sergeant-major type of respect. Which Grunter ignored. When she walked by him he would slap her on the buttocks and give her a caress or two if she couldn't escape him.

The boarding house was a large and old residence. The colonial-style verandas had been enclosed to add bedrooms. But there was

13

only one bathroom, and a pecking order among the men – the new man last. When finally it came Larry's turn a ploughable ring ran around the tub and the hot water was gone. He made do with a Grunter lick and a promise but in the morning he'd be first. So he vowed.

At the door Gladys nearly smothered him with her bosom while she proffered motherly advice on how to avoid the sinful pits into which, apparently, his workmates were already falling. To escape he promised that yes, he'd be careful, and that no, he wouldn't drink too much. (Anything if she'd let him loose.) He was the last to arrive at the pub.

He entered through the foyer. He saw Mac holding up a corner. The cigarette peeping from Mac's whiskers had long since drowned. He was in fine story-telling fettle. He spotted Larry, beckoned him over, and began telling a yarn in a fake Scottish accent – fake because he'd been brought to New Zealand as a bairn.

'There was this wee Scottish lass, she asked Jock wha' he hae under his kilt. Jock took her hand and he said, "Here, I'll show you." She felt aroond a wee bit, but quickly she pulled her hand back, and she said, "Ach Jock, 'tis gruesome!" to which Jock answered, "If you'll put your hand back you'll find 'tis grew some more!"' Mac laughed so hard the butt fell from his whiskers.

The story had been told and retold in that bar perhaps a dozen times, but it was new to Larry. Mac's put-on Scottish brogue reminded him of Scotland and Moira. He pictured Moira's stiff-necked father. What would he say if he saw his once intended son-in-law in this company? Probably, 'I told you so!' Larry laughed, and happy that the new man laughed at his joke, Mac sprang for a round of drinks. Larry sprang for another. Another round came from somewhere. And again. And again.

Bless 'em all, bless 'em all
The long and the short and the tall
Frig all the sergeants and w.o.1s
Frig all the corporals and their friggin' sons…

They sang until the proprietor told them to hold it down. When they didn't, he invited them to leave.

They resumed the celebration at the boarding house.

Gladys said, 'You ought to be ashamed of yourself, the things you got up to last night!'

Larry opened his eyes enough to see her. She held a tray. On it, a teapot, cup, milk and toast.

'And yesterday I thought you were such a nice lad. Taking me piana apart like that!'

Piano? What piano? Oh! Piano!

'Where did you learn to play like that? I could have listened to you all night except that me neighbours kicked up such a rumpus about the noise. And I didn't like it when they poured that beer in me piana! Pouring beer in me good piana!'

He closed his eyes.

'Come on... sit up! I made breakfast specially for you. Them others don't get nothing. Pouring beer in me piana!'

He struggled to sit.

'Why, you still got your clothes on!'

So he had. He wiggled his toes. But not his shoes.

'Shame on you! You hang around with them lot and you'll be just like them, you mark me words. Now, I'll put the tea on the dresser. Don't let it get cold. And when you finish, you get your bath while there's hot water. Them others won't be up for hours yet.'

When she left, he staggered down the hall to the lavatory. He dragged his way back. A bird fluttered in his stomach. He should eat something. He ate a mouthful. The butter had melted into the toast. Enough! He undressed. Got back into bed.

So this was civilian life. Well... he had a job, and they were good men to work with. Even old Mac was okay. Certainly, he'd been a character last night, when he'd warmed up. They all had.

A GI ran down the row of huts, yelling, 'It's over! The war's over!!'

15

The bells atop the Catholic church tolled. Not able to accept what he had heard, Larry ran to the orderly room. 'Is it true? Is it over?' 'Sure is, buddy. Came over the radio a few minutes ago.'

The sergeant lifted his sidearm and fired into the officers' mess, and that convinced Larry that the war was over. The air raid sirens turned on and stayed on. From the ships anchored in the harbour there came a tremendous mayhem of whistles and fog-horns, and light and heavy gun bursts. Grown men cried. Americans, Australians, New Zealanders, French, they passed the bottles, fired into the air. A day Larry would always remember.

Home! His foot touched the road. The school band belted out a vigorous but discordant 'Invercargill March'.

Haumoana. Home.

His family. There they were. They came running. His sister, Clarice, led. She threw herself at him, slobbered over him, pushed him to arm's length, measured him with her eyes. 'You've grown!'

His father, wheezing air from lungs seared by World War I mustard gas, pumped his hand. 'Wel... welcome... ' He hugged his son to him and said with his body what his lungs wouldn't let him say with words.

His mother reached up, pulled his head down.

'Oh, Larry!' She kissed him and cried, and he hugged her, and he cried – though he tried not to. They held each other. Home!

His father stepped back. Blew his nose.

'You've... you've... grown, boy!'

'He shaves!' Clarice said. 'My baby!' from his mother.

The town moved in. So many people who knew him. But who were they?

The house overflowed. Were they all his relatives? Five years made such a difference to those who had been eleven and twelve when he left. Five years – was it not twenty?

His mother made tea, his father opened bottles of Speights. They drank to his health, swamped him with questions. How was it in the war?

A cousin asked him how many Germans he had shot. He hadn't shot any, he was in the air force, he answered, rather lamely he thought.

'He flew Spitfires, silly! Didn't you, Larry?'

'No. I worked on radar.'

The next morning, the four of them, his mother, father and Clarice, were alone. Thank God the others were gone. It was not easy being a hero, especially since he wasn't a real hero like his cousin Jack who had left a leg in Mersa Matruh.

Over the breakfast table he answered their questions as best he could. But how to describe a convoy of ships, as wide as the eye could see, converging on to an enemy shore, to those to whom thirty Jersey milk cows on two hundred acres was a horizon? How to explain PPI tubes in a radar system, and their advantages over separate range and azimuth tubes? His sister wanted to know about Moira in Dundee, and had he met any Italian girls. His mother wanted to know if he remembered Mrs Huggins.

He described to his father an LST; its shallow draft. It ran up the beach, disgorged its tanks. He and his crew had fitted a radar antenna gantry to the bow of one to warn of approaching enemy aircraft.

'You don't remember Mrs Huggins?'

'Mrs Huggins? No, Mum, I don't remember Mrs Huggins.'

'You don't remember Mrs Huggins! Larry – for goodness sake – she was here before you were born!'

'I'm sorry, Mum, I don't remember…'

'I don't understand you…'

'He doesn't remember,' his father said.

'You say that they catapulted Hurricanes off LSTs. They couldn't land back there, could they? Where did they land?'

'…Larry, I'd like you to go and see the poor old thing. She's always asking about you, and she can't walk well enough to come here.'

'Mum, I don't remember Mrs Huggins.'

'But Larry…'

He borrowed his father's car, escaped to the pub at Clive. Hori Herawa, army, back a month; Jack White, navy, on leave. They drank furiously. Larry drove home late that evening. The grocer, Tim Arnett, sat at the kitchen table.

'Welcome back,' he said. 'Sorry I couldn't be at the train. I couldn't leave the shop.'

A servile mouse of a man, Larry thought. He hadn't liked him before the war, he didn't like him now.

His father said, 'I was telling Tim about the Hurricanes. Where did they land them?'

'If we hadn't captured an airfield, the pilots had to ditch them in the ocean. They…'

'Larry, we saved our rice rations. I made you a rice pudding. But now it's all dried out.'

His sister said, 'Phew! You smell like a pub!'

'You were in those landings, son?' the grocer asked.

'A couple.'

'…if you had come home at the proper time the rice wouldn't be dried out like this. I did everything I could to keep it moist…'

'Mum, don't worry about it. To be honest, I can't stand the stuff. I lived on it over there…'

'You always liked rice! It was your favourite pudding!'

'Leave it be, Ethel,' his father said. 'If he doesn't like rice, he doesn't like rice.'

'I don't know what's come over him! He doesn't like my rice; he won't see poor old Mrs Huggins! He comes home at all hours smelling like a pub… You've changed Larry, that's all I can say.'

The grocer said, 'We're putting on a reception for the returned men. You'll be here on the fifteenth?'

'I don't know. I've just arrived.'

'Of course he'll be here – won't you, Larry?'

'Mum!'

He left on the twelfth, by bus and train for Wellington. The city should be better. Uncle Forbes had sons in the air force. He would understand. But Uncle Forbes didn't understand. Neither did Aunt Hilda. Aunt Hilda said it was a shame what the war had done to the men.

It was better in Christchurch. Johnny lived in Christchurch. Johnny of England, and Malta, and Italy. They roamed New Zealand, drank, sought women. Six weeks, then back to Christchurch.

Before the war, Johnny had been an electrician at the abattoir in Belfast. Larry couldn't even remotely imagine anyone wanting to return to a job in an abattoir. Only the post office could be worse. Yet, one morning, after a gigantic drunk, Johnny said that he thought he'd get his old job back. They said that they wouldn't hold it much longer. Thus, he justified his treason.

'How did it go?' Larry asked that evening. He expected a tale of bored woe, but Johnny answered, 'Not bad. Better than I thought, actually.' That night, his conversation concerned the job.

Larry left for Auckland. In a pub, he met Mr Mudgway, the engineer in charge of the transmission line project, the 220,000 volt line that would bring electricity to Auckland from the new dam under construction at Karapiro. Mudgway offered him a job operating war-surplus, type 19 radio sets.

And now he was at Gladys's.

He pulled himself up and slid out of bed. He'd take that bath before the others used up the hot water.

A CALM, CRISP MORNING. THE promise, a cloudless, good-to-be-alive day. The gang's two trucks pulled into the work site not far from the giant dam.

The dog Kuri had been on the chain over the weekend, thrown scraps of food by whoever happened to be around. The one time he had been taken to Gladys's he had battled with her big hound, winning the battle by at least two hundred yards. Not that Grunter's dog lacked courage; he was merely prudent. He had proven his courage by leading the race between the wheels of a passing vehicle. This morning he celebrated freedom by trotting random, widening circles, sniffing and wetting each worthy bush, until his course took him into the tea-tree outside the clearing.

Soon thereafter, from the tea-tree, came a series of excited, shrill barks – the kind the dog made when he spotted rabbits – followed by angry snorts that were not of his making, and the snap and crackle of breaking branches. The dog re-entered the clearing half a dozen lengths ahead of a head-down Captain Cooker, and a dozen little Cookers trying to keep up with mum. Plainly, the dog had it in mind to win this battle too.

He headed for Grunter who ran for the trucks with his cohorts. They left the dog Kuri to fend for himself. He ran under a truck, out the other side, around and around the truck, back under the truck. Finally he leapt on to a mudguard, barking shrill defiance from its safety.

Mac drove up in his 4x4. He heard the laughter. He opened the vehicle door and strode purposefully to the truck.

'I turn me back for five friggin' min...'

The pig shifted attention.

Mac stood between vehicles. He opted for the 4x4, but the pig cut him off. He ran for the truck. The crew shouted encouragement. As if it were a hand grenade, Rangi hurled a tucker tin at the beast. The sow turned her attention to the new foe and while she tarried to eat the sandwiches Mac ran to safety.

'Pae kare, boss, you oughta be an All Black!' Grunter said. Mac answered, 'The show's over, you bastards! Start hauling that cable!'

Larry said, 'What would you like me to do, Mr McKenzie?'

'What would I like you to do? I'd like you to get up that friggin' tower, that's what I'd like you to do. Think you're on bloody holiday or something?' He turned away to discourage further discussion. But then he spotted something he hadn't noticed before.

'Boots!' He pointed to Larry's shoes. 'Boots?'

'You hard of hearin', laddie?'

'No, but...'

'You work here, you work up them towers like the rest of 'em – except for him,' he nodded to Grunter, 'and you don't climb towers in shoes!' He turned to Rangi. 'Break him in. And for God's sake don't let him break 'is friggin' neck or we'll never hear the end of it.'

He headed to the 4x4.

Rangi winked. 'She'll be right, sport. Nothing to it!'

Going back to camp that evening Larry got the truck to stop at a Cambridge shoe and boot shop. He bought hobnailed boots.

The next morning, he watched the men climb the spikes that protruded from a tower corner. Doesn't look too bad, he thought. But when the men strolled nonchalantly along horizontal members between corners, seventy feet up, carrying sacks of clamps, ropes, and blocks and tackle, the post office job looked pretty good all of a sudden. Rangi called down: 'Give it a go, sport. Nothing to it.'

'What the hell...' He climbed to the twenty-foot level, looked down. It seemed a hundred.

'You're doing great.'

He looked down at fifty.

'Oh, my God!'

'Come on, you can make it sport. Once you get to the cross-arm it's a piece of cake.'

He breathed deeply, pulled himself up a step, another step, another, not letting go one step until he had a grip of the next, while Rangi called down encouragement.

'Loosen up!'

If he loosened up he'd fall. Of that he was convinced. He reached the arm, pulled himself on to it, and clutched at a diagonal brace.

'Whew!'

'I told you, sport, nothing to it.'

'Tell me how I'm going to get down,' Larry said.

'No problema,' Rangi answered, using language he'd picked up in Italy. 'Same way you got up – one foot at a time. Capito?'

Larry had not learned Italian. 'Up you too!' he said.

The cables had been laid on the ground. The men fitted blocks around them and hauled them up to the insulators. Soon the tractor, a couple of miles down the line, would pull the cables through the blocks. The engineer would adjust the sags by shouting his go-stop orders to the flagman on the tower. The flagman would relay the orders to the tractor crew. When the sags were set, they'd clamp the cables to the insulators and remove the blocks.

This day, his first day up a tower, Larry had been told to watch, and keep out of the way.

At ten, the billy-boy called up, 'Smoko time! Come and get it!'

The men slid down the diagonal braces. Their hobnails rang tattoos against the steel. Half an hour later, they climbed back up, passing Larry still coming down. He dropped the last six feet, poured tea into his pannikin, and told Mac that he was climbing no more bloody towers that day.

The next day the climbing came easier, and the next easier yet. At the end of the week he was ready to work.

Mudgway had set the sags. Rangi showed Larry how to slide down the block and tackle, position himself on the cable, fit the clamp around it, and bolt the clamp to the insulator. Easy, he said.

Larry attached his safety strap, and very, very gingerly, slid himself down. His grip on the rope whitened his knuckles.

'Loosen up!' Rangi called. 'Loosen up!' Rangi had a perverse sense of humour, Larry decided. His feet felt for the cable. Ah! He slid to a sitting position. Yi, yi, yi!

'How's that!' he called to Rangi.

'I told you, sport – nothing to it. Now put the clamp around the cable. Bolt it up. And, e hoa, remember there's men below. Yell, "Timber!" if you drop something.'

Larry put the clamp in position, tightened the nuts. How easy it had turned out to be. 'What now, boss?' he called. Pride overlaid his voice.

'Move to the other side.'

'Righto, boss.'

He stood on the cable, unclipped the safety strap, clipped it around a cross-arm member, and began the climb up the tackle ropes. He backed down, tried the insulator. Half-way up, he could move neither up nor down. 'Rangi!' His voice strangled.

'What's up, sport?'

'I'm stuck!'

Rangi climbed down from a higher cross-arm. 'Well, so you are!' he encouraged.

'Rangi!'

'Okay, sport. *No problema*. I've got your weight. Ease back down, I've got you. Easy now. Easy. Okay? Now tell me, what made you climb the bloody insulator, for crissake!'

'I tried the tackle ropes...'

'All right, sport. Wrap your mitts around the ropes and climb. I've got your weight.'

He reached the cross-arm.

'Call it a day, sport.'

Rangi sang encouragement:

Haere mai! Ev'rything is ka pai!

When Larry reached the ground he ran for the tea-tree. Only bile came up.

Mac opened a warm Waitemata.

'If you're gonna spew, a beer will give you something to spew on,' he said.

Grunter said, 'Bloody good job, mate!'

Mudgway said, 'You push those boys too hard, Mac. Got to give them time.'

'Bullshit! What else do I do with him?'

23

'Soon as I can find another operator we'll get the radios going. Meanwhile, let him learn at his own pace.'

Mac walked away muttering about bloody wirelesses. He called to Larry from the 4x4. 'You got mail. You can get it when we knock off.' He turned to the others.

'Back to work, you bastards! You think this is an old men's home?'

LARRY LEFT THE TABLE. Other times he may have lingered over the tea or joshed with the men, but this evening he had letters. He carried a pork chop – with meat on it – for the dog Kuri. The dog sniffed at it, walked around it, picked it up, and carted it under Larry's bed.

'Out!' Larry ordered. He wouldn't have minded the dog inside but he stank. Grunter should bathe him. Actually water wouldn't harm either of them.

A letter from the United States Consulate! Another from the New Zealand Post and Telegraph Department. One from his mother. He puzzled about the fourth – from Great Britain. Who would be writing to him from Great Britain? It had been forwarded and re-forwarded. His mother had sent it on.

He opened the letter from the American Consulate.

```
November 13, 1946
Dear Mr La Salle,
In reference to your application to emigrate to
the United States of America, I have enclosed
```

the necessary forms you are required to fill in.
Note that you must furnish three copies of your
birth certificate, three each of the documents
showing your education...

He scanned the many and various requirements, stopping at the last paragraph.

...so that there is no misunderstanding, I must
repeat the information I gave you during your
visit to this Consulate. At the present time a
strict quota system exists that limits the
combined number of applicants from New Zealand
and Australia. Because preference is given to
those who have married American citizens and to
those who have proven skills and abilities deemed
of benefit to the United States, your chance of
obtaining early admission to the United States
can only be stated as slim. I will, however,
forward your application to the appropriate
quarters when you have correctly submitted the
necessary information...

He had known it wasn't going to be easy – they'd made no bones about that. But seeing it in writing was disheartening. If he couldn't get into the United States, then what? With his lack of education in a country too small to sustain an electronics industry, what chance of an electronic career?

He'd been buoyed up until this. From the gang's bantering he knew that they'd approved him. He'd passed a kind of test today, though Rangi had had to help him to climb back to the cross-arm. From what he had heard, not everyone had the daring (or stupidity) to become a linesman, and he had dared to try. Tomorrow he'd do it without Rangi's help. He opened the letter from the New Zealand Post and Telegraph Department.

15th November, 1946

Dear Mr La Salle:

In February of 1941 you were given leave by this
department to join the Armed Forces of New Zealand
for the duration of the hostilities. As the war
is over and our inquiries have shown you are no
longer a member of the Armed Forces, I must
respectfully request that you notify this department as soon as possible of your intentions
regarding your employment.

Yours faithfully,

J. G. Watford,

Postmaster-General

He put the letter down. Go back to the post office! Sort mail! The telephone exchange! (Number please? Two-four? Through. No, I'm sorry, there's no reply to three-six.) Send telegrams! Well, perhaps that part wasn't too bad. Certainly it had been better than the telephone exchange. The telegrams were sent by morse code. He had developed quite a skill with the morse key and clicker. But day after day... year after year...

Before the war, he had learned the morse code so that he could become a radio amateur. He'd built a transmitter and a receiver and had conversed with other amateurs around New Zealand, and later in America. That's when he had first become interested in America, and Americans. He thought to himself, now that he was more or less settled, he'd get back on the air again. He'd do that. He hadn't noticed the smell until he heard the thump, thump from under the bed as the dog Kuri scratched.

'Out, you bloody mongrel!' Larry wielded the broom to move him. 'Back to Grunter's!' He shouldn't feed him, he knew.

He looked over the remaining two letters and dreaded what his mother's letter might have to say, leaving home the way he had.

The English letter puzzled him. Who could it be? But his mother was his mother. He opened hers first.

12th November, 1946.

Dear Larry,

I've lain awake at nights wondering about what it is that the war has done to you. You were always such a considerate boy. But the way you left when you did, not waiting for the home-coming they were putting on for you even, that is not the way I brought you up. Your father says that it is the war and I know that he was pretty funny when he came back after the last one, but then he had been wounded and gassed.

Your poor sister cried and cried when you left. Can't you find time to write to her and tell her you're sorry, even if it is only a note?

Poor Mrs Huggins was so disappointed when you didn't go to see her. She always asks about you. Poor old soul, she isn't much longer for this world.

Larry, your old friend John Carpenter died. You must remember him. He's the one who got you started in wireless...

He stopped reading. No! Not old John. Old John who had shown him how to make his batteries from zinc, carbon rods and sal ammoniac solution. How to wind the coil for his first crystal set. How to solder. How to read schematic diagrams. He felt the tears close. Why hadn't he gone to see him?

He went to the cookhouse for a tea refill. The dog Kuri followed. Back at the hut, the dog stood at the door, dared to put his nose inside. He wagged his ragged tail.

Larry's father had scorned his 'playing around with all this newfangled stuff,' his radio. Why wasn't he hoeing the potatoes and why didn't he help with the milking? Until that day – Larry smiled when he remembered it – that day when he'd built his first tube radio with a 201A tube old John had given him, and he'd tuned in KFI of Los Angeles. His father hadn't known then the momentousness of the occasion. He'd come striding purposefully to the door.

'The cow trough's empty. Can't you hear them mooing for water?'

'In just a minute, Dad. Listen – America!' He handed the headphones to his father.

His father was in no mood to dilly-dally.

'Pump the water!' he repeated.

'Dad. Please! I'll pump the water as soon as you've listened.'

Grudgingly, but without actually entering the shed – that would have been a concession he wasn't up to – his father held one earpiece to an ear. Larry held the other.

'Good evening, ladies and gentlemen...' An American voice. His father straightened, not believing. The headphone cord tightened. The radio pulled off the bench and fell to the floor. 'Son, I'm sorry... I didn't mean to pull it off.'

'I know, Dad, it's all right.'

'I got such a surprise!'

'Dad, it's all right.'

'Can you fix it?'

'The tube's broken. But I'll get another one somehow.'

'I'm sorry, son. Look, you'd better get your dinner before your mother gets upset. I'll pump the water.'

'Thanks, Dad.'

'Son?'

'Yes?'

'Was that really America?'

'Yes. Los Angeles.'

About a year before this, old John had talked to his father, had told him that he should be encouraging his son in his hobby. Radio was a coming thing, he prophesied. For a while his father had been enthusiastic. He had given Larry use of a shed that had been used for ripening bananas. Because it was insulated it became very hot. The ceiling was four feet high at one end and about five at the other. Visitors didn't stay long. His father had helped him to put up the antenna. But the radio kept Larry from his chores. His father had threatened to nail the door shut.

Poor old John, blind from cataracts and there were so many things he wanted to do. When Larry mowed his lawn, old John would call out.

'Sonny, can you come here for a minute? I need you to wind a coil. Here, tie the end of the wire to this nail. Roll the wire out. Keep it tight. Walk back up to the nail. Roll the wire on to the former as you go. One hundred and eighty turns. Don't cross them.'

...Clarice is getting married. You didn't stay around long enough to meet her beau. He's such a nice boy. Larry, I'm asking you, please, for Clarice's sake, come to the wedding. Robbie, her hubby-to-be, and Clarice, they want you to be the best man...

Larry put the letter down. Clarice getting married! She was just a kid. But of course he'd go. He'd have to buy a suit, though. When was the wedding? He scanned through the letter. The fifteenth of January. The Hydro crew took their Christmas and summer holidays then. He could make it.

He was half aware that the dog Kuri was further through the doorway, but he was too engrossed to do anything about it.

He heard shouting and ribald laughter from one of the huts. It sounded like they were having fun. Drinking beer and playing cards, probably. He'd join them. But first, the letter from Britain.

12th August, 1946
Dear Larry,
I don't know whether you will receive this because I don't know where you are. I wrote to New Zealand House in London to get your address... He skipped to the meat.
...why didn't you write? I worried so much about you. I imagined all kinds of things. Then, when we heard about our invasion in North Africa, I just knew that you had to be part of it, and that explained why you hadn't written. But months went by and not a word. Why, Larry? Why didn't you write? Was it because my father insisted that we live in Dundee when the war was over?

29

...I joined the R.A.F. I tried to get into radar the same as you but they put me into administrative work... the war has changed so many lives. I found it so very difficult to settle down when I came home. I do miss the rush and bustle of London and the many things to do and to see there. It's so cosmopolitan. All those people from all over the world, from places that were just names before. I found it so romantic when you talked about New Zealand. Today I would not have a problem about going there. (Especially with this horrid weather of ours!)

I did intend that this should be a short note to find out how you are, but somehow I can't seem to stop myself. You were my first beau and you will always be special. I think of you so often and I wonder what you are doing... Larry, I may be getting married soon. His name is Ian MacDougall. He is a doctor at the hospital. But please Larry, write to me, tell me what you are doing. We can be friends...

Getting married! First Clarice. Now Moira. Well, she'd be much better off married to a doctor, he told himself, though something inside him cringed at the thought of it. Why hadn't he written to her? He had kept putting it off. Yet she couldn't be blamed for her father.

He noted that the dog Kuri had curled on the sack that Larry put his feet on when he got up in the mornings.

'Hey! Off there, you miserable fleabag! Outside!'

Then he shed his mood. 'Come. Let's party.'

He poked his head into Rangi's hut.

'Who's got a beer?'

'Well... if it isn't me old mate. The bloke that climbs friggin' insulators,' Grunter said.

And Rangi said, 'What-ho, sport!' He passed a bottle. 'Park the bod. Join the group.'

Larry took a long, slow swig. He grinned, lifted the bottle again.

'Down the bloody old hatch, you blokes,' he toasted.

LARRY HAD PHONED HIS mother from the Cambridge post office. Yes, he'd be at the wedding. Yes, he'd be the best man. Should he get a navy blue suit? Transportation would be no trouble, he was buying a motor bike. Yes, he would be very careful.

He wrote to the Postmaster-General. He wrote that he regretted that he had decided to resign from The Post and Telegraph Department. He was lying. He was elated.

He had not replied to Moira. He so much wanted to, but what to say? Would she understand why he hadn't written? He hardly knew why himself. And she was getting married. He would have to think about it.

Over drinks, in a corner of the Hamilton Arms, Larry learned that Rangi had operated tank radios at Mersa Matruh. Why then couldn't he operate the war surplus sets Mudgway had acquired? The problem was, could Mudgway find his replacement – someone with his climbing experience?

Mudgway did. His name: Speed Kau Kau.

Speed was a Maori, a giant, arms and legs like tree trunks and, like most of the Maori at Bruntwood, musical. A ukulele was as much part of Speed as a wristwatch. He had the ability, too, to sink vast quantities of beer and plonk or, in a pinch, gin or whisky – whatever was mustered. The men who knew him called him a dag. Women liked him, too. He had a following of them.

Speed rode his spluttering, pre-war Harley into the Bruntwood yard, braked in a shower of stones, revved the motor to an ear-splitting loudness, and blew the horn.

Grunter recognised the arrival. He sternwheeled from his hut. 'Me old mate, Speed!'

'Pae kare! Grunter!'

Larry came out of his hut to see what the commotion was about, as indeed did everyone else. When they realised who the visitor was they lined up to shake his hand, for his fame as a climber, a drinker and a womaniser had preceded his arrival.

The occasion demanded and got rightful celebration. But around nine o'clock the booze ran out. As Mac was away, Grunter jimmied open his hut door and purloined his supply of Scotch – two bottles, all there was – and when that ran out, he and Speed took off on the Harley for more.

Around midnight they returned without the Harley, with the booze in sacks, calling to all to come and get it. But Larry pulled the blanket over his head. Celebration or no celebration, tomorrow was a work day. He wondered at his workmates' prowess with the bottle. Was there something the matter with his own ability?

Sometime later, when all but Speed and Grunter had turned in, one of the two jimmied open the cookhouse door. They borrowed eggs, bacon, butter and bread. And probably because Speed would not brave the odours in Grunter's hut, and because his own was yet devoid of furniture – except for his bed – they took their loot to Mac's hut. The door was open anyhow. They brought firewood from the stack of resinous old pine roots at the side of Mac's hut and lit a large fire in the tin chimney. Soon the food was cooked and eaten down to the bacon rind. The dog Kuri ate the rind. Only then did they wind it up and go to bed. Meanwhile, Larry dreamed. He was back in Italy, on a beach near Naples. He had just made the acquaintance of a passionate, near-nude *signorina*. But before he could improve his knowledge of her, bladder pressure forced him to visit the shed they dubbed the dunny. Then he smelled smoke, saw the fire, and ran to the fire alarm – a length of railway line hung from a wire near the cookhouse door. He beat on it with an iron bar.

The turnout was rapid, but when they saw that it was only Mac's hut that burned they prepared to turn back in, until Rangi pointed to the firewood stacked against the hut wall.

'If that catches fire the whole camp will burn!' he said.

They moved the firewood and let the hut burn. There were plenty of huts. And what difference would a bucket or two of water make at three o'clock in the morning?

WHAT SPEED AND GRUNTER didn't care to mention when they came back with the booze was that at a fairly sharp bend before a small bridge within a mile of the camp, the Harley rode up on the gravel, turned its handlebars forty-five degrees from true, crossed two gravel berms, and sped down the bank into the creek. And there it submerged and remained. A miracle that neither man was hurt. A greater miracle that not a bottle was broken.

Only when they rescued the bike from the water two days later, did the truth come out. But Speed was good at fixing bikes. He dismantled it, dried it out and reassembled it. But it took time. Meanwhile, he was camp-bound. Not that it mattered. When he couldn't go to the action, the action came to him. The action in this instance was two delightful young nurses from Rotorua. Not real nurses, nurses in training – a distinction that bothered Speed not a whit. They were female, alive, healthy, and had come to see him.

They had borrowed a Model A Ford. The Ford purred into the yard twenty minutes after the men had returned from their toil, as Larry came from the shower shed. The vehicle slid to a halt in a spray of stones that beat against the huts. Larry tightened the towel around his waist and waited curiously. The two young things – no more than twenty-two or twenty-three – stepped down. They saw him. One said, 'Why... hello there!' She grinned impishly. The

33

other pulled his towel by a corner. He spun a half turn before he recovered possession.

'Hey! What the hell?'

'Hello, cutie,' said the first one. 'I'm Mary and this is Winnie.'

'We're looking for Speedy Kau Kau,' Winnie said.

Before Larry could point to Speed's hut, Winnie had slipped her arms around his neck.

'No hurry,' she said.

'I saw him first!' Mary protested. She tugged on the towel.

'Well!' Speed's leer was one you would expect to see on a spider when a fly hits its web.

'Welcome to Bruntwood,' he said. 'Come to my hut. We'll knock the top off a couple; make some music.'

'Who's your friend?' Mary said.

'Larry La Salle. Back from the war.'

'A returned soldier! La Salle? How'd you get to be French, sweetie?' Mary asked.

'My grandparents,' Larry explained.

'Luv-el-y!'

'I got to get dressed.'

'Oh, you poor dear,' Mary sympathised. 'Let's get you dressed. Which is your hut?'

'Wouldn't waste me time gettin' dressed, mate,' Speed said. Mary poked her tongue out at Speed and took Larry's arm.

In the hut he tried to slip into his shorts behind the towel.

'Here, let me hold the towel,' she said, whisking it away.

He'd been standing on one foot. Grabbing for the towel he fell on the bed.

She parked beside him, ran a hand through the hair on his chest. 'French, eh?'

He tried a kiss. She responded. A second kiss. She stiffened, pulled away.

'Dirty bastard!'

What, he wondered, alarmed, had he done to earn such non-factual nomenclature? But she'd been talking to the dog Kuri, who was practising aerobics on her leg. While Larry roared with laughter, she chased the dog out the doorway.

'Did you see what that filthy bastard did? I hope that's not *your* mongrel!'

Larry slipped into his shorts and pulled a shirt over his head.

'He belongs to one of the other fellows,' he said through the cotton. He was still laughing when his head appeared.

'The dirty bastard!'

But Mary had a short attention span.

'Well, well! He got his clothes on!' Given a few minutes he sensed she'd have got them off again, but the sound of a ukulele claimed her attention. She grabbed his arm.

'Let's join them,' she said.

It had been five years since Larry had enjoyed such a sense of well-being, such complete conviviality. That he had a young woman beside him whose sole aim in life, it seemed, was to take his clothes off added spice to the enjoyment, though she embarrassed him with her boldness. She played with the hair on his chest and blew into his ear. She held him close when they sang.

He wished they had a piano. He knew a couple of songs that were all the rage when he was in America. During a lull he took the uke and strummed a few chords, then he sang 'Dance with the Dolly with the Hole in Her Stocking'. When they had learned that, he taught them 'Rum and Coca-Cola'.

One o'clock in the morning. The party wound down. They had to work the next day. Mary said, 'What else do you do apart from playing the uke, sweetie?' Before he could answer, she took his arm and said, 'Shall we find out?' She led him from the hut and back to his.

The dog Kuri made signs to follow.

'Bugger off!' she ordered.

She closed the door to keep him out.

THERE HAD BEEN SUMMER rain. The tea-tree exuded a fragrant smell. A Captain Cooker snorted somewhere. A bellbird tinkled in the far-off trees. It didn't seem right to start the bulldozer.

Larry helped them push a spool of cable on to the cradle. Speed attached the cable's end to the Caterpillar and gave the 'Go' signal to the flagman. As it turned, the spool squeaked and moaned, and the flange scraped against the cradle, creating a clackity-clack sound. Grunter stood at the brake handle.

A crew moved ahead of the Caterpillar cutting fences and readying planks to protect the cables where they crossed the roads. When the cables were run Mac usually stationed men at the roads to halt the traffic, but this part of the country was not settled, and traffic was rare. Mac dispensed with the road guards.

The cable fed smoothly. Grunter left the brake to refill his pannikin from the tea billy. The tractor approached a steep gully. The driver looked for a place to cross. He yelled to his flagman to signal that he was slowing.

The tower to the rear of the tractor was inhabited by a flagman who had spent the last few years in the Middle East driving trucks for the 2nd NZEF. He was not accustomed to the quiet of back-country mornings, the only sounds the drone of insects, the distant chugging of a tractor. He was understandably enthralled when an inquisitive fantail inspected his presence. Next, a white-eye landed on the cross-arm. Seeming to prefer monocular views, it peeked at him with first one eye and then the other. The flagman held his fingers out invitingly.

'G'day, little birdie.'

He missed the 'Slow' signal.

Grunter heard the clackity-clack change tempo. He ran for the brake. Before he could reach it, the spool's flywheel action spewed several turns of cable on the ground and, while Grunter got rid of the pannikin, several more.

'Stop!' he screamed. 'Stop 'em, for crissake!'

They had stopped. Grunter meant that he didn't want them to resume pulling until he had wound the turns back. With the communication system out of operation, the tractor driver didn't know Grunter's thoughts. He took up the slack at the exact moment Grunter stepped into the mess. Grunter heard cable whip through the grass. He danced a dance that clearly put him in Bolshoi Ballet class. The renegade turns snapped and tangled around the spool. The spool lifted from the cradle, dragged along the ground, and nearly ground Grunter beneath it. The bird watcher heard Grunter's yells. He saw the flagman's 'Stop' signal. What was he supposed to do? The cable had stopped. He did nothing.

Mac sat in his 4x4 going over a list of needed materials. He heard the yells. He yelled too when he saw what had happened. He yelled all that day, and in the evening he came into Grunter's hut and yelled – brave of him, it was pirau season.

Rangi interceded with logic. 'Boss, if you'd been using the radios, it wouldn't have happened. Wait till Mudgway hears about it!' And because the cable had to be cut and spliced to eliminate the damaged length, Mac wasn't excited about Mudgway hearing about it. Later, he reappeared at Grunter's door, a pannikin of Black and White in his hand.

'Tomorrow… you better take them wirelesses out. But we'll have to put flagmen at the roads.'

'Whatever you say, boss.' Grunter scratched himself down his trousers and released a pirau belch that sent Mac reeling back to his new hut.

'The shit these people eat!' he grumbled.

FOR A MONTH LARRY had pondered how to answer Moira's letter. It was dated months ago; she was probably married already. Should he explain why he hadn't written? And what if her husband should read her correspondence? She had said so little about him, only that he was a doctor.

The evening was balmy. The crew had finished dinner. They sat outside around a table made from a cable spool. Some drank tea, some beer, Mac his usual Black and White.

'It helps me digestion,' he had answered Larry's inquiring look one previous evening.

They talked about what they could be doing, or should be doing, with their lives. An old-timer, an inveterate gambler, said that he'd like to meet a nice widow lady, marry her, and settle down. The man gambled his butter ration, he gambled his firewood, he gambled his pay away before he earned it. A perpetual money shortage kept him confined to camp. Mac fired back, 'You'd have to win her in a bet, else how would you get her?'

'I'm saving to buy a farm,' said one. 'You should do well; your hut's a pigsty already,' retorted another.

Grunter wiped foam from his lips, belched, and said, 'I like what I'm doing now, though I've known better foremen.'

Mac replied, 'Get stuffed, you bastard!'

Larry sipped his tea and wondered if he should talk about his plans. Was there a chance that Mac would take the conversation as a personal affront? He went ahead anyway.

'I've made application to emigrate to America,' he said quietly.

The men showed scepticism.

'The next paddock will have shit in it too, mate,' Speed offered sagely.

38

Mac said, 'You must be off your rocker, laddie, to leave a cushy job like this one. You won't find one like it in America.'

'Ten bob it's a sheila,' Rangi ventured.

'A quid you're right,' Grunter agreed.

They turned the conversation to rugby.

'I've got a letter to write,' Larry excused himself.

8th December, 1946

Dear Moira,

I should have written this four years ago. I had no real reason not to except that I needed time to think. Then, when I'd had time enough, I kept putting it off. Your letter has made me realise how selfish I have been. I do hope you will believe me when I say now that I'm truly sorry...

He stopped writing to read what he had written. Words! Powder-puff words. The truth was, he had not had the courage then – and he didn't have it now – to tell her that their plans had smothered him, nor that he had not been sure that he had loved her. That perhaps it was the perception of love he had loved. They were young – he young enough to think of the war as his chance of a lifetime, and she too young to understand her father's dominance. And now, if he did find the courage, how could he write these things to another man's wife?

The dog Kuri scratched at the door. Again Larry censured himself. He must stop feeding the dog.

He bent to the task of writing.

You were right when you surmised that I'd been sent to North Africa. We disembarked near Algiers and set up base on the aerodrome at Maison Blanche. Our unit installed radars in trucks, in aircraft and ships, and we operated shipboard radars during the amphibious landings into Sicily and Italy. Later, we were transferred to Italy.

The voyage home was everything I ever wanted. Ship to Nova Scotia, train to New Jersey (three months in New Jersey), train to San Francisco, ship to Auckland. Leave. Then air to New Caledonia. Then the Americans dropped the atom bomb. I liked America. Had I been able to, I would have stayed. I have promised myself I will go back.

There's a problem though. Years ago the American Congress instituted an immigration quota system based on the ethnic backgrounds of its people. New Zealand fares badly on the list. Short of developing a skill they desperately need, and I can't think what that could be, my chances of obtaining acceptance are remote — unless I should meet an American girl as desperate for a husband as I am to get there! None the less, I have applied.

New Zealand is a farmer's country. No electronics industry worth mentioning exists. Hundreds of ex-radio and ex-radar returned servicemen are trying to get into the radio business. I'm lucky to have found a job operating radio equipment for the New Zealand Hydroelectric Department...

Moira had been a wonderful listener. He had liked that about her. She hadn't always understood, but she had listened. He smiled when he remembered that. She called him Larr-ee, her voice rising on the *ee*, and rising too, at the end of a sentence. 'Larr-ee, I dinna ken wha' it is ye're talking aboot!' He had loved to listen to the sweet lilt of it. Music. Often he heard the music and missed the matter. 'Larr-ee, are ye no' listening to me?'

He wrote about Grunter, and Mac, and Speed, their work; how they used the radios. He wrote that he had resigned from the post office, and had been measured for a suit for his sister's wedding.

As he finished, he knew he *could* have written to her from North Africa or Italy.

The dog Kuri scratched on the door. Without thinking, Larry opened it. The dog made a tentative but alert exploration into the hut. Larry noticed him.

'Out!' He sped his exit with a precisely aimed boot.

He hadn't written about the difficult let-down into civilian life. Nor that he had roamed the country, depressed, a lost soul, seeking he knew not what. But he wrote that finally he'd found a home, was settling in, had friends and plans. Only yesterday he'd made the decision to set up his amateur radio station. Until he could go to America, he'd bring America here. Subconsciously, he heard the singing from Speed's hut: 'Haere Mai'. 'Rum and Coca-Cola'. 'Don't Fence Me In'. They especially liked the tunes he'd brought back.

He put the pen down. A few minutes only, he resolved.

Rangi said, 'What-ho, sport. Park the old bod.'

Grunter said, 'It must be a sheila – the time you took!'

'Me cousin married two of 'em. Got two years,' Speed said.

THE VELOCETTE PURRED INTO the yard. No one heard it. Speed looked up as it passed.

'Well I'll be…'

He removed himself from his bed, though not from the bottle he held, and ambled to the door. 'An egg beater!' he hooted.

'Not a Harley,' Larry apologised, 'but better than walking.' He extolled its features: electric start, coil ignition, hydraulic shocks,

41

246cc. Though a two-stroke, the oil didn't have to be pre-mixed with the petrol. His first motor bike!

He unstrapped a cardboard box from the pillion seat, laid its contents on the bed. Soldering iron, vacuum tubes, aluminium chassis, transformer laminations, sundry components.

But first, a place to work.

The hut's furnishing was scant: a narrow, wire-wove bed against a side wall, and a wooden box that doubled as a table and clothes chest. The hut's end, opposite the door, was taken up by the chimney, a rude affair made from battered sheets of corrugated roofing iron nailed to a wooden four-by-two frame and mortarless bricks stacked about three feet high around the inside circumference. This type of fireplace yielded horizontal heat only if stoked to a point just below burning the whole place down, and unless the hut door was open – defeating the fireplace's purpose – it sent choking smoke swirling about the hut, soiling clothes, blankets and the inhabitant.

An unlikely but highly important item of furniture was a bucket of water kept near the earthen hearth. It served to dampen the fire's enthusiasm when it threatened the main structure – which it often did in the winter.

A small casement window – no more than two feet square – allowed a smidgen of light through the wall opposite the bed. A naked, fly-blown light bulb suspended on a twisted, frayed cord completed the ensemble.

Though not the Ritz, in Larry's eyes it eclipsed the tents he'd inhabited and shared during the war. And it had a wooden floor!

The previous occupant had papered the walls with newspapers to keep out the draughts. Now they were yellow from smoke, but interesting reading when there was nothing more exciting to do.

It was summer. No fire burned in the grate.

Larry stood at the door. Where to build his work bench? Under the window? The sun would shine in his eyes during the after-noons, at weekends. But where else? He sat on the bed, visualised the bench. Six feet long; low enough so that he could work at it while sitting on the bed; two-feet-six wide. He constructed it from used equipment cases, tapping into the light's ceiling rose to obtain the electricity.

The heart of an alternating current radio is a power transformer. He wound one after he'd built the coil winder. At first the formula escaped him. Was it eight turns per volt on an inch square core of laminations, or nine turns? It came to him: eight turns. Eight times 230 turns…

Eight more days and it would be Christmas. Early in the morning he intended to leave for Haumoana to attend Clarice's wedding. Thinking about his family, he ached to see them. And this time, he swore, he'd not upset them.

The Model A slid to a stop, scattering the gravel. Sensing it was Mary, Larry put tape over the winding to prevent the transformer from unravelling and wrote down the turns count.

He rose to meet her. She grinned impishly. He noted her form through the light summer frock and was stirred.

'G'day,' he said shyly.

'Is "G'day!" all you can find to say to me, sweetie? I thought you'd be happy to see me after I was so nice to you last time.'

He took her hand. 'Salutations and all that good stuff.'

He kissed her palm, kissed up her arm.

'Hey! You and your Frenchie stuff – but I didn't say that you have to stop!' She tousled his hair, slipped a hand into his shirt.

'Aren't you gonna close the bloody door?' she said. About midnight, someone strummed the uke. Speed and Winnie sang 'Rum and Coca-Cola'.

'Come on, sweetie, let's join them,' said Mary.

He was roused from a deep, alcoholic sleep. What had awoken him? He peered at the alarm clock. Three! Mary nudged him. 'You hear me?'

'No. What?'

'I'm going with you.'

43

'Where?'

'To meet your mum and dad.'

He tried to sit up but his arm was under her waist.

'You can't do that!' He dreamed up reasons why she couldn't and patiently explained them. But when Mary made up her mind, it was useless to argue with her. She'd gone back to sleep anyhow. He freed his arm, went to the dunny.

She lay as he'd left her, not quite on her back, mouth half open, making little snoring sounds. She's a beauty, he told himself, but…

He climbed in beside her. Her little snores – snorts really – filled him with a rare comfort. A sudden and odd sense of protective love overwhelmed him. But they'd have to talk about Haumoana. Perhaps by morning she'd have forgotten. Anyhow, how could she get away from the hospital? With that thought, he fell into a deep and untroubled sleep.

At ten, he awoke to Mac's yelling voice; Mac banging on doors. 'Git them bloody women out of here! Turn me friggin' back and you've turned the place into a friggin' brothel! Stone the bloody crows!'

Speed's voice: 'Get stuffed, boss!'

Mary had been up. He remembered her coming back, climbing over him to be against the wall, snuggling into him; like nestled spoons they lay. He remembered too that he must talk to her – but in the morning.

Now it was morning. Perhaps she'd forgotten.

She lay nude, awake, watching him. His interest freshened. 'There's time,' she said, noting his attention.

Winnie banged on the door.

'We gotta go! Old Starch is gonna be madder than a wet hen.' She referred to the hospital matron whose face was stiffer than her uniform.

'I'm going to Hawke's Bay,' Mary answered. 'Tell her I'm sick.'

Larry sat up.

'Hey! You can't!'

'Why not?'

'The matron will sack you.'

'Good! I'm sick of the bloody job anyway.' She called back to Winnie. 'Tell her to stick her job you know where.' She turned back to Larry. 'Now, sweetie… where were we?'

At Tarawera, she had said, 'Sweetie, I've got to pee.'

She had washed her underwear before they had left. 'Jeeze! You can't go in like that! Put your pants on, and your bra!'

'They won't be dry. Sweetie, you're going to have to buy me more when we get to civilisation.'

He put the bike on its stand, opened the haversack strapped to the luggage carrier and handed her his jacket.

'Put it on! And don't bend over!'

While she sought the lavatory, he ordered sandwiches in the tearoom. She returned carrying his jacket and, he noted, she wore the bra. He looked down.

'No,' she laughed and poked a little tongue at him. He sighed and thought of her meeting his mother.

They bought underclothes in Napier.

'I've never been to a wedding,' she said. 'What will I wear?'

He thought. Everyone would be dressed up to the nines. What was she going to wear?

'My sister will have something,' he said.

The way Mary stood, walked and spoke, captured the male interest. Whatever they were doing, men paused to inspect her. She was sex, bold sex, and they liked it, though it scared some. It had scared Larry at first – until he got some of it. Most men looked though if their wives were with them only their eyes moved.

Of course, women were different. Their immediate reaction was to feel threatened, especially if they had husbands in tow. Larry introduced her to his family.

'This is Mary. Mary, my mother, my father, my sister Clarice.'

His father looked carefully, grinned uncertainly, and said, 'I should have known he'd pick a beauty.'

His mother said, 'Why didn't you tell us you were bringing someone, Larry? My goodness! And me in my old clothes!' She straightened her apron. 'You might have phoned, Larry.'

His sister, in love, about to be married, saw only her brother's friend.

'I'm pleased to meet you,' she said. 'Don't take any notice of Mum, she welcomes you.'

'Well, don't stand out here,' his father said. 'Let's go inside.'

Mary's dress, daring by Auckland standards, was positively shocking by rural Haumoana's. Not only was it short, it was form-fitting, and indiscreetly tight around the hem. When she walked – glided – the insides of her knees rubbed together, and her rear wobbled frantically. High-heeled shoes (red) augmented the condition. Larry's father came behind. Larry wondered at his thoughts.

When they had left the Tarawera Hotel the men had flowed from the bar to watch them leave. Self-conscious this once, Mary had held her dress down while she climbed on the bike. But the dress went up anyhow – to the fulcrum point. A drinker blew froth over his mate.

The top of her dress was modest, her bosom not. Larry's mother had a propriety problem finding a place to put her eyes. When she spoke to Mary she looked at Larry. His father also made a feature of looking at Larry when he spoke to Mary.

They talked about the coming wedding and Clarice's husband-to-be. They talked about the people who would be coming to the wedding, and of those who could hardly wait to see Larry again. They wanted Mary to understand that their son had friends.

Larry leaned back in the chair, clasped his hands behind his head, and let the chatter flow and meld around him like creek water over and around a rock. He was enjoying it. Bored, Mary glanced at her watch. He saw and winked, rose from his chair.

'We'd better be getting along,' he said, and that markedly changed the tone of the chatter.

'Getting along! But you only just got here!' his mother protested.

'Sorry, Mum. I've got to get this girl to bed. It's been a long day.'

'To bed! But where are you going to sleep?'

'At her sister's – in Napier.'

'Her sister's? I thought you'd stay here. Mary, you're very welcome to stay here.' She finally looked at Mary.

Larry wondered if Mary had a sister. He caught her eye, dared her to expose him. 'What do you think?' He bit his lips to keep from laughing.

'You wait till I get you outside!' Mary said under her breath. Aloud, 'I'm sure my sister won't mind if I stay here. With all her kids, we'd be in the way anyway.'

'Oh, thank you, Mary. I'll make up the beds.'

'We'll ride over and let her know,' Larry said.

YOU BLOODY STINKER! YOU rotten, rotten stinker,' Mary scolded when they were outside. 'How could you do that to your own mother?'

'What about all those kids your sister's got?'

'You started it. Anyhow, where are we going?' She climbed on to the pillion seat.

'You'll see – if it's still there.'

It was – the Clive Arms. He pulled up under the street lamp. A bored constable stood a lonely vigil in the front. He looked them over. Mary slid from the bike, her finesse considerable and showy. The constable awoke.

'Hello,' he said, addressing them both, looking at Mary.

'Hello to you, too,' she answered sweetly, pausing at the footpath's edge where the street light shone best.

'G'day,' Larry said.

As a trained officer of the law the constable noted everything about Larry and, as a man, he noted even more about Mary. But work came first. He turned to Larry. 'Where you from, son?' He was not unfriendly.

'Haumoana.'

'Haumoana! Do I know you? What's your name?'

'La Salle – Larry.'

'La Salle! Dick La Salle's boy! Well I'll be damned! Last time I saw you you were a knee-high whippersnapper. Weren't you in the war? You just got back?'

'August.'

'Well… welcome home. You boys did a great job. And this is your girl? Wonderful. You going in there?' He indicated the hotel.

Larry nodded. By law, the pubs closed at six. Was he going to deny them entrance?

'It's the side door. Tell them to keep the noise down. Good night.'

'Thank you,' they answered together. Mary smiled at him.

'If they don't want to let your girl in, tell them O'Haggerty said that it's all right,' he called after them.

The Clive Arms was an old building. A carry-over from English tradition, the public bar-room was the working man's bar. Here, a man could swear and spit on the sawdust floor if he felt like it (but good manners decreed that he refrain from too much blowing and snorting so as not to annoy the majority).

But because the law forced the pubs to close at six o'clock in the evening, at four o'clock, or soon afterwards, the public bar turned into a frenzied mêlée of workers competing for and stock-piling drinks – the six o'clock swill. Publicans slid glasses under the tap without turning it off and propelled them down the bar on a film of beer, with just the right momentum to halt them before the appropriate customers. It was a lusty, man's world; women were refused service.

The local businessmen hung out in the private bar. They sat on bar stools or at tables. Here, a businessman could bring his wife and friends. Unescorted women were asked to leave.

When the public and private bars closed at six an after-hours bar catered to the illegal clientele and was raided on rare occasions by out-of-town police. (The local constable was likely to warn the publican, hence he was not asked to participate.) And here, too, women were not welcome.

Larry brought Mary into the after-hours bar. The drop in noise level acknowledged her presence. The drinkers nodded and shuffled about to get a better look at her. The proprietor looked up from the pump to see what had engendered the silence.

'I'm sorry, miss, we can't have ladies in here, you know.' His voice brooked no disagreement.

'Who sez?' Mary responded promptly. Her eyes shone with challenge.

'I'm sorry, miss, but that's as it is.'

'Try putting me out!' she snapped.

To defuse the situation, Larry broke in. 'Constable O'Haggerty said that it would be all right. He's out front.'

'Does O'Haggerty run this bloody place or do I run it?' the proprietor fired back. 'I say…'

'La Salle! You old bastard!' The greeter was a man of about Larry's age. He pushed through to grab Larry's hand. 'You old bastard!' He turned to the bar.

'Me bloody old school mate.' He turned back to Larry. 'Gee, it's good to see you, and you made it back in one piece, I see.'

Larry noticed the folded sleeve.

'Shit! Where'd you lose that?'

'Monte Cassino.'

'Shit!' This didn't happen to people you knew. 'Guess I was pretty lucky,' he said.

He turned to Mary.

'Mary, this is Tom Mainson. Tom, Mary. As you heard, Tom and I went to school together.'

'Hello, Tom,' she said. 'I'm sorry about the arm.'

'That's all right. I'm getting used to it.' He turned to the proprietor.

'Harry! Taihoa on the bullshit. Serve these two before I come around there and knock your bloody block off.' He turned back to Mary.

'You're a good-looking sheila. If you get a yen for a one-armed bloke, let me know.'

'That could be interesting,' she speculated, getting laughs. Larry went for the drinks.

'It's been paid for,' the proprietor said grudgingly. He nodded at the crowd.

Larry nodded at them. 'Thanks.' He lifted his glass. 'Down the hatch,' he said.

'We owe you boys,' someone toasted.

'Hear! Hear!' others agreed.

'God bless you all,' Mary said.

Others trickled in. Ronnie Page – he'd been a rear gunner in the air force, three years an unwilling guest of the Germans. Bill Conlan, army. Jimmy Smythe, navy. Fritz Berkham – his grandparents came from Germany; he had fought Rommel's army in the Middle East. O'Haggerty came in to quieten them down. He ceded defeat and went home. Jimmy Smythe left and returned with his girl.

The proprietor complained. 'Look here! I can't have this! First thing you know all the women will want to come in!'

'And what's wrong with that?' Mary challenged. And Jimmy's girl wanted to know what was wrong with that. And Tom Mainson.

The proprietor grumbled that the habits these men brought back would ruin the country. He didn't harp on it though, lest he lose their business.

Next morning, around eleven, Larry parked the Velocette against the kerb.

'Come on, you Jezebel, let's face the music,' he said.

At the door he called to his mother. He poked his head tentatively inside, expecting – he was not sure what. Five years ago she'd have lit into him, but now... and with Mary along...

'Hello, Mum.' He grinned contritely. 'Sorry we're a little late...'

'Little! This is little? Middle of the next day he arrives and he says he's a *little* late!'

She was a petite woman; small, round face, angular body. She stood with one hand on a hip and the other extended in front, palm up. She spoke to an invisible audience.

'His bed made up! His tea in the oven because I thought he'd be hungry! And next day he walks in larger than life itself and says that he's a little late! Oh, the Lord help us all. Well... now that you're here, you may as well sit down. You too,' she said to Mary, who lingered outside. 'I'll make some tea.'

Larry mouthed a silent 'Whee!' and winked at Mary.

His mother plugged in the electric kettle.

'Well...' she said over her shoulder, 'what's the excuse this time?'

This is more like it, he thought. She won't be content until she worms it out of me.

'We stopped in Clive,' he said.

'Clive? What's in Clive that time of the night?'

'The pub. Decided to have a drink.'

'Ah,' she said. 'They still allow boozing there at night. What's the good of having laws if people disregard them?'

She brought the tea to the table.

'Mary, have a scone.'

She poured the tea.

'Larry, I don't know what's come over you, drinking all the time. Mary, I hope he's not teaching you all those bad things. He wasn't like that. All the boys who came home from the war are the same. Never out of the pub. His father says they'll get over it in time. I hope he knows what he's talking about. But the pub didn't stay open all night until eleven o'clock this morning, did it? You went on to your sister's?'

Larry cut in. 'No, we…'

'It was Mary I was speaking to, Larry. Since when were you named Mary?'

'Look, Mum, there's nothing to hide. I was going to tell you. I met Tom Mainson. We got into conversation. It got late.'

'You didn't answer my question.'

Twenty-five I am, he thought.

'We stayed at his house. Quite proper and all that. His parents were there.'

'Ah,' she said. 'And they don't have a telephone, I suppose?'

'It was late.' It's like I've never been away, he thought. Tom's parents had given Mary a room to herself. Larry slept on a second bed in Tom's room. He had whispered to Mary, 'No nooky tonight, my love,' and she'd whispered back, 'Who said you were getting any?' She had tweaked his cheek mischievously. They'd had too much to drink anyhow.

'Ah, here's your father,' his mother said. 'He's been to the post office.'

His father looked them over shrewdly. He saw the tea and the scones on the table and recognised that if there had been a war, it was over.

'They stayed at the Mainsons' in Clive,' his mother said. 'You know, their boy lost his arm in Italy.'

'Well, they're safe, that's the main thing. It's good to have you home, son. And you're very welcome also, Mary.' He was careful not to let his eyes dwell too long on Mary.

The wedding day. Larry paraded in front of the mirror – his first suit, excepting, of course, his air force uniform.

Mary was stunning in Clarice's Sunday best frock. When they'd selected it, he'd thought, they can't! She'll look like a nun. But no. Mary looked like Mary, overtly sexual and appealing as ever. Small ruffles lined the neck discreetly hiding what Larry thought attracted so many men's glances. But no, they looked as before. Even the groom looked her over and, as Larry instinctively knew, liked what he saw.

Things had gone well over Christmas and New Year. If they were not coming home at night, Larry had been careful to phone. He never said that they stayed at Mary's sister's – just Napier. Sometimes they stayed at the Mainsons'. One night they slept on the beach at Cape Kidnappers, right on the sand. Another night they checked into a hotel as Mr and Mrs La Salle.

Larry envied his sister. Today she started a three-week honeymoon. Tomorrow Mary and he returned to the Waikato, he to work. Mary? Well, there was no knowing what Mary's impulsiveness had done.

'Don't worry about it, sweetie,' she had said. 'It's been worth it. You know' – she looked at him quizzically – 'if I were the falling in love type, you'd be the bloke I'd fall in love with – now, don't go reading anything into that. I said, "if"! Besides' – she paused – 'you're the jealous kind. Your jealousy would get on my nerves after a time.'

Clever Mary, he thought. It's true, I get jealous. It's the way men look at her.

Suddenly, he realised that he hadn't thought of Moira since he and Mary had been in Hawke's Bay; not once.

Clarice and her father came down the aisle and she stood beside her husband-to-be. Mary's eyes shone as much as Clarice's.

'...I declare you man and wife. You may now kiss the bride.'

Clarice and her husband prepared to leave. Larry's mother cried and laughed and cried, and she hugged them all.

'Thank you, thank you for coming, Larry – and Mary, you too. I'm so proud of her – Clarice, I mean – and he's such a nice chap. He will be good to her, I know. And Larry, you look so nice in your new suit, doesn't he, Mary?'

Clarice hugged them both.

'Be careful you two don't catch the bug,' she warned with a twinkle. Looking meaningfully at Mary, she said, 'He's not getting any younger, you know.'

They walked, that evening, along Haumoana's beach.

'They're nice,' Mary said.

'Who?' Larry answered, coming back from his thoughts.

'Your parents, your sister – your family.'

'It was touch and go when they first saw you, your tits popping out of that dress!' He smiled. 'Dad couldn't keep his eyes off them!'

'Don't be silly.' But she considered his words. 'I was expecting them to be different somehow. You're lucky to have parents like that.'

Later she said, 'Larry, what's a Jezebel?'

'You, my sweet,' he said, 'you.'

They stopped at Tarawera for lunch. Mary needed to pee. What appeared to be the same drinkers stood at the bar. Their glances followed Mary to the dining-room.

'Your admirers are waiting for a re-run,' Larry chuckled.

'This time I'm walking up the road before I get on,' she said. 'And next time I ride your bike, I'm wearing slacks.'

'Such modesty!' he chuckled.

It was evening when they drove into the yard at Bruntwood. The dog Kuri barked a welcome. Speed came to the door.

'Hey, welcome back,' he said, looking them over. To Mary, he said, 'Winnie covered for you much as she could, but the last I heard old Starch said if you weren't back by the sixth, you're out. Hey,' he said to Larry, suddenly changing the subject, 'if I wasn't so bloody tired, I'd celebrate you coming back. Wasn't sure that you would, seeing as how you had her along. If it had been me,

I'd have stayed gone.' His attitude conveyed that he had missed the great chance of a lifetime. But when Speed was down, he was up in seconds.

'Hey, maybe I can stand another beer.'

'I'm worn out, Speed. Been a long day.' It was true. The pumice road was potholed and rutted, and slippery where it was wet.

Turning to Mary, Speed said, 'Well, if he kicks you out, you come and see me, love.' He grinned wickedly and returned to his hut.

There was a sadness with them this night. Neither wanted it to be over.

'You know something, Mary?'

'What?'

'I wish it didn't have to end.'

She snuggled into him.

'But it has to end sometime, sweetie.'

'Why?'

'You know it does. Now, shhhh, and hold me.'

FEBRUARY, THE SUMMER HEAT waning, the autumn rains nearing; a time of deep contentment, when the juices slow and thoughts of the approaching damp and cold of winter make one thankful for the present.

This morning Larry lay on his back, hands under his head, a twig of tea-tree in his mouth. A just-right sun filled him with comforting warmth. The faint whine of a distant sawmill rose above the drone of insects.

As the days passed, his thoughts turned to a future he could not envisage. The evening work with the radio equipment progressed, but to what purpose? And while he saw Mary on her days off, and she was, each time, the same old bubbly Mary, without her saying so he knew there was to be no deeper involvement. Life, he was beginning to feel, had no motive beyond living.

The Department of Scientific and Industrial Research had a job opening. A winter in Antarctica, part of an international geophysical research project. The job was for a radar mechanic with his particular qualifications and experience. He weighed the pros and cons.

The pros were: a few months back in electronics, a foot in the door, perhaps toward something more lasting.

The cons were: a cold, cold winter, little prospect of any follow on – so they had written. He had to face up to it that with his lack of a degree it was unlikely that they would find another use for him.

The sound of tools and sundry equipment bouncing up and down on the tray of the 4x4 told him that Mac was coming.

'That all you got to do, squat on your bloody arse?' Mac scolded.

'There's nothing doing on the radio; I'm waiting for them to call.'

'Well... they got a hold up at number twenty.'

Mac took out the makings, rolled a cigarette. Between the pulling of loose tobacco from the ends and the ritual of the lighting, he said, 'What's this I hear about you going to the South Pole?'

'I haven't said that I'm going. I'm trying to make up my mind.'

'Bloody stupid idea if you ask me. Freeze the nuts off a steel bridge down there. Where's your brains, laddie?'

'You know better than I do, Mac, this job's going to peter out soon. Then what?'

Mac drew on the cigarette while he contemplated.

'You're right, of course! You do what you think best, laddie. Look at me; for years I've been saying I'm gonna get out but I haven't. Now what have I got to look forward to? I don't have a home I can call my own. I don't have a family. Nothing. An old men's home's what I'll get.'

That evening, Larry connected the feed line to the antenna. By hauling on the halyard, he raised it between the poles. He had been receiving signals of a sort, on a piece of wire tacked around the wall, but interference from the power lines had made the reception noisy. The new antenna should cure that problem.

The Voice of America came clearly through the loudspeaker. A baseball commentary: 'Strike one! Three hits, no errors!' He could feel the commentator's presence.

The fever was upon him. He wished his father could hear it! A far cry from the old tickler coil TRF on which he had first tuned in America. He turned the dial. The BBC, Radio Australia…

Rangi poked his head into the hut.

'What you got, sport?'

'A shortwave receiver.'

'Sounds good.'

'All right for starters but it needs a better dial mechanism. It's a bitch to tune.'

'You'll get there,' Rangi said, his faith unbounded, his interest quenched. 'Got a beer back in the hut if you're interested.'

'Thanks, but not now.'

The wireless nut, they had begun calling him. It wasn't that he was antisocial, but the boozing wasted his time and left him with hangovers. One beer was all right – even two – but three… four…

On one of her visits, Mary had said, 'Sweetie, the time's coming when you're going to think more of that bloody wireless set than of me.'

Speed bought an accordion. Grunter played the uke, Rangi the guitar. But the accordion hurt the dog Kuri's ears. When Speed picked up the accordion, the dog moved to Larry's hut. If Larry didn't tune in high-pitched heterodynes the dog was content. But not Larry.

'You stink,' he chastised, chasing him out. But the dog's 'thump! thump!' on the step as he scratched, Larry found comforting.

He had until Friday to decide about Antarctica.

He consulted with the dog Kuri. 'What do you think, you miserable apology for a mongrel, should I take the job or shouldn't I take it?'

The dog stood on the doorstep. He wagged his ragged tail and awaited further intelligence.

Larry made his decision. No Antarctica! Not that he wouldn't have liked the experience – five years overseas had not slaked his thirst for adventure. But if he took the job, in a few months he'd be back to where he started. By staying, at least he'd be here if something came along.

And there was Mary. Perhaps Mary had more to do with his decision than he was willing to admit. But instinctively, he knew his decision was the right one.

A week later he signed up for a course in mathematics – two nights a week. One of the nights coincided with Mary's day off. 'I don't see you enough as it is,' she complained, 'and now this.'

'But if I don't, I'll be a peasant for the rest of my life.'

'What's wrong with the job you've got?'

'Nothing – except that it's just a job. This is a new age, Mary. Technology won the war; technology will win the peace. I don't know how I'll do it, but I'm going to be an engineer. And I… I'm sorry, Mary. I didn't mean to get carried away.'

She linked his arm.

'My! You are a one! Soon I won't be good enough for you. Well, I'd better make the most of you while I have you. Come on… shove the radio!'

By mid-March he'd finished the transmitter. It hadn't been easy without test equipment. Though it wasn't the first transmitter he'd built, it was the first since the war. The night the transmitter was ready to test the ether was full of atmospheric static.

'Calling CQ, calling CQ. This is ZL1AAX, calling CQ.' He switched back to receive.

'ZL1AAX, this is ZL1XLN…'

The signal boomed from the speaker. From the ZL prefix he knew it was a New Zealander and, from the numeral one, from the northern part of the country. Not distant, but a contact!

'The name is Mac,' said the voice. 'I'm located in Hamilton…'

The dog Kuri looked for the voice.

Hamilton! Only thirty miles away!

'…I'm receiving you loud and clear on a very noisy night. How do you receive? Over.'

'Hello there, Mac…'

Mac lived half a mile from Gladys's place. To celebrate the contact, they arranged to meet at the Hamilton Arms, the pub of earlier conviviality, on the next Friday evening.

Larry was there when Mac – the new Mac – arrived. The old Mac, dour of face, not yet warmed up, supported a corner where the bar met the wall. His remoteness, tilt of shoulder, intentness upon his beer, hinted that this night, for the time being anyhow, he preferred his own company.

The crew held space down the bar; Grunter and Speed well along as usual; Rangi slower to get going and careful about it; Jock Pene, the truck driver, young, not quite sure of himself, about to get in over his head; and men from the other gangs. Larry stood at the edge of the group, his eye on the entrance.

It was the usual Friday night swill – the bar awash. A timid person ran the risk of dying of thirst before he found a way over or through the drinkers.

Larry, on his second drink, waited. A giant of a man entered the room. He shoved his way down the length of the bar. Those irritated by the shoving nodded genially when they saw the size of him.

'Beg pardon. Beg pardon.' The man, for all his size, was a gentle person.

Larry rose to meet him. 'You must be Mac?' They shook hands.

'Let me get you a drink,' Larry said.

'I'll get them. I've got the reach,' Mac grinned.

They chatted about radio and about the war. Mac had been a radio operator in the merchant navy.

Soon they moved into an electronic world from which the others, dropping by occasionally, felt excluded. They moved on. The smaller Mac, warmed up now and ready for company, joined them.

One eye shut against his cigarette smoke, several days' beard, sweat-stained hat without a band, and clothes which, had he been married, would have long ago been burned, hardly conveyed the impression of a successful man. He shuffled his feet while he waited for an opportunity to speak.

'G'day,' he put in at first hint of an opening. 'My name's Mac.'

If the Big Mac made judgement of the smaller Mac's appearance, he didn't show it. His hand went out.

'Also Mac. James McKenna, actually. My parents were from the Old Sod – as the name probably tells you.'

'Ah,' said the smaller Mac, 'a bloody Irishman!' He removed his hand. He opened his shuttered eye and scrutinised the son of the Old Sod.

'You're a big bastard, I must say,' he said, taking a swig and licking the suds from his moustache. He contemplated how far he could push it.

'My name's McKenzie. From the land o' the heather where men are men and the other bastards went to Ireland!'

You're an old bastard yourself, Larry thought, hastening to intervene.

'Cut it out, Mac! The other Mac here is a friend of mine. Mind if I call you Big Mac? Old Mac here, because he's the foreman, thinks he has the right to abuse everyone.'

'Just call me Jim,' Big Mac said, 'and don't let it bother you. I've been called worse.' He turned to old Mac.

'Here, let me get you a drink – that's if you'll condescend to drink with an Irishman. I warn you though, I'm not just an Irishman, I'm an Orangeman to boot!'

'An Orangeman! A Protestant! Stone the bloody crows! I don't know why, I thought you was a mick. Why didn't you speak up, laddie? I'll be honoured to drink with you. When you get back I got a story to tell you aboot a wee Scottish lass...'

Larry sighed and looked at his watch. He could have been doing so much. But Mac – Jim – was good company. And there was tomorrow.

He blew the froth from the refill.

THEY HAD HAULED THE cables through the pulleys. Mudgway took readings with the theodolite. When he'd set the sag, he gave the go-ahead to clamp the cables. A simple but exacting job, and time-consuming.

This day the sky stormed to the east. Rangi sat high on tower number twenty-one, clamping a cable. Mac arrived in the 4x4.

'I don't like the look of the weather,' he called up. 'Call it a day! And keep the ground-sticks on.'

The new line ran parallel to the older 110,000 volt line. The old line induced voltage into the new line. To prevent electric shock at regular intervals ground-sticks grounded the cables to the towers. And supposedly, the ground-sticks minimised the risk of shock from lightning.

'Won't be long, boss. This, and the one on the other side, to finish.'

The second 4x4 drove up. Grunter and Speed got out.

'I don't like the look of it, boss,' Speed said. He nodded to the east. 'Blacker than the inside of a cow.'

'Yeah, I've told him. He's winding it up.'

In the east, lightning zigzagged across the sky, quickly followed by thunder.

'Hey! Call it a day!' Speed called up the tower.

'In a mo', sport.'

Rangi unclipped the harness, walked the cross-arm to the other side, and slid down the rope to the cable. He sang.

Oh haere mai, ev'rything is ka pai!

'Not to worry, boss, ev'rything's ka pai...' He tightened the nuts. His attitude was, he'd fought the Germans, what was a little lightning?

A zigzag flash covered the sky to the east. A blue fire licked along the length of the transmission line. A blue-yellow halo effused around the tower. The air smelled of wet baby napkins.

The dog Kuri ran from the tea-tree. He hid among the foot pedals in Grunter's truck.

Mac called: 'You okay up there?'

No answer.

'Get him down!' Mac ordered.

Speed grabbed a block and tackle. It became apparent how he had earned his nickname. His hobnails beat a rat-tat-tat-tat up the steps.

He reached down from the cross-arm. 'Gimme your hand, mate.' If Rangi heard he gave no sign.

Mac got his binoculars from the truck. 'That's the whitest Maori I've ever seen!'

Speed tried coaxing.

Mac yelled up: 'Lower him down, for crissake.'

In spite of his girth and weight, Speed had the dexterity of a monkey. He slid down the tackle rope, past Rangi's clamped hands, and on to the cable. Reaching under the cable, he unscrewed the clamp nuts Rangi had put in place, took out the bolts and climbed back to the cross-arm.

'Lower away!'

The pulleys squeaked and clacked. The ropes slid through Rangi's hands. If they burned, he gave no sign.

They pried Rangi's fingers from the rope.

'Give him water,' someone said.

From Mac: 'You'll choke him. Get your hands under his arse.' They lifted him to the bed of the 4x4.

Speed leaned over the tailgate, his ear to Rangi's mouth.

'I think he's breathing!'

'Let's go!' Mac urged. He climbed into the cab. Larry held Rangi's head.

The truck bounded over the ruts and potholes. The treatment did something. Speed banged on the cab.

'He's come to!'

Speed leapt to the ground and lowered the tailgate. He leaned over.

'You all right, mate?'

Rangi spewed. The stream hit Speed in the chest, ran down his trousers, on to and into his boots. 'You friggin' bastard!' from Speed.

'Come off it,' Larry scolded, 'he couldn't help it!'

Mac poured a pannikin of water from the canteen.

'Drink it up, laddie. You gotta have something to spew on.' Rangi swirled a mouthful and spat it over the side. 'Jeeze!' he said.

Mudgway drove up.

'For crissakes, Mac, thought you'd have more sense than to put a man up in a storm!' He turned to Rangi. 'You all right, boy?'

Rangi nodded.

'Mac, what's come over you?'

'I told him to git down, I...'

'If they hear about this in Auckland my balls'll be in the wringer. For God's sake! You got to watch this sort of thing Mac – if you mean to stay with us.'

Mac fished for the cigarette butt and angrily threw it down. He shouted: 'Stone the bloody crows! I told you, I told him to git down...

'Now look, Mac, I'm not going to argue with you in front of the men. You've been at the game long enough to know better!' He stamped back to the truck and drove off in a cloud of angry dust.

Little veins pulsed in Mac's forehead. His mouth munched until he found voice.

'Stone the bloody crows!'

His anger grew. 'Bunch of friggin' bastards I got saddled with! Next thing you know I gotta wipe their bloody arses!' He turned to Rangi. 'When I tell you to come down off the friggin' tower, you bloody well come down off the friggin' tower. And if I tell you to jump from a friggin' tower, you jump from a friggin' tower! You hear me?'

'Boss, it coulda been worse,' Speed cajoled. 'He coulda been fried.'

LARRY HAD STARTED DREADING Tuesday and Thursday evenings. The mathematics class had become hard going. At the end of the third week, as he was leaving the classroom, the teacher, Wally Binden, intercepted him.

'Larry, give me a minute. Take a seat.' Binden had been gassed in World War I. Though he wheezed and coughed, he was a cheerful man, but short on patience with anyone he thought was wasting his time. Larry decided that he was about to be booted off the course.

When the room emptied Binden dropped into the next chair.

'Larry, tell me, why are you taking this class?'

Larry squirmed uncomfortably on the hard seat. Though, on occasions, he wondered if his aspirations weren't too ambitious, criticism and difficulties served only to drive him onward.

'I'm working toward becoming an electronic engineer,' he said, trying hard to keep defiance out of his voice.

'A commendable goal, and of course you'll need to be proficient in mathematics – which is what I'd like to talk to you about. But one thing first: I want you to know that I'm here to help you, not to criticise you. When you're having problems it's my job to help you overcome them. Now, what's your background in maths? How far did you go in school?'

Larry considered Binden with fresh interest.

'I had to leave school when I was thirteen. The Depression. You see…

'Ah yes… the Depression. Too many people affected by it. But you were on technical work in the air force. How did you manage to make it through their schools? From what I hear, they were not easy.'

'No, they were not easy, but I had help from other airmen, I memorised formulae, and my other marks were pretty good. Fortunately, outside the classroom, the work was of a practical nature.' Maths doesn't help much when someone's popping pellets at you, he had nearly added, remembering in time that Binden would personally have known all about that.

'Well… now things are clearer. The gaps in your knowledge had me puzzled. You're good with logarithms, yet you have a problem with trigonometry. But of course, if you haven't learned the basics… Fortunately we can rectify that. So let me see… I tell you what, if you can come in on Monday evenings I'll give you a couple of hours. We'll start at the beginning. I'd only be in the pub making the old lady unhappy, anyhow,' he added with a wry laugh.

Larry didn't believe the pub story. Binden was being a bloody good bloke. The problem was, Monday evenings were the only nights Mary had free and they had arranged to start spending them as man and wife in a hotel. So it got down to priority. He accepted Wally Binden's offer, but with a feeling of unease.

Late on Saturday afternoon, he drove to the hospital. He prowled the wards until he caught a glimpse of Mary tending a patient behind a screen. How different she looked in uniform, how business-like, he thought. Not a hint of the passion tense within her. He waited around until she saw him.

'Sweetie!'

The immediate smile! But then she looked about nervously.

'Sweetie, we're not supposed to…'

'I know – but something's come up. I wondered… Could you switch your day off to Wednesdays?'

'Bloody damn!' Her glow vanished.

'I've got a class now on Monday evenings.'

'Sweetie… I don't know…'

'Nurse Peterson!'

Mary turned. 'Yes, Matron.'

'Get on with your work, please.' The matron looked Larry over with a dubious eye then departed in a flurry of crackling starch.

Mary watched her leave, shrugged her shoulders, and turned back to Larry.

Suddenly she smiled again. 'Okay. Wednesday. I'll do it somehow. And sweetie – thanks for coming.'

Larry took her hand, astounded as usual at the speed at which Mary made decisions.

'Thanks, Mary.' He pretended to kiss up her arm. She pulled back quickly and looked about for the matron. He grinned and winked.

'Wednesday,' he said.

THE DAYS GREW SHORTER, the nights colder. The air had a fierce nip to it in the evenings, enough to deter the motorbikers from foraging far from the camp, unless with good reason. One colder than usual evening, Grunter stoked his fire with resinous pine roots, closed his door and crossed the yard to Speed's hut, not noticing that he had locked the sleeping Kuri inside. Above the noise of the orchestra tuning up, Larry heard the dog's frantic barks and came running. When he opened the door the dog beat the smoke out.

The wood around the fireplace had caught fire. Holding his breath, Larry entered and grabbed for the bucket of water kept near the fireplace for such emergencies, but the dog Kuri had emptied it during the summer. Fortunately, Grunter had forgotten to empty a second bucket he used these cold nights to avoid trips to the dunny. His mates had been harshly critical of that bucket, but now he was vindicated.

Except for that moment of excitement, the months had grown monotonous. When the trio practised their music and on the evenings Larry was not at night school, he studied or worked at his bench. Subconsciously he listened to their music. At times he came close to putting his tools down and joining them. But three nights of evening classes, Wednesday evening and most of Sunday with Mary, and the rest of the week poring over the study papers, left him no time for frivolity.

The power line neared completion. The next job, Mudgway told them, would be in the Wellington area. The gangs followed the jobs. Must he go with the gang, Larry wondered. There had been no further job offers, and no future in this one. So why hadn't he taken the job in Antarctica? He was moody. Mary impatient.

'For goodness sake! Something will come along,' she rebuked him.

Easy for her, he thought. Nurses can get jobs anywhere. Her training would soon be complete; she'd be a fully fledged nurse.

The following Saturday he awoke deep in depression, asking himself what was the point of all his study. There were no jobs. He picked up the homework papers, threw them into the fireplace, dressed, climbed aboard the Velocette, and rode. Around noon he found himself on the beach at Tauranga and didn't remember riding there. A chill, cutting wind blew off the sea. He rode again, wasted the day, and returned to camp in time for an over-the-air schedule with Big Mac. He turned on the radio. But before it had warmed up he turned it off, whistled the dog Kuri to come, and walked to the bridge. There he threw stones into the creek, and at the dog when he rolled in cow dung, as was his habit.

What to do?

He walked slowly back to camp and opened a bottle of Waitemata. Tomorrow, he'd tell Mac he'd move with them to Wellington.

The defeat ate at him. He opened a second bottle.

His depression eased enough to think about the schedule with Big Mac again. He turned the radio on.

Mac answered his call with, 'Where you been, e hoa?' His voice hinted excitement. 'How'd you like a job fitting out a fleet of fishing vessels with communication equipment?'

'Say that again!' Larry said. He dared not believe it.

'A friend of the family north of Auckland owns a fishing fleet. He wants someone to fit his boats out with radios.'

'He's got the equipment?'

'That's where you come in.'

'Mac, you're off your rocker! Where will I get that kind of equipment – and the money to buy it?'

'Build it.'

'Do you know the problems I had finding the components for this rig?' But he thought quickly. 'How many radios?'

'He didn't talk numbers – give him a ring. I told him you'd call. And if money's a problem I'm sure you can get something up front. Don't be timid about asking – no one else can supply him.' It was true. Everything was in short supply so soon after the war. And money was not an immediate problem. During his five years in the air force, part of his pay had been withheld by the government until he returned. The main problem, as far as he could see, would be where to obtain components, and where to build the equipment.

The fleet was based at Leigh, a township a few miles east of Warkworth, its owner Jake Watson. Larry phoned him the next evening, after he'd mulled the idea over all day and still found it absurd.

Larry explained about his evening classes, and his job. He said that he was prepared to leave his job, but only when the line was completed. They depended on him to see it through, he added.

'Hey… I don't expect you to walk out on them. But if you can get up here for a day or two, I'd like to talk to you about the project,' Jake said.

Larry hung up, wondering if this could be the beginning of something. How many other fishing fleets needed communication equipment? Would there be a market for amateur equipment? But where would he get components? From what he had heard and read, the government was unsupportive of small manufacturers. Which bolstered Mudgway's claim that farmers shouldn't be running the country. 'Better to run it with lawyers like they do in America,' he had said. 'You know already that they're crooks.' Larry wished Mary were here. While she didn't understand his aims, or half the time what he was talking about, usually her arguments made sense, or made him think. And there was nothing negative about her.

He waited for her on Saturday night – actually, early Sunday morning – when she came off the midnight shift. She surprised him when she put a hand on his shoulder – he had been indulging in further depression and hadn't heard her come.

'Hello, sweetie.'

Just her 'hello' and he warmed up inside. His doubts weakened.

The previous days, his thoughts had been of nothing but Jake's proposition, but as he weighed the pros and cons his enthusiasm had waned. Mary perceived his gloom.

They lay together. 'Something's on your mind, sweetie? What is it?'

He told her, explaining the many reasons why he shouldn't take the work and the few why he should. 'The problem is, I just can't walk into a shop and buy components. I believe – and old Mac agrees with me – that it will be years before the government will allow what they call non-essential products to be brought into the country. They want farm machinery and transmission line cable

– all that sort of thing. I should go to Australia. I hear it's better in Australia and, unlike America, they don't require a visa.'

She sat up. 'Australia! You're not serious.'

'I've been thinking about it. I spoke to a fellow in Sydney over the radio. He said that there's all kinds of openings over there. He said...'

'You're crazy! On the strength of one man's report you'd go to Australia!'

'Well...'

'And you say that I'm impulsive!'

'Well...'

'Listen, my little Frenchman, what you're proposing is utterly ridiculous and you know it. You have an opportunity to get started in something here and you'd throw it away for pie in an Australian sky! I don't understand you.'

This was Mary! And she should cover herself up when she lectures, he thought. She saw the direction of his eyes and crossed her arms.

'Behave! And you listen to me!' She pulled her knees up and girded them with her arms. 'I'll ask for a couple of days off. We'll go to this... wherever-it-is place and talk to this Jake. We'll look around Auckland for components. There's got to be somewhere to get them. And...'

She stopped speaking because he had kissed her.

She pulled away. 'Not until you've promised you'll see this man.'

'You know something?'

'What?'

'You're all right.'

She reached up to pull him to her. But paused.

'You haven't promised.'

'I promise.'

He kissed her again, nuzzled her neck and breasts.

'Stop fooling around,' she said. 'I've never known a person to waste so much time.'

SOON AFTER DAWN LARRY picked Mary up for the ride to Warkworth. She had dressed in slacks and a heavy cardigan. A brightly coloured scarf covered her head and was tied under her chin. 'You look beautiful,' he said, and he meant it.

She poked a little tongue at him.

'Compliments so early!' She climbed on to the pillion.

In Auckland she yelled into his ear, 'I'm hungry.'

'There's a Tip Top up the road...'

'A Tip Top! You're taking a girl away for the weekend, remember!' She talked into his ear. 'Crayfish and oysters, or no lolly tonight, my lord!'

Her smile was impish. He yearned to pull her to him. She may be wrapped up like an Eskimo, he thought, but it doesn't hide that something about her.

At the table he said, 'Big Mac gave me the address of a surplus dealer not far from here. Rumour has it he's a crook, but he's supposed to have equipment. Think he's worth a visit?'

'Try him, but if rumour says he's a crook you be careful, sweetie.' She squeezed his hand.

He felt the moment one of precious accord. He held her hand between his until she said, 'Are we going to eat or are we going to hold hands all day?'

Bernie Steinmetz was a war surplus wheeler-dealer who dealt mostly in radio equipment, but piles of bayonets in cracked leather scabbards, and rubber rafts, and mess kits, and water canteens, everything in higgledy-piggledy heaps about the floor, indicated that he dealt in money, too.

Bernie's dress matched his warehouse. The buttons of his partly fastened waistcoat didn't match the button holes and his top trouser buttons were left undone to accommodate his paunch. His shoes were missing the laces. His razor had missed patches of beard. He came toward them, washing his hands with air.

'Ah! May I help you?'

'I'd like to look around if you don't mind,' Larry answered, bewildered by the store's confusion.

'Not at all, me boy. Now… if you need help, you just let me know.' He continued his hand washing.

Larry poked among the heaps until, next to a pile of ammunition cases, he came upon a stack of New Zealand-made, war surplus radio equipment designated the zc1. Why not surplus equipment, he asked himself. He called to Bernie for prices.

Bernie had the business shrewdness of a Kasbah Arab. 'Make me an offer,' he proposed.

Larry was taken aback. He had fully but mistakenly believed that he had left that kind of bargaining overseas.

'No, the price!'

'Not so fast! You see…'

'Forget it!' Larry turned to the door.

'How many would you be wanting?' Bernie compromised.

Larry explained about the fishing boats. 'But the radios will have to prove suitable. If I could try one at the base and one on a boat, I would know. But first, how much are they?'

'I know what you're saying, but it's hard to be specific. You see, it depends on…'

'On what?' interrupted Mary.

'On many things…'

'Like what?'

'Well…'

'Like what you think you can get for them, eh?'

'Well, not exactly that. You see…'

'You want the business or not?' Mary demanded. She glared fiercely.

Bernie knew he'd met his own kind. He grinned.

'Well! Ain't she a spitfire! But let's not get upset about little things. I'm sure that we can work something out.'

They did. Bernie would supply two radios on consignment, with two weeks to test them, then Larry would either pay for them or return them. After that, Larry would pay thirty-three per cent down and the rest on completion of the installation, the time not to exceed three months.

As they were leaving, Bernie addressed Larry.

'A word of advice, boy. You let the lass do the negotiating with that boat fellow. You stick to the technical end of it.'

Larry mumbled his thanks. Mary blew him a kiss.

At the kerb, Larry, heretofore always proper in public, threw his arms about the negotiator. He hugged her tightly.

'You little beaut!' he said. 'Where in the hell did you learn to do that?'

'Do what?' she stalled. But she was pleased with him.

'Remind me to reward you,' he said with a grin.

'Here?' she answered, laughing.

'But what would you have done if he'd told you to go to hell?'

'Why would he do that? He wants the business, doesn't he? Sweetie, I don't see how you made it through the war without getting yourself killed! But do you know something?'

'What?'

'You're all right.'

He was content.

THE FOLLOWING AFTERNOON, LARRY and Mary, on the Velocette, passed the Puhoi exit, climbed the bush-girt hills, wound down through the stands of ponga ferns, and descended into Warkworth where Larry was to meet Jake Watson.

They entered the Warkworth Hotel, a stately, two-storey kauri building surrounded by a colonial-style veranda, its curved roof decorated at the eaves with wooden curlicues. The building was separated from the road by a green lawn, a huge Norfolk Island pine, and a neat, white picket fence.

'Here we are, my love,' he said, pulling the bike on to the footpath beneath the Norfolk pine.

In their room he said, 'Well, Mrs La Salle, it's time for your reward!'

'Mrs indeed!' but she kissed him and took off her cardigan.

They were to meet Jake at five-thirty. They came down the stairs at four-thirty which gave them an hour to explore Queen Street – more than enough time.

Nearly opposite the hotel was a veranda-fronted butcher shop, its parapet blazoned by a sculptured, painted Holstein bull that, probably for reasons of propriety, lacked the essentials such animals need to earn their keep. Though its body stood parallel to the parapet, its head was turned so that it commanded a broad view of the street below, through eyes the artist had painted large, life-like, and cleverly wistful.

Several times, Mary looked back.

'It's eerie, but those eyes follow us,' she said, shivering a little.

'Come on!'

'They do!'

He glanced back but failed to see what Mary saw.

They walked hand in hand past the fish and chip shop, the drapery, the garage on the corner of Mill Lane, the newspaper office on the opposite corner, to the bridge crossing the Warkworth river, and they stood at the rail.

'It's a nice little town,' he said, voicing his observation. 'Pretty,' she answered, 'but probably dull.'

He didn't know why, but her opinion disappointed him. But then, he allowed, after Rotorua, it probably would be dull. And that caused him to ask himself what she did with her spare time in Rotorua. They walked back to the hotel in silence; a little excitement had left his day.

As arranged they waited in the private bar. A man came in, looked around, and turned to leave.

'Mr Watson?' Larry said.

'Sorry. I didn't realise you'd not be alone.' He proffered his hand.

'This is Mary Peterson.'

'Mary. Pleased to meet you.' His eyes indicated approval.

They ordered drinks and chatted, and Larry told him about the zc1s. He explained that not only would the zc1s provide immediate coverage, they should yield valuable information towards a new and simpler design.

Jake showed immediate interest. An hour later, he agreed that he was prepared to give the zc1s a trial, especially if it meant that he could get an operating system sooner.

Then he asked, 'When your work with the Hydroelectric Department is done, I was hoping that you'd want to move to Warkworth – I mention that now because there's a building close by you may wish to look at before you return.'

Larry thought, move here! Then, well... why not? He liked what he had seen, and he would be near the work. Odd, until this moment, he had not considered that aspect. But Mary?

'Mary's in her final year of nursing,' he answered. 'I'd like to discuss it with her first.'

'A nurse, that's wonderful. You know, there's a maternity hospital here in town – they're always looking for nurses.'

'I'm hoping to work in maternity,' Mary proffered, and Larry was confident that everything was going to be all right after all.

Jake said, 'If you ride out to Leigh in the morning I'll show you the boats, then you'll get a better idea of things. If you can be there at eight...' He drew a map. 'Now what about some dinner?' he said.

'He's nice. I like him,' Mary said later, in their room. 'And I think you can trust him.'

But Larry's mind was on something else. It wouldn't wait.

'Mary, would you join me here?' He asked knowing full well that, really, what he was saying was, 'Mary, will you marry me?' though he wasn't sure that that's what he wanted yet.

Watching her face, he thought he saw it tense.

She started undressing before she replied. 'Sweetie, I'm awfully tired. Let's talk about it tomorrow if you don't mind. I worked last night, remember?' She finished undressing, climbed into bed, turned her back to him, and soon he heard her little snores.

He blamed himself that he had jumped the gun. He knew Mary well enough now to know that Mary did as Mary wanted. Unlikely she'd allow herself to be steered in a direction she was averse to taking.

He undressed and climbed in beside her. His desire was to put an arm around her, but a small resentment held his arm. He turned his back to hers and dreamed about fishing boats and factories and a house to live in. They should explore the beaches before they went back to Bruntwood, he decided. Haumoana beaches were stony. He wanted to live where there were sandy beaches. He'd teach their children to fish and swim. He'd buy a boat and they'd go sailing. And the last he remembered, he wondered why in the hell he was dreaming about children when he wasn't married yet.

WHITE FROST COVERED THE ground right down to the river.
'Brrr!' shivered Mary. 'I thought it was supposed to be warm in Warkworth?'

'I thought so too. Maybe this is unusual.'

They walked to the Bridge House for breakfast. On the bridge, leaning heavily on a crutch, was an old, white-whiskered man. He stared short-sightedly as they passed, pivoting on his crutch.

'Oh hip!' he called at them.

Larry stopped.

'I beg your pardon?'

The old fellow rolled a wad of spittle and let fly a stream that landed at Larry's feet.

'Oh hip!' he repeated.

'What the hell was all that about!' Larry exclaimed when they'd passed.

Mary laughed. 'The town's full of them,' she said.

'Full of them?'

'Crazies! Haven't you noticed? Half of them don't even speak English!'

'Oh come on!' But he remembered that last night in the bar some customers had funny accents.

At breakfast he said, 'I wonder where the building is he spoke about?'

'You mean Jake?'

'Yes. He said it was right in town here.'

'You're thinking quite seriously about coming here, aren't you?'

'Not really – not yet. But I have to think about the future.'

'Wonder what the hospital's like?' Mary said.

Larry put his fork down.

'Oh Mary!'

'Just wondering,' she said.

Jake was waiting for them. He saw Mary's cheeks, blue with cold. He saw the sweater.

'God! You should have something warmer than that on these cold mornings – on a bike! The wind must cut right through that thing. Here, come inside. Sit by the heater.'

It was an office of sorts. An electric heater burned in a corner. Jake moved oilskins from a chair and made to move the chair nearer the heater, but Mary waved him away.

'I'll stand,' she said. 'The seat on that bike isn't designed for gravel roads!' She smiled and stood close to the heater.

The men talked... and they talked. Mary brought the chair over and sat. She had trouble staying awake.

They inspected one of the boats and Larry worked out the antenna installation.

Back at the office, Jake said, 'Well, what do you think? You think you can manage it? I'm quite sure that if this works out all right there'll be others. I know the people up at Waipu. They have the same problems as we have, and I'm sure they'll be interested. They're a bunch of tight-arsed Scotsmen so they'll want to see a system working before they'll spend a penny, but once they see the worth of it, I'm sure they'll want in.'

'It'll be two months before I can leave my present job,' Larry answered, 'and it'll take a while to get moved.'

'But you'll do it?'

'Why not!' Larry spoke enthusiastically. But then, remembering Mary, he added, 'Mary's the one with the business brains. What do you think, Mary?'

'Some people spend all their lives thinking,' Mary replied. 'Others do it.' A typical Mary answer, Larry thought.

Jake waited for more. When it wasn't forthcoming, he said, 'Well put, young lady! Well put!

'Now here's what I suggest: Right near the pub in Warkworth there's a lawyer named John Arrf – that is A-R-R-F. He's the son-in-law of an old Puhoi Bohemian named Fritz Kler. For your information, Fritz owns half the town. The old fellow is getting on – must be in his eighties now – so John is handling his affairs – as much as the old man will let him. See John and tell him I sent you.'

They found the upstairs office. The sign on the door read,

JOHN V. ARRF

BARRISTER AND SOLICITOR

Mary said, 'What a funny name! How terrible to be a Mrs Arrf!' She was laughing when Larry knocked on the door.

'Come in!' said the voice.

The voice wore round, wire-rimmed glasses and a rumpled suit that had seen many a good meal.

'Hello, I'm Larry La Salle. Jake Watson suggested I see you. And this is Mary Peterson.'

'Ah…' answered John, his eyes on Mary's bosom. 'Ah yes… Jake.' He extended a limp hand. Larry smelled gin. The old bastard boozes on the job, he thought. He was tempted to squeeze the fish in his hand, but settled for light pressure.

'Please take a seat, both of you. Oh! Just put those books on the floor. Been meaning to put them away. Now, what may I do for you?'

Larry explained that he needed to rent a small building and he gave the reason why he needed it. He added that he also needed a place to live, a small bachelor's place, if he knew of anything that was available. He couldn't afford anything too expensive – not beginning a new business. Just the bare essentials.

'Ah!' said John again. 'And the young lady?' his eyes on the young lady's bosom.'Well…' What to say? They should've talked about it! He was ready to say that they weren't sure yet, but Mary broke in.

'I'm a nurse in my last year of training with three months to go,' she said. 'I'm going up to the hospital later to see if they'll have any openings. So you see, we can't answer your question yet.'

Larry warmed inside; would he ever know this girl?

'Ah!' said John. He took a flask from a jacket hanging on a rickety coat stand.

'I have a condition,' he explained. He didn't explain what the condition was. He took a spirit glass from the desk drawer and filled it.

'Ah!' he said again, and downed the conditioner in a swallow. It must have helped the condition for suddenly he smiled. He had just the buildings, he said. The description faltered when he got to looking at the top of Mary's dress and he lost his place, but he conveyed a passable picture of what the buildings were like, aided by only one additional glass of conditioner.

'Come. I'll take you to see them.' He sprang from the chair, grabbed his jacket, and took the stairs two at a time. 'Come on,' he called, 'they're not far.'

The first building was a disused bakery. A modern bakery stood alongside. The older building contained three brick ovens, each of which featured two cast-iron doors. John opened a top door. 'Here's where you put the loaves.' He opened a lower door. 'And here's where you put the coke.' He pointed to wooden paddles on wall brackets, each eight or nine feet long. 'You slide the bread in and out with them.'

Larry wanted to say that he wasn't going into the bakery business, but John was wound up. When there was danger of his running down he nipped conditioner from the flask.

'It needs a little fixing up,' he explained, coming back to the purpose of the visit, and he showed them where the roof leaked over the ovens. But a nimble chap like Larry shouldn't have any trouble nipping up on the roof and fixing it.

Behind the bakery was a small, old cottage. It appeared to be held up by the ivy that grew over it. Larry's foot went through the porch floor. John brushed that away as one of those things that a bright young chap could soon fix with a hammer and nail.

The inside showed evidence of the need for a nimble chap to nip up on the roof here, too, but by and large Larry liked what he saw.

'What kind of rent are you asking,' he ventured.

'Ah!' said John, 'a good point!'

Mary moved in. 'Come on, give us a break. This man's been at the war. A nice man like you wouldn't take advantage of him now, would you?' She put a hand on his arm. 'Be a good sport,' she coaxed further.

'Ah!' John said. 'Whatever gave you the idea that I wouldn't be anything but ethical? You see, I don't own the buildings. They're owned by a Mr Fritz Kler, who just happens to be my father-in-law.' At this point it was apparent that John found the conversation depressing, his face lost some of its former conviviality. He took the conditioner from his pocket, held it to the light. It held only a drop.

'Ah!' he said, his look crestfallen. Then, 'Let's go back to the bakery.' He set out at a brisk trot.

He opened an oven door, and using a paddle, brought forth a bottle of Gordon's gin. He downed a sizeable portion. 'Now the rents...' and he suggested a sum that set them both agog.

'You darling man!' Mary said. She hugged him to her.

'No need to start paying until you get here,' he said, 'but that's between us girls!' He giggled like one.

Out on the street, watching them walk up the pathway, was the old man of the crutch.

'Oh hip!' he said.

'Hello, Percy,' said John.

'He's not the full quid,' he explained as they walked back to the office. 'Years ago he was in an accident at the cement works. He's harmless enough though.'

'Sweetie! I've never seen anything like this place!' Mary said later.

'Nor me,' Larry answered, laughing. 'But you know something? I think I'm going to like it!'

'Oh hip!' Mary said.

They were asleep, cuddled into each other, when the shooting started; two explosions close together, then two more. Then more. They could see nothing from the window. Larry climbed on to the veranda.

'I can't see anything,' he reported, 'just a man pushing a wheelbarrow.'

He was on his way back to bed when the street light was blown out.

'Someone shot the light out!' he said.

'Didn't I tell you they're crazy? But come to bed. Sounds like it's all over now, whatever it was. Besides, it's cold. Come on...'

APARTY CELEBRATING THE COMPLETION of the transmission line began in the Hamilton pub. It ended at Gladys's at three o'clock in the morning when the constable, responding to complaints from her neighbours, broke it up. It sparked anew at Bruntwood, and continued during the loading of the trucks until they pulled out for Wellington. The dog Kuri, his feet on the tailgate, barked a shrill goodbye. Sitting on the Velocette ready to leave, Larry, who intended to spend the rest of the day and the night with Mary before he rode to Warkworth, sadly watched them go. At that moment he came close to changing his plans and going with them.

But then the dog Kuri leapt from the truck. He landed heavily and rolled, picked himself up and ran limping back to Larry.

The men yelled at the driver. The truck stopped and backed up.

But when Grunter tried to catch the dog he ran off. I'm not going, was his message and Grunter left without him. Yet, when Larry wired an apple box to the Velocette's carrier behind the pillion seat and plopped the dog in it, he stayed. Except that he didn't seem to like the wind in his face or eyes – he turned his back to it at speed – he acted content enough. He barked his pleasure during the ride to Rotorua.

Mary decided that it was the wind in his eyes he didn't like. Next morning she tied a rubber band to a pair of cheap, child's, white-rimmed sunglasses and stretched the band around the dog's head. He was a curious sight and drew many a look when, driving through Rotorua next morning, Larry left for Auckland.

Larry's first stop was at Bernie Steinmetz's warehouse. Bernie looked up from the loading platform.

'God in heaven! What've we got here!'

'He doesn't like the wind in his eyes,' Larry explained.

'Don't tell me you traded that beautiful girl you had with you last time for this sausage material!'

Larry laughed. 'Hardly! I'm on my way to Warkworth. Mary will follow when her training's completed. Would you mind if I left the dog here for an hour? I have to go downtown.'

'It's all right with me. Better tie him up, though. If he wanders out to the street he'll get run over.'

Larry drove to the American Consulate. He didn't get past the Consulate's secretary.

'I'm sorry, Mr La Salle, we have no new information. Don't lose heart though. Hang in there.'

Hang in there! A surge of depression suddenly blemished what had started out as a day of new hope and fresh ambition.

On the way back to Bernie's, he speculated about what he would do if by some chance his application were approved. And what about Mary? He couldn't take Mary with him if they were not married.

As he turned into Bernie's street, he wondered if the wily Bernie would wriggle out of the deal they had made without Mary there to keep him in line. But when Bernie gave his word, it seemed that he stuck with it. Larry signed the invoices on the understanding that the equipment would be put on the first bus to Warkworth.

Riding the Velocette into Warkworth's Queen Street and noticing that people turned to stare, he experienced a sudden thrill of importance. Perhaps they had heard that he was starting a factory in Warkworth. Prolonging the pleasure, he rode the length of Queen Street and back before parking the bike in front of John Arrf's office. Only then did he realise that it was the dog Kuri they were staring at. Obviously, Warkworth dogs didn't wear sunglasses. He ordered the dog to dismount, but the dog refused to leave the box until Larry removed the glasses. Then the dog ran to the nearest post and without fanfare, marked his territory.

John Arrf had little to say this day. Larry paid the rents and received the keys. Strange fellow, Larry determined, shaking Arrf's limp hand on the deal.

Old Percy stood at the entrance to the lane that went to the cottage. The excited dog made an exploratory inspection of the old man's trousers. Percy lifted his crutch. Tail between his legs, the dog moved to a lilac bush.

Larry surveyed the cottage's interior. A bed of sorts. Instead of slats, a sagged mattress made from coiled springs and connecting wires. A hundred children must have been conceived on this bed. He took tools from the bike's toolbox and tightened what would tighten.

Head down and rear end up, he didn't see the visitor until his shadow crossed the room. Before he could straighten, Percy's 'Oh hip!' caused him to do it involuntarily; he bumped his head on a shelf.

'Percy! Do you have to sneak up on a bloke like that! You scared the shit out of me!'

Percy rolled a ball of spit, turned his head toward the dog Kuri and shot, but didn't connect.

Larry looked for a broom. Some water, he thought, and the floor will grow mushrooms.

He turned to the door.

'Move, Percy. I have things to buy.'

Percy stood aside. When Larry looked back, as the dog tried to leave the room Percy poked at him with his crutch.

At the furniture shop, Larry checked out the mattresses.

'You the new man that's moved in across the road?' asked the salesman, a skinny little dark fellow.

'Yes,' Larry answered tersely. There was a prying aura about the pinched sparrow of a man that Larry instinctively didn't like. 'Pleased to meetcha,' the salesman said, ignoring the curtness if, indeed, he had even noticed it. 'I see you picked out a double mattress.'

'That's what people usually put on a double bed, I believe,' Larry answered curtly. 'And now, perhaps you'll be good enough to give me a hand to get this thing across the road.'

Larry's next stop was the hardware shop. He bought a broom, an electric kettle and dishes. While the young lady brought them to the counter, he studied her figure. 'Add to that a bucket and scrubbing brush,' he said. He was tempted to add that if she were free after work she'd be welcome to help him clean up his cottage, but Mary intruded upon his thoughts and he asked for Jeyes Fluid disinfectant instead.

'I hope you'll like Warkworth,' she said. Larry sensed that she was eager for conversation, but Mary was still in his mind. He took the hardware back to the bakery and returned to the grocer's.

The grocer was a bald-headed, rotund little man with a round, round face and a sham smile. He said, 'Ah, Mr La Salle, I've heard about you. Pleased to meet you at last. And is your sweet little wife with you? I'm told that she's a dear, dear girl.'

'She would be, no doubt, if I had one,' Larry said. 'Now, I'd like a pound of bacon, a dozen eggs...'

He cleaned the cottage then started on the old bakery. But no matter how often he swept, within minutes, a coating of fine, white dust – flour he presumed – covered everything. Among the sweepings were hosts of black seeds. Closer inspection showed that the bakery supported a population of mice. Supposing that the mice had left other residue, Larry washed off the benches with Jeyes Fluid. Even Kuri was subjected to a long-overdue bath.

Remembering his visit to the cottage with John, he inspected the oven for the lawyer's cache. A sudden shadow fell across the floor. He turned to the doorway. 'Percy! You've got to stop this creeping up on a bloke.' Later, he met the Auckland bus and signed the receipt the young clerk gave him. She smiled.

'You're Larry?'

'Yes, that's right.'

'I'm Beverley. It's nice to have someone new in town. It's been pretty dull since the Americans left.'

What Americans, he wondered.

Old Percy watched him unpack the radios, but except for a random 'Oh hip!' he watched in silence. The right kind of supervisor to have around, Larry thought.

He ate pork and beans on toast that evening, washed the cottage floor for the third time and now, tired, he undressed and slipped between the new sheets, on the new mattress. Though he had placed a flour sack on the floor for the dog, the dog opted for the bed. Twice Larry kicked him to the floor. The dog waited. When the master slept, he returned to the bed.

Larry dreamed of Mary, who somehow turned into Beverley from the bus depot. His hand was down the neck of Beverley's blouse when she turned back into Mary. She said, 'If I catch you doing that again, buster, you'll be deader than a dodo!'

LARRY HAD INSTALLED ZC1 transceivers in five fishing boats. He worked on radio number six.

Old Percy stood at the door, impassive and silent – except for his once-in-a-while 'Oh hip!' Once he'd called out, 'Me boy! Me boy!' Taken by surprise, Larry had glanced up from the bench, but the old man's face contained nothing but a look of placidity and not a thing to suggest that he had said a word. Squeezing past him, Larry bought pastries from the new bakery. He passed one to the old man, who ate it without a word. Larry handed him another and he ate that too. It became habit then, each day, around three in the afternoon, to feed him.

Larry drank tea with the pastries. One day he put his cup on the bench near the door. When he remembered to get it, the cup was empty. He wasn't sure – did it have something in it when he put it down? The next day he made two cups. He put one by the door. The old man leaned his crutch against the bench, took the cup in both hands, and drank greedily, making great slurping sounds. After that Larry regularly made two cups. A problem was the old man's attitude toward the dog Kuri. He'd wait until the dog was in the doorway then lash out with his crutch. It was a game the dog won four times, but on the fifth, the crutch caught him on the rump and bowled him over and over. Larry looked up in time to catch a malicious grin on the old man's face, but in moments it was gone. Had he imagined it? 'Percy! You get the hell out of here! Out! Go home!'

The old man swung his crutch.

'You old bastard! You'd hit me, would you?'

Larry took a bread paddle from the wall. He poked it at Percy. 'Out!'

Percy left. Larry heard his 'Oh hip!' from the corner.

He coaxed the dog from behind the ovens.

'You can come out now, you miserable fleabag.'

The dog understood the endearing address. He came, but to play it safe he kept his tail – what ragged part there was of it – protectively between his legs.

Larry rubbed him between the ears and that night didn't chase him off the bed. And set a precedent: the dog slept there every night after that.

As usual, the old man showed up the next morning.

'So!' Larry said. 'You hit my dog again and I'll belt you. You understand me?' He handed him shortcake.

He didn't mean it, of course. Why would he hit a crippled old man, only three bob in the pound?

Since the beating, the dog no longer played the game. If he wanted out when Percy was at the door, he whined at Larry's feet until Larry escorted him out, telling Old Percy, 'Out of the way! Let him through.' Old Percy made tentative fending-off motions with his crutch, but he let him be.

Beverley Plenkovich from the bus depot was dark-haired, slender, a shyish girl, without Mary's boldness and – Larry couldn't help noticing – without her bosom. Yet, she had an aura of femininity he couldn't stay away from. He made excuses: 'Anything for me today?' to which she'd answer, 'I don't remember seeing anything – but let me look.' Not that so many boxes or parcels came that she didn't remember them.

It was Beverley who told him about John Arrf's problems: his wife, his father-in-law, Old Fritz, and booze, and how every six to eight months or so, convinced that the sign of the bull was under Old Fritz's orders to spy on him, John shot up the butcher shop. The last time he had threatened to shoot the constable. The constable warned the father-in-law that he was losing patience with the errant lawyer. If it happened again, he would lock him up and charge him.

Old Fritz was losing it of late. When he had tried talking to his daughter, she turned on him, calling him senile, a stupid old man. The sooner he was dead and buried the better for everyone.

That night, Fritz went to bed an hour earlier than usual. Somewhere between midnight and seven in the morning when his daughter took his tea in, he died. The funeral was the greatest event to happen in the area since the Japanese surrender. People came from everywhere – Bohemians from Puhoi, Dalmatians from Dargaville and Henderson, and the locals. The Maoris came too, most of them old and crippled with arthritis, one of them blind – fellow sawyers from the old days. Then, from all over the country, came the descendants of Fritz Kler, perhaps a hundred of them: thirteen children, grandchildren, great-grandchildren and one great-great-grandchild.

The morning of the funeral, John Arrf hustled into the old bakery building.

'Pardon me. I have to get something,' he apologised to Larry. He slid a bread paddle into the number two oven, withdrew a bottle of Gordon's gin, gulped down an impressive portion, and filled a silver-plated flask he took from the inner pocket of his jacket. Then he was gone. Larry looked in number two. Two bottles. He opened numbers one and three. Two bottles in number three.

Fritz Kler had specified that he was to be buried with his fellow Bohemians at Pukapuka, near Puhoi. The service was in Warkworth.

The cars parked all the way up Church Hill and beyond. After the relatives were seated, the friends were ushered in. John had argued with his wife about where people should sit. She had wanted the respectable people, those who came to the funeral in modern cars and three-piece suits, to sit at the front. John sat his father-in-law's Puhoi cronies in the front – men who walked with canes made from bush supplejack, and wore the same suits they'd worn to funerals and weddings for the past forty years or more. He sat the Maori pit sawyers who, more than anybody, had helped old Fritz make his fortune, next to and behind them. The 'respectable' people he let fend for themselves.

The church was filled and people stood about the entrance, among them members of the Plenkovich family: Mr and Mrs Plenkovich, daughter Beverley of the bus depot, two younger sisters and four brothers – four little bastards, it was rumoured. It was natural that, as Larry knew few people in Warkworth, he should gravitate towards Beverley. They got into light conversation. Only when people emerged from the vestibule did they realise that the service was over.

By the right of dominance, the youngest child, John Arrf's wife, was to follow the hearse in their car, an immaculate, pre-war English Rover with a wooden dash and leather bucket seats – as rightly befitted the daughter of one of Northland's wealthiest. John opened the door for his wife, probably the only time since their marriage that he had done so. A possum jumped from the interior. Mrs John Arrf screamed and fainted, conveniently as it happened, into her husband's arms.

John took out his handkerchief and, with an exaggerated flourish, wiped off the Rover's leather seats. He inspected the subterranean depths against further – probably Plenkovich – surprises and bade his recovered spouse to enter. There was nothing he could do about the skunk-like smell the possum had left.

The death of the father-in-law put new life into the son-in-law. When they arrived home after the funeral and his wife attacked him about the possum, he turned his back on her, went to the garden shed, and returned with his shotgun. He poked it into one of her ears.

'The next bloody time I fire this, it will be to blow your bloody brains out!' he said. Having made his point, he opened the cupboard, withdrew a glass, and emptied his flask into it. He stood defiantly in front of her while he drank it.

BEVERLEY WATCHED WHEN MARY stepped down from the bus. She turned away when Mary planted a soft and lingering kiss on Larry's lips. She went inside so that they could not see her tears, and pretended that she was busy with papers.

Mary rented a room near the hospital, not a real room – a boarded-in veranda. It came equipped with a tiny sink, a miniature hot plate, a single iron-framed bedstead without a mattress, and nothing else. She shared a bathroom with the landlady and the family.

The veranda's floor had a three-inch slope to it which would have prevented the rain from puddling in the days before the wall was built. Mary found herself walking with a list. If she dropped something it rolled under the bed. When she crawled under the bed to retrieve an earring, she found several coins and what she thought was a suppository, but it might have been something else as the ants had been at it.

Larry brought her suitcases from the bus depot.

They looked at mattresses. The salesman, the same skinny little dark fellow who had attended Larry previously, followed them about the shop. He coughed into his hand, a prelude to his saying, 'May I be of assistance?'

'No!' Mary said, not looking up.

'Later perhaps,' Larry said, wondering at her abruptness.

'Don't be nice to him!' she demanded, not caring if she was heard. 'He's a bloody tippy-toes!'

Larry looked at her in surprise.

'A tippy-toes?'

'A tippy-toes! A fairy! Don't you know a bloody fairy when you see one?'

He hadn't known. 'Come on, Mary!' He wished she'd lower her voice. 'How can you say that?'

'You can't tell…!'

She let his hand go and returned to business.

'This will do,' she said, deciding quickly as usual.

They bought sheets, blankets and utensils, and Mary moved in. Later, in the private bar, Larry brought her up to date on what had happened in the town. He told her about John Arrf, explaining about the shots they'd heard the first night, and that John's father-in-law had died, leaving everything to his children in a trust he had appointed John Arrf to manage.

He didn't mention that he'd taken the Plenkovich girl at the bus depot to the firemen's ball held in the Patriotic Hut the Americans had used on R and R during the war. Nor that he had walked with her along the river front afterwards. Like the dog Kuri, he had an innate sense of self-preservation. He told her that he'd sold radios in Waipu and contacted a company in Auckland that made VHF radios for taxis and police cars, and that he was trying to get the Northland franchise.

They went to the cottage. The dog Kuri ran excited circles

around her and jumped for attention.

They made love. Larry told her that he had missed her and he meant it. She held him. 'And I missed you too, sweetie,' she told him. They took turns at kicking the dog off the bed.

When they slept the dog jumped back.

EXCEPT FOR THE DAYS he travelled to Waipu or to Auckland, Larry's life had settled into a routine. Whether Mary spent the night with him depended upon her shift at the hospital. They tried to be discreet. He'd take her home in the early hours, before it was light or, if she'd been on the late shift, he'd pick her up when she came off duty in the early morning. She'd sleep at the cottage until noon, leaving at one or so in the afternoon when she thought people were too busy to notice. He hinted that if they were married, she wouldn't have to be sneaking out like this and they'd get more sleep, but she turned the conversation to something else.

Beverley was frostily polite since Mary came. Her being so polite made Larry penitent. But there was nothing he could do or say that would make things different.

There had been a dangerous moment, late one afternoon, when he'd walked with Mary. The dog Kuri ran ahead. Beverley backed out from the depot's front door to close and lock it. She didn't see them. The dog ran to her. She bent to pat him. She saw Larry with Mary. The smile froze on her face. She pushed the dog down and walked quickly away.

Mary looked quizzically at her back.

'Boy!' she said. 'If looks could kill!'

Once, they had gone to the depot to pick up equipment. When they came out, Mary said, 'What did you do to that one, sweetie?' His look was genuine; he was surprised at how discerning this Mary of his could be, not at the question. Fortunately she misread him.

'All right now, don't get upset! With that French blood in you I'd be surprised if you hadn't got up to something before I got here.' She said it with a shake of her head that set her hair swirling. She thrust an arm through his.

During the evenings he worked on the radio that one day would replace the ZC1s. Around ten he talked to Big Mac over the radio. Others joined them, turning the contact into a sort of miniature, technical brains trust. Through the day he made notes of his technical problems, findings and conclusions. He discussed them with the group. One evening, a member of the brains trust said, 'Why don't you put some of that material into an article and send it to *Break-In*?' *Break-In* was a New Zealand radio amateurs' publication.

He started an article, but halfway into it felt that he didn't know enough about writing. He enrolled in an evening class.

Every morning Percy stood in the doorway and accepted tea and whatever else he was given. His stays were erratic. Sometimes he'd stay all day, on and off talking to himself; other days, he'd leave at noon. If the dog was at the door when Percy came, he'd wave the crutch threateningly and move closer, waving and prodding, until the dog moved.

He was gentle to Mary. He moved to let her through – something he never did for Larry, unless he was ordered. She responded with a smile and a 'Thank you, Percy'. After she had gone, he usually held an animated conversation with himself, though what he said was gibberish.

Mary loved the work at the hospital.

'Larry, it's so wonderful to see a baby born. Sometimes I have to say to myself, "There has to be a God!" '

She wasn't religious but she was tolerant of those who were, though sometimes she baited the Mormons who came to the door.

She was a happy girl and Larry was in love with her.

Mary had worked at the hospital four months when she turned up at the bakery one day at a time when she was usually on duty. She shooed Old Percy from the doorway and closed the door. Larry looked up, surprised. He could tell from her face something was terribly wrong.

'Mary! What is it?'

She threw her arms about him.

'Oh Larry!' she said. 'Larry…' She put her head on his shoulder and sobbed.

'Mary! For goodness sake! What's the matter?'

'I'm pregnant!'

The possibility of this happening had flitted through his mind, but he'd reasoned that if she became pregnant, she would marry him. So now they'd have to talk about it.

'Oh, Mary!' He hugged her in return. 'What's so bad about having a baby? I love you and now we can get married! We'll find a better house…'

'No!' She pulled away.

Larry had long had a curiosity about her past; she had to be hiding something. The assertive 'No!' made the anger well up within him. He forced himself to be calm.

'Look, we have to talk about things whether you like it or not! You've been putting me off for too long. Let's go to the house. We'll sit like two sensible people and talk about it. I'll make tea.'

Old Percy was at the door.

'Go away, Percy!' Larry knew it was wrong to take his frustration out on the old man, but for the life of him he couldn't help himself. Percy shuffled back down the lane to the road.

They sat on the bed.

'Mary, why won't you talk about things?' He held her and smoothed her hair. 'Whatever you say, it's not going to stop me loving you.'

'There's nothing to talk about,' she said.

'You're going to have a baby and there's nothing to talk about?'

He shouted. 'What's the matter with you?' He pulled away. She pulled him back.

'Don't! It's not you. I love you, Larry – believe me I do – although I swore I'd never let it happen to me – it just happened. But marriage! People change when they get married. My mother and father fought like a cat and dog. And look at the Arrfs.'

'But what about my parents? Look, you're upset. Give yourself time to think about it. It's not the worst thing that can happen to two people who love each other – to get married. Now what do you say?' He lifted her chin. 'Think about it, huh?'

She looked at her watch. 'I have to go!'

'Mary, you're impossible!'

He took her back to the hospital on the Velocette.

'Think about it,' he said again, when he let her off.

'Yes, sweetie! I'll think about it!'

He watched her walk up the steps, through the doors. She didn't look back.

RITA TOMLINSON AND HER mother lived in a cottage on the road behind Queen Street, a stone's throw, more or less, from the cottage in which Larry lived. Larry had seen Rita playing with other children and he'd noted her beauty, her skin blushed with Polynesian, her eyes dark and expressive.

A few days after she had disclosed her pregnancy, Mary said, 'I've told you about Ngaire. She works at the hospital with me. That's her daughter, R: you've seen playing out in the lane. It's time you met her.'

They visited Ngaire and drank tea. Larry was enamoured of

her beauty and thought that he had never met a more ethereal person. Later, Mary told him that Ngaire had looked after Old Percy without payment, in his hut down by the river, when he had contracted pneumonia a few years back.

Mary avoided talking about the wedding date. The last time Larry had brought it up, she'd turned on him.

'Stop harassing me.' She flounced out the doorway. He was reluctant now to mention it again. Six weeks after she had told him that she was pregnant she said that she was taking the bus to Auckland to get a few things. Larry worked in Leigh that day. He didn't get back until nine.

Rita saw him pull in. She came running.

'Mum wants to see you,' she said, 'it's urgent!'

Larry hurried through the lane to her house. He knocked at the door.

'Oh Larry... Mary's in Greenlane Hospital in Auckland. She...'

'Hospital! What happened?' His mind was a sudden turmoil. What could have happened?

'She lost the baby. Go and see her, Larry, she needs you.'

Mary lay white and still.

'She's sleeping,' the nurse whispered. He waited in a chair, dozing, but alert for the sound of her waking.

It was near dawn when he heard her.

'Hello, sweetie,' she said.

He took her hand.

'Mary!' So inadequate, but it was not in him to say more. Even resting in bed she seemed possessed of a sureness he didn't have. He leaned and kissed her forehead.

'Sweetie,' she said, 'I'm sorry.'

'Sorry! You couldn't help it, darling. These things happen.'

She closed her eyes. Never had he been more consumed with love.

'I love you,' he said. He kissed her again. She smiled. Then she slept.

The doctor came.

'Are you her boyfriend?' he asked.

'Yes,' Larry answered.

'Well, just wait outside for a moment. I'll be with you.'

Later he said, 'Let's take a little walk, shall we?'

They walked to a lounge at the end of the passageway.

'You know we've had to report this to the police... It's the law, you know.'

'The police! I don't understand...'

'You are – or you were – the father, is that right?'

'Yes, of course – we're getting married. But what's this about the police?'

'You didn't know it was an abortion?'

'An abortion!'

'Yes, an abortion. She's lost a lot of blood.'

'An abortion!' He thought quickly. 'She said she was coming to Auckland to get a few things. An abortion!'

So that's why she wouldn't talk about a wedding!

'Look... I know nothing about an abortion and, by God, she must have known that I wouldn't have gone along with it! An abortion!' He was angry now.

'Listen, young man,' the doctor held his arm, 'she's a sick woman. Let her rest. You go on home now and get some sleep. When she's back on her feet, you can sort your differences out. All right?'

Larry nodded. He didn't want to stay anyway. He didn't remember riding home. He knew that he must have ridden through the main part of Auckland, when people were going to work, but he had no recollection of it. He remembered thinking that today was rent day and that he mustn't forget to pay it, but when he arrived at the cottage, he lay on the bed and slept.

Since Mary's coming, the dog Kuri could not be sure that he'd be welcomed on the bed. This day he sensed was different. He jumped upon the bed, confident he could stay, and snuggled against his master.

The dog Kuri scratched and whined to be let out. Larry had to

97

force him from the door in order to open it.

'I know how you feel,' he sympathised, realising that he had the same urgent need. He looked at his watch. Five o'clock! He'd slept all day! No wonder he felt drugged. He barely knew what he was doing. A shower might clear his head.

The cottage boasted an enamelled cast-iron bathtub on decorative legs shaped like lion's feet. When Larry had first rented the cottage, he'd rigged up a shower head and curtains. This afternoon he elected to shower with hot water and rinse off with cold. While he soaped and rinsed, he thought about Mary's duplicity, and because he hadn't put the curtain inside the tub, the water ran down the curtain to the floor. It ran under the tub and out into the kitchen.

How could she have done it? And he'd been stupid enough to believe that she loved him. He stepped on to the wet floor and cursed. He mopped the floor with the bath mat and a towel and the flour sack that was the kitchen mat. Then he pulled on his underpants and trousers. In the kitchen he plugged in the electric kettle. When a shadow fell across the doorway, he cursed again. He was about to call out 'Not now, Percy!' but it was Ngaire. She saw his mood and was uncertain.

'How is she?' she asked, wary.

'Ngaire! I thought it was Old Percy. She's all right, I suppose. The doctor says that she'll be okay.'

'Oh, thank goodness. I was worried.'

'You knew that she had an abortion?'

'Only after it had happened.'

She paused.

'Larry, truly, I'm sorry, but for both your sakes, don't be too hard on her. She's a troubled girl in spite of her bravado.' He remembered his manners. 'I'm sorry, Ngaire. Come in. I've just put the kettle on. Please, take a chair.'

He poured the boiling water into the teapot. 'But why didn't she talk to me about it? That's what I don't understand. I know she's dodged the issue, about us getting married, I mean, but I thought that… well, with a baby coming.' He broke off. 'I know

I don't have much to offer…'

'Oh Larry! Don't start blaming yourself! Really. You have to realise that Mary isn't your everyday girl. Mary's ambitious. I wonder if you know how ambitious she is?'

'She killed our baby! I can never forgive her for that.' The dog Kuri barked. 'Go away, Percy!' Larry yelled, without looking up. The shuffle moved away. He heard the 'Oh hip!' when Percy reached the street.

'Maybe she thinks it's all right, but I call it murder,' he said.

H E HAD WONDERED HOW he would bring Mary home. He didn't think she would be well enough to travel on the bus, and obviously he couldn't bring her on the Velocette. He was pondering the problem when he called on John Arrf to pay the rent.

'I'm sorry I'm late,' he apologised.

'That's all right, my boy,' John replied, 'I understand. This is a small town, you know.' He left the rest unsaid and wrote the receipt.

'I want you to know that you have my sympathy, and…' He saw Larry's ire. 'Now let me finish! How are you going to get her home? If you don't have the means, it'll give me pleasure to drive you down and back. We can put cushions and blankets in the back for her.'

Larry was overwhelmed. After all he'd heard and thought about the man. And as far as he could see, there were no strings.

'It's the least I can do,' John said, and Larry felt remorse that he had looked for a catch.

Mary looked stunningly beautiful. Small roses had come back to her cheeks. Her overall pallor suited her.

Ngaire had given him clothes from Mary's room. He recognised the dress as the one she had worn to Hawke's Bay, and when she was dressed in it, he wished that he could clap his hands and go back to then. Instead he said, 'You look beautiful, Mary.' In spite of what had happened, he meant it.

John Arrf said, 'That she does, my boy!'

Mary's eyebrows had lifted when she'd seen John.

They took her to Ngaire's.

'She's going to need a week of complete rest,' Ngaire had said, 'and she won't get it if she has to fend for herself.' To lessen the nature of her generosity, Ngaire explained that she had holidays due.

Larry saw Mary each day. They talked generalities. He so wanted to ask her 'Why? Why?' but something about her forbade it. He was surprised, then, that on the fourth day after her return, she broke into tears and said, 'I made a perfect arse of myself, didn't I?'

He felt midway between saying, 'Yes, you did!' and, 'It's all right, sweetheart, I forgive you.' Instead, he said, 'These things happen.' He knew full well that they were just words, non-committal and dishonest, that they covered his true feelings. He would never forgive her.

Her face hardened. He sensed then that there would be no further opportunity to bring them together, to recapture their old closeness. But for the life of him, he couldn't bring himself to say anything different.

He turned to his work. Though he often hated his evening classes, he realised when the course was over that he had learned from it.

He wrote an article. It was printed as he had written it. He surged with confidence and began a second article.

On the air, Mac said, 'Hey! I liked your article. A nice presentation. You should try for the American magazines.'

'You're kidding!' Larry answered, but that evening, as he lay in bed, he thought about it. Perhaps he'd try.

Three weeks after she had gone back to work, Mary came to

see him. It was five in the evening. He was working on a radio he had to install the next day.

'Sweetie, I'm cooking you a dinner. Don't be too long out here.' She was the old Mary. He knew that there was more than dinner in the offing.

'I'll be in as soon as I've fixed this radio,' he said. His inclination was to forget the radio but he had promised it.

The problem proved difficult. When he looked at his watch, he was startled at the time.

The meal was covered with an inverted plate. A candle burned. A note beside the plate said, 'I once told you that you'd like your bloody old wireless better than me.'

To hell with the meal, he thought. She could have called him. But then he thought, I'll ride up and tell her I'm sorry. He blew out the candle, put the dog Kuri in the apple box and started the bike. He drove up the hill towards the boarding house, slowing to a stop at the school. He turned around. 'To hell with her!'

He spoke to the dog, 'Kuri, let's take a ride.'

They rode to the Sandspit.

Near the boat loading pier, at the water's edge, he threw the dog a stick, and when it was returned he threw it into the water.

Why hadn't she called him as once she would have done? Was it over between them? How he missed her. But how he hated what she had done.

It was too dark to continue the game with the dog. He put the dog back in the box, and headed home.

He took the covering plate from the meal. His favourite vegetables: carrots, parsnips and silver beet; and a lamb chop. He picked at the carrots but couldn't develop a hunger. He took the plate to the door and set it down. The dog Kuri wagged his ragged tail and began with the chop.

He walked to the pub. Except for John Arrf, the customer side was empty. Larry had heard that since Old Fritz had died John often came in. He wondered if John still had his binges.

'G'day, my boy,' John greeted. 'Still working hard?'

'Yes,' Larry answered, 'but not tonight.'

'Well, I'm sure you know the old adage about all work and no play making Larry a dull boy. Don't overdo it.'

'Not tonight!' Larry answered, raising his glass.

The proprietor was impatient. After Larry's second drink he said, 'Gentlemen, let's not get started in on a session. It's late.'

Larry rose from the stool. 'I have to work tomorrow,' he said.

'Don't we all,' John agreed, finishing his glass.

Outside, John pointed to the butcher shop's wooden bull. 'You know, I used to think that the old man – my father-in-law that is – put that beast up there to spy on me.'

Larry laughed. 'Mary says that its eyes follow her.'

John turned sharply.

'She does, does she! Very perceptive of the girl. Very perceptive indeed.' He was silent until Larry turned down Bakery Lane.

'Good night, my boy,' he said.

'Good night,' Larry answered.

John continued up Queen Street. Larry turned and stared at the bull, dimly illuminated by the street lamp. To him, the eyes were paint on wood. But, he remembered, not everyone saw the same patterns in colour-blind test charts. Obviously, John and Mary saw something up there that he didn't.

He turned down the lane to the cottage.

'Come on, fleabag,' he called. 'Time to call it a day.'

He dreamed that he was shooting at the bull with a rifle, but suddenly the bull was Mary. She screamed at him. 'For God's sake! Why are you shooting at me?' He awoke startled. It was so real. In the morning he couldn't shake off the feeling that he had shot at her. Passing where Bakery Lane joined Main Street, he slowed. He had to look at it. And of course it was whole. Not that he really expected anything else. But he was relieved, none the less.

THE NIGHTS WERE WARM. This night, a hint of rain threatened the air. The sounds of the bush – fronds chafing against fronds, the hum of myriad insects – and a full moon, made the evening mysterious and beautiful.

Larry stood at the bridge, peering into the water. The water was turbulent near the waterfall.

Old Percy's crutch scraped along the footpath.

'Percy! What are you doing out so late?'

The old man scratched his whiskers. He answered Larry's question with a vacant, placid look.

'Time you were in bed,' Larry told him.

The dog Kuri had retreated to the other side of the bridge. He waited, alert.

Percy turned and shuffled back. Opposite the Ford agency he called out an 'Oh hip!' Then, except for the insects, Larry had the evening to himself.

He watched the eddying waters, silvered by the moon. He missed Mary. God, how he missed her. He remembered how it felt to have his hand on the soft skin of her thigh. He thought of how, when he'd just dozed off, she'd ask, 'Are you awake?' and he'd reply, 'I am now! What is it?' And she'd start to tell him something, but fall asleep before she had finished.

Reluctantly, he returned to the cottage; the dog Kuri stayed close to his feet. He wondered how the gang was getting along in Wellington. Windy Wellington they called it and, in his experience, cold Wellington too. He was pleased he hadn't gone with them – in spite of what had happened between him and Mary.

His sleep was deep, beyond the dreaming stage. He was slow to emerge from it.

'Move over,' she said. 'Do you want all the bloody bed?'

'My God! What time is it?'

'A woman climbs into his bed at two in the bloody morning and he wants to know what time it is!'

He awoke.

'Oh, Mary! I...'

'And all he wants to do is talk!'

When he awoke in the morning, she was gone.

He tied equipment to the Velocette's luggage rack while Percy watched. Ngaire's little girl hop-scotched her way to school and he thought, 'Ours would have done that one day.' Then he thought of last night and he warmed all over.

He made tea and brought a cup out to Percy. He had no pastries this day so he toasted two slices of bread and opened a can of smoked oysters. He spread the oysters on the toast. Percy wolfed his down as fast as the dog Kuri wolfed his food. The way he smacked his lips afterwards, too, sounded like the dog Kuri.

Turning his thoughts to business, Larry thought about a van, but vehicles of any sort were in short supply and, in spite of what the government said to the contrary, a black market existed. If you asked to put your name down on a dealer's list, he laughed. It was said that if you offered the dealer enough inducement – the kind that crackled – he'd stop laughing. But where would he get the inducement? It was all he could do to keep ahead of the bills as it was. Not that he wasn't making money, but the growth of the business, and the need to stock a growing inventory, kept him perpetually broke. It would have to be a used vehicle – very used.

He was scheduled to go to Leigh this day but Mary's visit had left him lazy and disorganized. Why hadn't she stayed longer? He rode to the post office. The first letter asked if he could come to Auckland to discuss the franchise.

His mother wrote that his sister expected a child. He was to be an uncle! And that reminded him again that he could have been a father.

He stopped at the bus depot. Bernie should have sent a zc1.

Perhaps because it was such a beautiful morning, but more likely because she had heard of his estrangement from Mary, Beverley smiled at him.

'Hello,' she said. 'There's a box for you.' He smiled back. He would have liked to linger. He sensed she was ready to forgive him, but Mary was with him still.

Later, John Arrf came by.

'You know, I've been meaning to pick up those bottles I left in the ovens.' He grinned conspiratorially. When he grinned he was transformed from the thin-lipped, mousy, accounting type, to a middle-aged, cherubic, almost jolly fellow. He wore horn-rimmed glasses now.

'I'll keep them in my office where it'll be easier to get at them,' he said.

While John talked, the dog Kuri pissed on his trousers. He kicked him away.

'The old lady's always sniffing at my clothes for signs of drink. I wonder what she'll make of this lot!' he chuckled.

He stacked the bottles on the bench.

'Larry, why don't you call in to my office after work and let's have one together – one evening when you're not so busy. I can even give you ice. All mod cons, so to speak!'

When he was gone, Larry took stock of the day. It's funny, he thought, how a smile from a girl at a bus depot, and a kind word from a lawyer – odd fellow though he is – can change your day. And the news about his sister.

'Hey! I'm going to be an uncle,' he told the dog.

While she smiled and seemed glad to see him, Larry recognised a carefulness in Beverley. He wanted to ask her could he take her to the end-of-the-month dance at the Patriotic Hut, but he wasn't sure enough of his reception.

Since the time she had climbed into his bed at two in the morning, Mary had twice woken him again in the night. She'd come with a voracious appetite he'd had difficulty satisfying, especially since each time he had been awakened suddenly, not readied by anticipation.

His earlier experience had been limited. Before Mary there had been no more than half a dozen back-seat wrestling matches, which usually, due either to his gross inexperience or the slow coming around of his partners, had taken so long to reach a conclusion that invariably there'd been no fulfilment.

Mary had changed that. Though she had kidded him about his supposed manly prowess, which she claimed was due to his French heritage, she knew and he knew that he'd been a babe in the bed until she'd taken him in hand.

His real fulfilment was afterwards, when they lay together, legs intertwined, and shared their thoughts, ideas, and the little experiences the day had engendered, before drifting into sleep.

He knew, the three times Mary had come to him in the night, that she came to slake desire, for though she had later crossed her legs with his and played with the hair on his chest, she deflected attempts at intimate conversation.

He had grown determined to tell her no, next time. He was not there for convenience. But inside, he knew he wouldn't do it lest he lose even this small part of her.

He wondered what it would be like with Beverley. She wore a reserved aura that suggested that she would never really open up. He couldn't imagine her climbing into his bed and telling him to 'Move over, lover!'

Mary had spoiled him. He no longer had the patience – or wish – to fool about with virginal preliminaries and tentative gropings. He knew that for some men the sport was in the getting. Some collected conquests like trophies, but he was not that kind of sportsman. If that's what it would take to get Beverley, then she'd remain a virgin. To be sure, he had sparred with her, and had enjoyed the sparring, but then he had been safe in the knowledge that he had Mary. The other was diversion.

He felt bad about that now; Beverley was too innocent, too naive, too serious, to be a diversion.

WHEN LARRY AWOKE, HIS head felt full of liquid. If he moved it side to side, he heard slosh, slosh! He put a finger into an ear and twisted. The ear popped. The other ear refused to respond to like treatment. He took two aspirins and put water on for tea.

It was not only his ears; his stomach was awry, which made it difficult to decide what to have for breakfast, yet he knew he should eat something. Last night's drinks had made this morning's stomach feel like a next-day bar must smell to a Baptist minister.

He was so busy enjoying how miserable he felt, he didn't notice the coughing from the floor until a major cough and strained puking drew his attention. The dog Kuri laid a long, turd-like extrusion on the linoleum. From where he stood, Larry saw grey hair and small tails protruding from the offering. It wasn't an invigorating sight first thing, but it proved that the mouse-catcher was earning his keep.

Larry and Kuri sometimes had a field day with the mice. Each had a mouse-catching area. Larry set his traps on the benches, the dog Kuri had a franchise to operate the floor. The dog sat patiently by one of the holes the mice had gnawed in the walls. When the mouse was halfway out his hole, snap! He disappeared down a different hole. Larry tried to keep track of the snaps to tally who was ahead, but he would become engrossed in his work and forget. This morning, the evidence clearly showed that the dog was ahead.

Larry went for the fireplace shovel. He returned in time to prevent the dog from re-ingesting the offering, and buried the mess in what had been a vegetable garden. He washed the floor with Jeyes Fluid and finished just as the dog laid down a second set of winnings. He cleaned that up and decided to forego breakfast.

Today's headache had nothing to do with the telephone. It had started with John Arrf. Larry had dropped in to explain that though he had nimbly climbed on the roof, he couldn't fix the leak. The corrugated tin roof had rusted through and the sheets needed replacing. The ceiling was in danger of collapsing. If John paid for the materials, he would perform the labour.

They struck a deal and, at John's insistence, celebrated with gin; Larry's over ice. John was in a celebrating mood this evening. He insisted upon seconds and thirds, which led to sixths and sevenths, possibly more. Larry taught John several seasoned wartime ballads, which they sang with increasing volume until the constable knocked on the door. He told them to keep it down. They switched to trading confidences. Larry talked of Moira of Dundee. John was reminded of Joan Burchett. She was the one he should have married, he said. How he wished for the 'good old days'. Larry, too, wished for the good old days, not long since, when he and Mary had been so happy with each other.

John asked about Mary.

'Rumour has it that you and your young lady have come to a parting of the ways. I hope…'

'You shouldn't listen to rumour,' Larry interrupted. He wanted to hear about Joan Burchett but he didn't want to talk about Mary.

'I'm so sorry. Was I impertinent, my boy?'

'Yes, you were!'

John paused to release air trapped in his stomach.

'The only excuse I can offer is that as a neighbour I'm interested in your well-being, so natcherly I'm interested in your young lady. Forgive me please.'

Larry was mollified.

'Itch all right,' he apologised, and on that note they wound up the celebration.

The dog Kuri preferred to lie where he could keep an eye on a mouse hole to the left of the door jamb, and at the same time watch the people using Bakery Lane as a shortcut to the road behind.

Most of the passers-by had at various times stopped to satisfy their curiosity about what was going on in the old bakehouse, and had voiced questions and pleasantries. The dog Kuri took pleasure from the visits, for the various poles and posts in the vicinity were passé. But the pedestrians had wised up. If he rose to greet them, he was greeted with, 'Piss off, you bastard!' When Percy came, the dog left the entrance for space under the bench, near Larry's feet.

The dog was an indication of what went on in Bakery Lane. If his tail thumped and quietened, it was a passer-by. If it thumped and he left the doorway, he was investigating a newcomer. If he put his tail between his legs and sought Larry's company, it was Percy.

This morning, his tail thumped.

The visitor was the baker, the former leaseholder of the old bakehouse, and leaseholder of the new bakehouse, the neighbour, Joe Montini.

Joe had been born in Wellington. His parents were born in Italy, which hadn't made life easy for him while the war was on. People he had considered good friends before the war had taken to referring to him as 'that wop' during the war. But the Italians came over to the Allied side and then the war ended. Joe was Old Joe again.

'Come in. Welcome to my humble abode.'

'Thought I'd see what you're up to,' Joe said.

'Not too much.'

Larry wondered about the purpose of the visit. He made tea preparatory to explaining the workings of his business, but soon saw that he had lost Joe's comprehension.

He noted, too, that the dog Kuri came inside. He correctly surmised that Old Percy was at the door. He took tea and a pastry out to him.

'So you're feeding the old reprobate.'

'I feel sorry for him.'

'Don't feel too sorry. Half the town's feeding him. I wonder sometimes if he's as stupid as he makes out. But that's not the reason I came. I'm told you're looking for a van. I have one for sale. It's not much. It's seen better days and it needs tyres, but it runs well. Things being as they are, a van's a van. I'm selling it because we no longer make deliveries. These days, people come to town to buy their bread, along with their groceries. It's yours for fifty quid if you want it.'

Fifty pounds was a lot of money. The average working wage was about fifteen pounds a week. But a vehicle, right after the war, if it had wheels, and a motor of sorts, was worth more than fifty pounds.

'Fifty pounds!'

'If you can't manage it right away, you can pay me as you can,' he said generously.

'It's not that, it…' He thought of Mary and what she would say if she heard his bargaining – or lack of it. 'I'll take it,' he said, 'and thank you very much.'

Percy said, 'Oh hip!' Larry looked to the door. John the lawyer stood in the opening.

'Sorry, I didn't realise you had a visitor. G'day, Joe,' John said, nodding. 'Look, I'll came back. Nothing important.'

'Odd fellow,' Joe said when John had gone. 'But that woman he's married to would make anyone odd. Strange… most of old Fritz's offspring are pretty good people, but something got coddled with that one. I can't say that I blame John for running around on her.'

'John runs around on his wife!' Larry was astounded. 'I would never have guessed it.'

'It's common knowledge. They say he has a doxy stashed in Auckland – but I don't know that first-hand.'

'Well, I'll be buggered!'

Larry arranged to pick up the vehicle as soon as he got tyres.

'If you have trouble getting them, see John. He can fix most things,' Joe said.

Though Mary found constant excuses not to go anywhere with him, Larry decided to ask her out one more time. The occasion was a prestigious one: the once-a-year Returned Servicemen's Ball. The dog Kuri had gone walkabout. Larry whistled and waited for him, knowing that in spite of the dog's initial lack of good manners Mary had become fond of him, and an inner sense told him that he would need all the help he could get this day.

'Sorry, I'm working,' she told him.

He knew from Ngaire that she wasn't.

'Okay,' he snapped. Grim-faced, he turned and left.

'Larry!'

He didn't turn back. He put the dog back in the apple box – forgot to put the glasses on – and rode to the Sandspit.

Larry sat on an upside-down dinghy.

'Come here, fleabag.'

The dog nestled his jaw on Larry's leg. Larry scratched him between the ears.

'Well… that's it! I suppose you'd call that the old heave-ho, eh!'

Perhaps it was for the best. He hadn't forgiven her and she knew it. No doubt, also, she found him dull. She liked the night life, and doing things, and going places. What had he offered her other than his bed? And possibly she was seeing someone else. A sudden mental picture of her in bed with another made him cringe.

He wondered if Moira had found him dull. Perhaps he was being paid in kind for what he had done to her.

The dog Kuri sat back on his haunches. He tilted his head first to one side and then the other as he waited to see what this was all about.

'I'll never understand them,' Larry said, thinking about the vagaries of women.

Finally, he said something the dog understood: 'Okay, let's find a stick. Time you were reacquainted with the water anyhow!'

The following day he asked Beverley if he could take her to the ball. He sensed that she liked him, and by now, possibly she had guessed the truth about his relationship with Mary.

'I'll let you know tomorrow,' she said.

The next morning she answered, 'Yes, I'll go, but please... not on the motorcycle. My evening dress.'

It wasn't just the evening dress, he was sure of that. She had seen Mary with him on the bike. They had cut an unusual picture, the two of them, and the dog in sunglasses. This much Larry guessed. As Joe had said, the van was old. Also, it was full of hidden flour which poured from the crannies after passage across potholes. Larry removed the rubber mats and hosed out the interior and for a while the dust abated, but it returned.

The morning of the ball he made a fresh assault on the dust. He took out the seats and beat them with a stick. The seats had played host to a congregation of mice while the van sat up on blocks during the war. Small volcanoes of flour and horsehair stuffing erupted from the holes they had made. The beating erupted more hair than flour. He covered the seats with printed cloth.

This particular model of Essex van was not esteemed for rugged body construction. Its frame was made from wood. The wood screws constantly loosened. A headlamp fell from the mudguard the second time he drove it. He backtracked three miles to find it.

What he hated most about the Essex was its gear shift. The lever was supposed to slide up, down and sideways in a slotted H. Most frequently the slide wouldn't slide unless Herculean pressure was applied to the lever. When it did move, instead of the gears meshing quietly with each other, they ground teeth on teeth in great volumes of protest. People turned to see who was mistreating what.

Larry removed the cover from the gearbox. Inside was a dough-like substance that appeared to be a mixture of flour and oil. After he had pried it loose and washed the slide with petrol less effort was needed to move the lever, but the gears grated still.

He had not had the time to repaint the van. It advertised that it belonged to JOE MONTINI – BAKER – WARKWORTH. But needs must prevail when the occasion demands.

He dressed in the suit he'd bought for his sister's wedding, shone his old air force shoes – he had meant to buy new ones.

Mrs Plenkovich opened the door.

'You must be Larry. Please come in. Beverley will be here in a minute.'

He was stunned when he saw Beverley. She didn't have Mary's voluptuousness, but she had a slim and regal shapeliness. He was captivated.

'Beverley! You're beautiful!'

'Isn't she!' her mother preened. 'Now, you two enjoy yourselves. And don't be too late coming home.' She smiled at them as she opened the door.

Larry had been overseas long enough to learn about opening car doors for women. Beverley rewarded him with a smile and climbed into the van as if it were a Rolls. The dog Kuri greeted her with a wet nose.

They danced through the evening, well into the morning.

On the way home, Larry hesitated at the entrance to the park by the river, but then he drove on.

'What's different this time, Larry?' Beverley said.

He turned about and followed the lane to the river's edge. The tide was incoming. The high water brought the wholesome smell of the ocean. The last time they'd been here, Larry tried to place a hand over Beverley's breast. She had taken it away. Eventually she had allowed it to stay but had strongly rejected further progression. He wondered if she would reject him this night.

He trailed a finger from the curve of her ear to the top of her gown, leaned forward and kissed her lightly. He caressed her back and shoulders through the evening gown, kissed her again, deeper and longer. He played with her throat, lowered his hand and cupped a breast. She shivered. She returned his kiss, bit at his lip. He moved his hand inside her gown, under her bra. She gasped. Her nipple hardened. He reached around to undo her bra.

Mary used to laugh at his attempts to undo her bra.

'A girl would be past needing it undone if she waited for you,' she had told him, undoing it in a twinkle. He had practised, the few occasions she wasn't in a hurry, and had found the secret. But the secret didn't seem to apply in this instance. Finally, Beverley unbuttoned the back of her gown and undid her bra.

He kissed down the curve of her breast, teased her nipple with his tongue, took it in his mouth. Then, unable to stop himself, he lifted her gown.

Beverley quickly stayed his hand. He cursed himself that he had moved much too quickly, and then came to his senses. Beverley was not Mary. And Beverley would never be Mary. Contrite, he said, 'Beverley, I'm sorry. I was carried away. Your mother said that we mustn't be late. I'll take you home'.

Beverley replaced her bra, buttoned the back of her gown, stood, and patted her clothes. Outside her house, she took his hands in hers, brushed his lips.

'Thanks for the evening,' she said.

L ARRY POSTED AN ARTICLE to *Popular Electronics*, an American publication. Not that he expected it to be published, but he had to try. The material wasn't original. The article was different only in that he wrote it for the average man – a man such as himself.

During the process, he'd discovered that the best way to learn about a subject was to write about it. In writing about it, Larry found that what he did *not* know was more than what he did know. Disheartened, he signed up for a further course in mathematics.

Twice, he took Beverley to the pictures. One Saturday, she rode pillion to the fishing base at Leigh. Jake Watson looked her over, quickly suppressed surprise when he realised that she wasn't Mary, and held his silence. Later, when the work was done, they rode to the cove. Larry had brought snorkels and goggles and he taught Beverley to use them.

One afternoon, a few days later, he tied a ZC1 radio to the pillion seat, put the dog in the apple box and started out again for Leigh. Riding from Bakery Lane into Queen Street, he saw Beverley locking the depot. On impulse, he turned and pulled in at the kerb.

'Good afternoon, young lady. May I offer you a ride on my velocipede?' His manner feigned regal assurance.

'To where?' she answered, smiling in a way that made his heart suddenly flip.

'I have to return a radio to Leigh.'

'And where would you have me sit?' she asked, inspecting the accommodation.

The radio occupied the pillion seat, while Kuri was in the apple box on the luggage carrier.

'Your choice; under the dog or under the radio.'

He sat the radio on her lap. Her skirt hitched above her knees and there was nothing she could do about it. He fought an evil urge to reach back and run a hand up her leg as he had done often enough to Mary. He let out the clutch and advanced the throttle.

The road was gravel in sore need of grading. Over a particularly rutted part his cheeks and body shook. He slowed and looked back to Beverley.

'You all right?' he asked.

'Ye-s-s-s, j-j-just kis-s-s me,' she stuttered, grinning roguishly.

He pulled into the grass verge, realised that this wasn't the place to start a romance, and pulled back on the road.

'Later,' he threatened over his shoulder. When he had completed the radio installation they rode to the cove. Not having brought swimsuits, they sat on the bank and threw stones into the water. Larry delivered the promised kiss, some accumulated interest, and was delving into the capital when she pulled free.

'You stay here!' she ordered, going behind an ancient and gnarled pohutukawa.

What is she up to, he speculated.

Before he reached a conclusion she dashed for the water yelling, 'Last one in is a rotten egg!' Her nude body cut the surface cleanly. She came up laughing, treading water.

'It's corker! Come on in,' she invited.

This was Beverley! It was a turn of events he would never have forecast, but she had started it. He took off his shirt. A sock. A second sock. His watch. He eased his trousers off, deliberately folded them, laid them carefully down. His intention was to eke out the show, but the problem developed that the slowness of the undressing put him in danger of displaying more than he had intended. He tore the jockey shorts off and dived in. Swimming underwater, he rose a distance behind her.

He eased down into the water, swam just above the weed, and came up under her. She was slippery and squirmy and put up a fight, but he satisfied the earlier urge to run a hand up her leg. As he contemplated further exploration the dog Kuri paddled between them. If petting was in the offing, he wanted in. Beverley broke free from a situation that had gone further than she had no doubt intended. She swam to the bank, ran to her clothes and dressed.

Going home, she held him tightly. The dog Kuri stood on his hind legs, his front paws against her back, and he maintained the position even over the most corrugated portions of the road.

Larry worked hard to keep the bike between the gravel berms, but he had time to reflect that he didn't know women. He had underestimated Moira, he didn't understand Mary, and now Beverley; he didn't know her, either.

They arrived at her house. He saw the living room window

curtain move and knew that they were observed. He wanted to kiss and hold her tightly, but instead he held her hands and wished her good night. She said, 'Thank you for a wonderful time,' then reached up and kissed him lightly.

He wanted to say 'Thank *you*,' but she was gone.

JOHN ARRF WAS AWAY from his office. The envelopes protruding from under his door indicated that he had been gone a while. His neighbour was an accountant. Larry asked him if he knew when John would be back.

'He's in Australia,' the accountant replied. 'He didn't say when he'd be back.'

'He gets around,' Larry said, envious.

Back at his bench, he worked on the new radio. Surplus zc1 radios were becoming difficult to obtain and those in service broke down frequently.

Old Percy stood at the door. The dog Kuri lazed under the bench. Larry had heard the dog catch two mice this morning. The score stood at two to zero, for the bench traps were empty when he had opened up.

He attached components to a breadboard – a radio chassis having nothing to do with bread – and soldered them together with hook-up wire, pencilling over the schematic diagram as he completed the connections. He hadn't seen Mary around and he wondered why. About a month earlier, he had met her unexpectedly at the grocer's. She had been laughing and joking with the proprietor, who fawned over her as usual. The grocer was unaware that she despised him.

'Hello, sweetie, how are you?' she had greeted him as he entered.

'Mary!' It was a while before he could say more. When he could, he wanted to tell her that he was sorry about everything, and that he missed her. Instead he said, 'I'm fine, Mary. And you?' So formal. He hated himself.

'I'm very well, thank you.' Also so formal. Why were they doing this to each other? She paid the grocer and flashed Larry a patent leather smile as she left.

''Bye, sweetie.'

''Bye, Mary.'

While he added wires to the breadboard, he asked himself why he had not tried harder to understand her. He remembered what he liked about her. There was a lot that he liked about her. Wasn't the joy of her goodness greater than the misery of her misdeed? Suddenly he was penitent. This evening he would ride up to the boarding house. Not that he expected that they would return to their old intimacy – enough if he could see her and talk to her sometimes.

When evening came, he plopped the dog Kuri into the apple box, rode along Queen Street and up the hill to the boarding house. Nearly there, his intention wavered. But then he was at the kerb. If she was home she would have seen or heard him come. While the dog Kuri sniffed and peed on the fence posts, he knocked at Mary's door. In the past he would have called out, 'It's me,' and entered. Tonight, he waited.

He knocked again.

'I'm coming!' a voice – not Mary's – called.

A buxom, middle-aged woman he remembered was the land-lady opened the door.

'Hello,' she said.

'I'm looking for Mary.'

The landlady peered short-sightedly at him.

'Aren't you Larry?'

'Yes. I was hoping that she would be here, but if she's working

118

it's all right. I'll come back.' Secretly, he was relieved that she wasn't there.

'But Larry, Mary's not here any more.'

'She's not here!'

He looked through the doorway into Mary's room. Was the landlady playing a joke on him?

'You mean that she's gone for good!'

'She said that she was going to Australia. I'm surprised she didn't tell you. I thought that you and Mary…'

'Australia… But where in Australia? Why…' He broke off. 'I can't believe it!' His mind reeled in confusion. He had to get away. 'Well, thank you. I'm sorry to have troubled you.'

'You haven't troubled me. I just wish I could have been of more help. But you know, that lawyer chap opposite the butcher shop can probably tell you more. He's the one that arranged it – from what she told me. Though why she would allow herself to get mixed up with the likes of him, I'll never know!'

Startled, Larry looked at her more closely. 'You mean John Arrf?'

'Yes. Arrf. That's him – what a dreadful name! He was here talking to her about it. But she didn't tell you?'

'Yes, well, thank you very much. I'll talk to John. Thank you again.'

He spoke his confusion to the dog. 'What the hell's going on, Whiskers? John in Australia! Mary in Australia!'

He went to the kitchen, brought back a beer, poured a little into the dog's scrap dish, filled his own glass.

'Fleabag,' he said, 'why don't we get drunk, eh?'

119

WHEN HAD MARY TAKEN up with John? He was twice her age, and married. His money? What else?

His head throbbed – not just from the booze, but also because he had tossed and turned all night. Visions of them together had kept waking him. He had dreamed that he'd shot John through the eyes. Only a short time back he'd shot Mary in a dream. His day seemed never to end. While he tried to work at the bench, his mind sought to cope with Mary's and John's duplicity – or had he jumped to a wrong conclusion? Yet, what other explanation?

Australia. Auckland he could understand, but Australia…

A fragment of last night rose in his mind. Beverley. She'd been with a girlfriend, walking home after the pictures. He had talked to her. But what had he said?

He looked at his watch. Five. She'd be closing the doors. He started the Velocette and rode over. The dog Kuri scurried to catch up. 'Hello, princess.'

Beverley placed her hands on her hips with a self-righteous 'Harrump' and said, 'I'm not speaking to you, Larry La Salle.'

'Come on, Beverley, we're going for a little ride.'

'We are not!' She turned away.

'Bev, I know I was awful last night and I want to apologise. If you won't come with me, I'll apologise right here, on my knees, and I'll yell it to the whole town.'

She yielded reluctantly.

'I'm expected home soon.'

He put the dog Kuri in the apple box. They rode down Hepburn Creek Road. At the highest point, he took her hand and pulled her up the bank. The expanse of the Mahurangi River and its wide estuary lay before them.

'This is where I'd build my house if I wasn't going to America,' he said.

'America!' She scanned his face.

'One day,' he said.

She relaxed.

'I mean it.'

She laughed. 'The best laid plans of mice and Larry...'

'I love this view.'

'It's beautiful.' She said it to appease him. She'd been born in Northland. Beauty was everywhere. 'But is this why you brought me here? Funny, I thought that you were bringing me here to apologise for your awful behaviour last night.'

'Patience, my princess; a kiss first.' He took her in his arms.

She resisted, zealously at first, then half-heartedly. In proper time, she yielded.

In proper time, too, she pushed him away.

'Some apology,' she said, flushed and flustered. 'Really, I don't know when you're the worst, when you're drunk or when you're sober! Well... perhaps you're a little bit nicer when you're sober – at least you don't call me Mary when you're sober!'

'I called you Mary! Really?'

'You weren't nice at all,' she said.

He wondered what else he'd said.

'I'm sorry. Something happened yesterday and I... Bev, truly, I'm sorry. It won't happen again. I promise.'

The dog Kuri scrambled up the bank, put his jaw on Larry's knee. Larry scratched him between the ears.

'I hope *you* weren't rotten to her too, you miserable apology for a canine.'

'No, he was a gentleman – more than I can say for his master.' Beverley took over the scratching.

'One out of two of us isn't too bad,' Larry answered. 'And now, my princess, my apology won't be a proper apology unless it's ratified with a kiss. If you'll just stop pulling away.'

'I prefer you drunk.'

'But I'm sober.'

'Just one then.'

'Whatever you say.'

LARRY TOWED AN INNER tube from which he had suspended a mash sack. He expected to fill the sack with crayfish, for at Leigh, after the war, there was an abundance of them.

He swam to the rocky point at the south side of the cove and threw the tube's anchor overboard.

Diving along the length of a reef, he spotted a broad array of cray feelers protruding from under ragged ledges and beady black eyes on short stalks tracking his movements. The crays scurried back into crevices when he approached. As he reached under to grab one something jabbed urgently at his scrotum, which – he didn't realise it then – dangled like fish bait through his wide-legged shorts. Once he'd seen a shark while diving and although it was said that in this part of the world they didn't attack humans, he now considered the possibility and it alarmed him. His first and immediate reaction was to clamp his legs together. His second was to withdraw his head from the crevice. The rapidity of the second action scraped a layer of skin from his forehead. The pain slowed his third reaction, which was to position his spear gun defensively.

But then he was relieved to discover that the poker was a fellow fisherman and that it was the business end of a spear gun that had prodded him. He was grateful to note that the spear gun wasn't loaded. Relief at the revelation made him bold enough to discover more about the poker who turned out to be smooth of limb and artistically curved about the upper torso. He concluded that the fisherman was a fisherwoman, especially since she had long hair, but as her face was covered with a mask and her mouth attached to a snorkel corroborating proof was not immediately evident.

She pointed a forefinger in the up direction, a direction he was about to travel anyhow because he was out of air.

She removed her mask.

'What do you mean by shagging about in *my* possie, eh?' she protested.

He studied the scrotum poker. She was oval of face with merry, light blue eyes. An impish grin played across her mouth. He fingered his scratched forehead.

'I'll fight you for it,' he answered, sportingly.

She weighed the proposal. 'You're bigger than me.'

An inner flash led him to anticipate that soon he might catch more than crayfish.

'There's plenty for both of us. But you watch where you poke that spear! By the way, I'm Larry.'

'Suzie,' she answered.

They set up a system. Suzie pushed the gun under the ledges to flush the crays, and Larry grabbed them around their backs as they came out. The females with eggs he let go. Soon they had filled the sack.

She swam to a rubber dinghy, climbed in, and invited him to join her. Larry had been raised to believe that it was good manners to bring gifts when visiting. He had seen a small octopus below. He dived for it. His intention was to introduce it down the front of Suzie's bathing suit, but the material was tight about its tenants and Suzie's flailing arms prevented the transfer. He dropped the creature around her neck.

He let her scream until she had been punished enough for her earlier, shameless behaviour. He removed the octopus and made a motion to place it in her lap, but she jumped overboard.

'I should have made a eunuch out of you when I had the chance,' she shouted from the water.

They headed back to shore with the sack of crays and as they entered the clearing Larry was dismayed to see people camped near the Essex. Though the evening was warm they had built a huge fire, and near a tent they had stacked crates of beer.

These were the friends she came with, Suzie said. They had arrived that morning, but had gone back to Warkworth to replenish the beer supply while she had sought to catch the evening meal.

They invited him to pull up a log and pop the top off a Waite-mata.

He accepted the beer and while Suzie detailed the technique they had used to capture the crays he released the dog Kuri from the van. The dog ran from bush to bush, and when he ran out of bushes he reconnoitered the area around the fire and dared to move closer when no voice was raised against him.

'Mangy looking bastard,' one drinker praised him.

The dog found the crays and worried at the sack until a claw took hold of his lower lip. Later, while inspecting the visitors' legs, he found Suzie's mug of beer. He had lapped up most of it before he was seen.

'The poor thing. He's thirsty!' Suzie said.

'Hey! The bastard likes beer!' her friend Fred said. Kuri went up in his estimation. He refilled the mug.

Between the 'Kia oras!' and the 'Down the bloody hatches', Larry concentrated on knowing Suzie. He coaxed her to a grassy bank near the water's edge.

Larry had long asked himself why the girls in his life liked to play with the hair on his chest. He had examined his face in the mirror; his nose was well shaped, his mouth well proportioned, and his profile handsome, but did they play with those? No. They went for his chest. And Suzie, without hesitation, proved to be no different.

This phenomenon, he realised, had its advantages. It gave him excuse to retaliate in kind. He put the thesis to the test and was rewarded with a series of passionate kisses.

He discovered, too, that the new girl was a biter. She bit his ears, she bit his nose; and they weren't nibbles – they were wholehearted bites. He wondered if they were meant to arouse him. He tried to tell her that he was already aroused, but between the kissing and the biting he found it difficult to be coherent. Speculating that he might find relief if he cooled her, he rolled them into the water. But this did nothing to alleviate things; now he was in danger of being drowned as well as eaten.

Fortunately Suzie's appetite was finite; the bites subsided to nibbles and eventually to sighs of what Larry hoped was contentment.

Back at the fire, they found sleepy drinkers, empty crayfish shells and a drunken dog. The dog saw them coming. He struggled to meet them but fell back down.

'You shouldn't have given him beer,' Larry admonished. 'It makes him sick.' The dog obliged and proved him right.

'Let's go to Warkworth,' he suggested to Suzie, 'and get something to eat.'

But first he stopped at the house to pick up a pullover. Inside, Suzie elected to postpone the meal and snack on an ear. He protested that the fish and chip shop closed in fifteen minutes and broke free.

Later, he discovered she liked to bite on toes too, but this was part of a ritual about one little piggy and two little piggies…

'Hey! That hurt!' he protested at the conclusion of 'ten little piggies', when she had given him a number ten bite.

'You shouldn't leave them lying around, honey!' she said, looking around to see what else was loose.

H<small>E COMPLETED THE PROTOTYPE</small> marine radio. Bernie Steinmetz had helped him to find the components. Each time Larry had left him, Bernie had said, 'Now you give my best wishes to that smart little girl of yours,' to which Larry agreed, wondering if the components would be as readily forthcoming if Bernie knew that Mary was no longer with him.

Tomorrow, he intended to install the prototype radio in one of Jake Watson's fishing boats.

Over the last two weeks, he had installed VHF radios in four taxis, two in Warkworth and two in Wellsford. He had recently contracted to install another in Waipu. Gradually this part of the business was building up.

He had sent further articles to several American magazines. *CQ Magazine* had replied that they liked his article and to prove it they enclosed a cheque for one hundred dollars. He pinned it to the bakery wall. Later he took it down, cashed it, and bought a single-lens reflex camera, his premise being that text *and* pictures should sell better than text alone. The previous night he had learned from the hotel proprietor that John Arrf was back. Though he had known that the day must come when John would return, the news that he was back turned Larry's heart to granite. But the rents were due. Not wanting to meet John, he rose early, walked to John's office, and slid the cheque under the door.

A week earlier, two days after he had met Suzie, he had taken Beverley to lunch at the Tip Top. He liked Beverley. What he especially liked about her was that she was naive and honest, completely free of guile. He instinctively knew that she had not led him on when she had swum nude at Leigh; her action was probably one of unconscious foreplay to a one-way walk down the aisle. But his horizon was America.

Suzie was neither a nest-builder nor a homebody. Her interests seemed to be sex and scuba diving – he hadn't yet determined in which order. Either way, she made for an exciting time. She was to arrive by bus from Auckland this Friday evening and wait at his house until his evening class was over.

When he arrived home, she was in his bed. He forgot that he was hungry and climbed in beside her.

'What took you so bloody long?' she complained before she bit his ear.

Later he started to tell her about his day, but her heavy breathing told him that she wasn't listening. Neither was she listening when he went to the kitchen and cooked bacon and eggs. She opened her eyes for a moment when he got back in beside her. 'Mmmm! You smell like bacon,' she said. One thing he was soon to discover about Suzie: besides going to bed early, she got up early. He seemed to have been asleep only a few minutes when she bit his shoulder. He sat up. The clock on the windowsill said that it was five o'clock.

'Who is the girl over at the bus depot?' she said between bites.

Now he was alert.

'The bus depot?'

She poked a tongue in his ear. He pulled away.

'Honey… I was just wondering.'

A week later, after a gruelling day in his office, John Arrf opened a bottle of gin. In Australia, at a business cohort's house, he had accepted gin poured over ice and by the end of the evening had decided that over ice was the only way to go. He was glad now that he had installed the refrigerator in his office.

After five or six, or maybe seven, gins – he hadn't counted – his mood had turned reflective, enough to speculate about the vagaries of his life. An inconsiderate client interrupted his thinking. He told the client to bugger off and put the 'DO NOT DISTURB' sign on the door. 'Now, where was I?' he asked himself, pouring another drink.

He had been back from Australia several weeks before he realised that Larry was avoiding him. He was surprised that the boy could exhibit such petty behaviour – it didn't seem like him. John had grown fond of the young fellow. He was ambitious, didn't mind work, and was destined to move up in the world – once he had learned how to use other people's money. John knew from experience that money was easy to obtain if you didn't need it, virtually impossible to obtain if you did, and that Larry must be feeling the pinch about now. He had toyed with the notion of investing in the business, but now… well, he'd wait.

On the surface, John was a bumbling person. But his looks were misleading. While he bumbled and dallied about giving replies to quotes or offers, the buyers raised their bids, scared they'd lose out.

It was John's meek and bumbling nature that so infuriated his wife. She had learned the hard way that his bumbling was a front, that he went his own mulish and merry way no matter what. He sat in his office this evening in a mood of growing resentment, at his wife because he was married to her, and at Larry because he thought Larry was avoiding him. Though he suspected that he knew why, in his view that made the reason no more just. Deciding to confront him, he left his office and set out for the cottage.

WHEN LARRY OPENED THE cottage door, John moved unsteadily to the kitchen table and sat down heavily. He put his hands palms down upon the table, leaned back in the chair, and said, 'My boy, why are you avoiding me?'

Larry trembled with anger. He gripped the back of a chair until his knuckles whitened. Then he forced himself to wait for the anger to subside enough so that he could speak coherently.

'What the hell would you expect me to do?' he replied through tight lips. 'Ah… yes… quite so.' John withdrew the flask from his inside jacket pocket and unscrewed its cap. 'I don't suppose you have any ice?' The unexpected question defused Larry's anger. He shook his head. What was this – John taking his drinks with ice now?

'What do you want of me?' Larry said, suddenly weary of his thoughts, resigned now to hearing what John had to say.

'My boy, I've concluded that we may be at cross purposes about something. Now, I admit to having taken a little nip or two this delightful evening, but at the moment my faculties are in good shape. So suppose you tell me what's troubling you.'

Larry pulled out a chair and sat. His mind probed for understanding.

'The name Mary doesn't mean a thing to you, eh?'

'Ah,' John sighed, 'so it is that. Well, I suppose that in a town this size I should expect someone to have misinterpreted my actions. But now, my boy, there's the matter of confidentiality between client and lawyer, so we're going to have to let the matter rest, I'm afraid.'

Larry stood.

'John, what kind of bullshit is this? Confidentiality, for God's sake! Listen! Do me a favour and get your arse out of here.'

The dog Kuri, sensing Larry's anger, barked at John.

John had lifted the flask to his lips. He stopped it midway.

'Larry, my boy, would it be too much to ask you what you think I may have done?'

Larry wavered. What if he were wrong? It was one thing to think things and quite another to speak them.

'You went to Australia with Mary, right?'

John took a long and slow pull from the flask, then wiped his glasses. Stalling, Larry thought.

'Yes,' John said at last. 'I did go to Australia with the charming young lady – but look, my boy, I want you to understand, it's not what you must be thinking.' He lifted the flask, studied it absent-mindedly, then sat it back on the table.

'All right, Larry. I'll betray a confidence – the action's warranted. You see, one day the young lady came to my office. She asked me if I could help her secure a nursing job in Australia. A small request. Through a good friend, I was able to assist her. Oh yes… and as I was going to Australia on business, I offered to escort her there. And I must say, she's a delightful travelling companion. But that's the extent of my involvement, my boy. No more than that.'

Larry pondered the explanation. It sounded feasible, but why did she not tell him that she was going? Why the secrecy? But then, hadn't she always been secretive? He rose from the chair and brought a beer from under the sink.

'John, what can I say?'

A few weeks ago he had felt like murdering them both, but now, hell… But he was glad that it was a job and not John that had taken her away.

Sweetie,

I know how you must feel about me and really, I don't blame you. Over here I have had a lot of time to think about things. But before I go into that, I want you to know that I didn't leave you for someone else. Nothing like that. You are the sweetest person I have ever known.

As you can see from the address, I'm in Sydney. I'm doing the same kind of work I did in Warkworth and I love it.

But my reason for writing is not to chit-chat. I want to tell you why I left. I owe you that.

Sweetie, I'm not cut out for marriage. The thought of it scares me. Married people change. Look at John Arrf and his wife, and the way they fight. Yet, once they must have loved each other. And if we were married, how could I do the things that I want to do now, and see the places I want to see?

My problem, sweetie, is that I fell in love with you. It's a complication I hadn't expected to happen.

When I have saved enough I'm going to England, and then, who knows? Perhaps one day we'll meet in America!

One last thing - John Arrf helped me to get the job. Please tell him hello and thanks.

Now sweetie, I want you to get on with your life. One day you'll go to America. I'd have been a hindrance. But don't marry before you get there or you'll never make it.

Forgive me. I love you lots and lots.

Mary.

USUALLY, WHEN THE SUN set in Warkworth, so did its people, but this Christmas Eve the shops were filled with last-minute shoppers. Balloon-carrying children drooled over toys in the windows and they hoped that Father Christmas would remember them. The town exuded a carnival atmosphere.

The shadows lay long across the road when two motorcycles tooled into Warkworth: Speed on the Harley, now fitted with a home-made, red-painted sidecar in which Grunter lolled, and Rangi on a new Triumph. In spite of a series of explosions, natural to the Harley when its throttle was retarded, few people turned to look; they thought the noise was part of the celebration. When the bikes pulled in under the Norfolk pine in front of the pub, and the riders disembarked, a few shoppers glanced at the big Maori with funny feet before they went their ways. The riders entered the public bar.

Mac had arrived on the four o'clock bus and immediately hit the pub. When the motorcyclists entered he was warmed up and with an audience, in the middle of the yarn 'aboot the wee Scots girl who asked Jock what he hae under his kilt'. He reached the punch-line and drank deeply while the audience laughed. Looking over his mug he saw his crewmen.

'Stone the bloody crows…!'

It was twilight when Larry and Suzie dressed and wrung out their swimsuits. They had put three crayfish and an octopus in a wet sack, placing the sack with the dog Kuri in the apple box. One crayfish was for Ngaire Tomlinson, one each for Larry and Suzie's dinner, and the octopus for old Nawhai, an ancient Maori woman with a chin moko, a near neighbour.

As Larry prepared to turn into Bakery Lane, he saw the Harley under the Norfolk pine.

'You'll never guess who's here!' he told Suzie.

He dropped a cray off at Ngaire's and put the others in the bathtub. When he walked to the pub he was accompanied by Suzie, the dog Kuri, and the octopus in a sack. He had Suzie restrain the dog while he threaded his way through the drinkers. As Grunter was the closest, he was given the gift meant for Nawhai – around his neck. The great cry from Grunter startled everyone, including the octopus. It fell to the floor where it received the dog Kuri's attention until Larry put it back in the sack.

Then came the greetings. Even the dog Kuri was given appropriate welcome. Grunter nudged him with a boot.

'You bloody old bastard! You been good, Kuri, eh?'

They showed no surprise that Suzie was not Mary. Women came and went.

At nine o'clock the shops closed, the people emptied from the town, and the publican announced that he was shutting down.

Larry had been given three one-gallon demijohns of home-brewed blackberry wine, which he had stashed in the number one oven. The wine turned out to be of the highest octane rating and conducive to such good music that he was brought to tears. He'd missed all this, and his friends. All of a sudden, going to America was one of the things he was not emphatic about.

They had sung 'Pokarekare' when Ngaire stopped at the open door.

Larry stood and said, 'Come on in, Ngaire.'

Ngaire said, 'Forgive me for intruding. They have such beautiful voices – I just had to come.'

Larry said, 'You're not intruding, Ngaire, and this is Christmas. Everyone, this is Ngaire.'

Rangi stood and took Ngaire's hand.

'Tena koe, Ngaire. Haere mai! Very welcome indeed!'

His eyes shone.

MAC WAS THE FIRST to flake out. He searched the cottage for a place to lay his weary body. Only the bathtub was unoccupied. Not noticing the crayfish, he pulled the plug and let the water drain. He rolled up the mat for a pillow and lay down to sleep.

While the others sang he slept. Once he yelled out, 'Spiders! Friggin' great spiders! Crawling all over me!'

Early next morning, Rita Tomlinson rode her new bike up and down the lane. She had yet to master the art of ringing the bell while she rode. She coasted to a stop outside Larry's house and pushed the bell lever back and forth.

The dog Kuri gave up worrying at a crayfish shell and bounded out the door. He added his yelps to the bell ringing, and Rita added her laughter.

Rangi heard them. He went to the window and watched.

It was said that the spinster, Lady Loomis, was an aged ewe trying to look like a spring lamb. Accurate assessment of her age was made difficult because of the layers of paint and varnish that covered the exposed parts of her, but general opinion agreed that she was between forty-five and fifty. Her real name was Jeanie Elizabeth Loomis. She was given the title 'Lady' because she thought she was one.

In addition to owning the cottage next to Ngaire's, she owned a female cocker spaniel she called Queenie.

Few people allowed dogs in their homes, but Lady Loomis was different. Not only was Queenie allowed in her home, she was allowed in her bed. At certain times of the year, however, Queenie was banished to the wash-house. When Queenie was in the wash-house, the dog Kuri was usually at the door to it, a phenomenon that irritated Lady Loomis beyond measure. When she complained, Larry chained the dog to the gate post by the cottage. Lady Loomis had complained the previous evening.

When, next morning, the Hydroelectric Department's line gang saw the dog tied to the gate post, although Larry had explained the reason for his privation, they revolted.

'Untie the bastard!' Speed said.

Rangi was on his way to see Ngaire. The dog Kuri passed him lickety-split. Rangi saw the dog's urgent destination and checked for witnesses before opening the wash-house door.

Queenie was slow to take advantage of the opened door, but not so the dog Kuri. Queenie protested his arrival – a regular rumpus Rangi described it later – until she saw the way out. They streaked around the house. Queenie led by six lengths. The second time around, Queenie led by four lengths. The third time around

Lady Loomis whacked at the dog Kuri with a cane. Though it slowed him down, it did not prevent his ultimate victory.

They disappeared. Lady Loomis scouted the area for them. A couple of hours later they reappeared – coupled. Lady Loomis whacked at the dog Kuri with the cane. The dog Kuri took a course through the seven-wire fence that separated the Loomis house from the road. But Queenie went under the lowest wire and the dog Kuri went over it. When they abruptly halted, Lady Loomis wielded the cane. The dog Kuri discovered his voice. Mac, walking, nursing a hangover, came running.

'Missy! Missy!' He caught Lady Loomis's arm. 'Do you want to kill the beast?'

Her face told him that he'd asked a foolish question.

'You can get into trouble for beating a dumb animal,' he said.

The dogs did a one-eighty.

Mac let go her arm. She raised the cane to him. He held his hand up in protest.

'Don't take on so,' he said. ''Tis only animals. And so she has some puppies. Is it not nature?'

'Puppies!' She looked at Mac with interest. 'You think so?'

'Well... I'm no expert on the process, ye ken, but I think that's the way they go about it.'

She lowered the cane.

'And who might you be?' 'Me name's McKenzie, missus. Alexander MacAllister McKenzie. They call me Mac. I'm here on holiday.'

'Indeed!'

She examined him minutely.

'I'm Jeanie Elizabeth Loomis. My good friends call me Elizabeth. You may call me Elizabeth. Now, tell me more about yourself, Alexander MacAllister McKenzie.'

SPEED AND GRUNTER WENT prowling. They put the Warkworth women into categories: those who they thought would, and those who they thought wouldn't. The poll showed a predominance of those who wouldn't. At the top of the 'who wouldn't' list was Beverley at the bus depot.

A 'possible' was the girl at the hardware store until their inquiries revealed that she had a boyfriend – the skinny, dark fellow who worked at the furniture store. Speed reckoned he was a tippy-toes though he had no idea how he knew. Grunter was of the opinion that he was a hermaphrodite, a word he'd heard somewhere that seemed to fit the man. But they were in unison that Warkworth had little to offer. Larry directed them to Orewa where, he said, they held dances nightly on the beach; they'd find hundreds – thousands – of willing women there.

They didn't find thousands – nor even hundreds – of willing women in Orewa, but they saw a few they hoped were willing.

While Grunter and Speed explored the pleasures of Orewa, Mac and Rangi found theirs in Warkworth. But because Lady Loomis and Ngaire were of proper dispositions, relationships were slow to mature. To boot, Lady Loomis was puzzled by the feelings Mac evoked within her, and that inclined her to intermittent behaviour. Mac plied her with port.

'Ye'd nae deny a mon a wee bit o' a kiss, would ye noo?' he asked, under the apparent impression that a brogue was irresistible.

She giggled and told him not to be silly – but not forcefully so. But just when he thought he had conquered, a picture of the dog Kuri coupled to her dog Queenie popped into Lady Loomis's mind. She thrust Mac away with the urgent direction that he leave her house this minute. Puzzled by her behaviour, Mac went to the pub.

Rangi was smitten with Ngaire. He wanted immediate marriage. Not Ngaire.

'You said yourself, your job takes you all over the place. Where would we live? My girl has to go to school.'

The answer came later in the pub. The man who drank next to Rangi worked for the power board. He offered Rangi a job.

Rangi waited for Ngaire to come home from work. He gave her the news and asked her to marry him.

Ngaire was used to being the provider and decision-maker. She wasn't sure about a changed format. But Rangi kissed her, a long and enduring kiss. She pushed him away.

Suzie was an accountant for her father, a building contractor in Auckland. She adjusted her hours to get as much time as she could with Larry. Larry had trouble getting his work done. She went with him to Leigh and Waipu. The first time Larry had taken her to Jake Watson's, Jake had raised his eyebrows.

'I can't keep up with you, my boy,' he'd said quietly. 'That's number three, isn't it?'

'Like radios, the newer models get better and better,' Larry countered.

Since the visitors had come, Suzie complained about the sleeping arrangements.

'What's the point in coming to see you if there's a dozen people in the room?'

He cleared out part of the old bakery and transferred the sleeping bags from the cottage. That evening, Suzie bit his ear so savagely he threatened to invite them back.

Old Percy didn't know what to make of the new people. The visitors swore and threatened him when he blocked their passage. Lately, if he saw them inside, he turned away.

Larry introduced John Arrf to the visitors.

'A funny bunch of jokers,' John appraised them later. 'I should take them home and let the old lady see what real men look like!

But tell me, Larry, did I see your foreman chap with that old prune, Loomis?'

When Larry answered yes, John said, 'Wonders will never cease! You tell him to watch his step. If she's like the rest of her brood she'll skin the socks right off his feet.' 'I'll warn him,' Larry replied, 'but as far as I know, Mac doesn't have anything worth taking. They could be a good combination.' But he found it hard to believe.

Suzie came from the bus. Larry sighed. How could he study? 'Hello, honey,' she greeted him.

'Hello,' he answered.

'My oh my! Isn't he pleased to see me!' She hooked an arm through his. 'Well, let's see what we can do to get you out of the mood you're in,' she said.

To toast the New Year, Larry bought champagne, Gordon's gin for John Arrf, Black and White for Mac, and on Mac's advice, port wine for Lady Loomis.

He and Suzie cleaned and tidied the bakery. Larry bought tinsel and crêpe paper and, with Suzie's help, hung streamers across the room. He put the gin bottles in the number two oven.

Old Percy stood at the door. Suzie gave him sandwiches from those she had made for the party.

By eight, not a soul had come. Larry opened two bottles of beer.

'Looks like it's just you and me, my scrotum poker,' he said. 'Happy New Year!' And he was thinking, I could have been getting so much work done.

'Oh hip!' Old Percy said.

'Listen to him! He understands. Give the poor thing a drink. It's New Year!' Suzie said. 'And stop worrying – the others will come. Everyone's having parties. They'll have stopped at some along the way.' I hope she's right, he thought, pouring Percy a beer, hoping he was doing the right thing, and saying to himself, thank God the holidays are nearly over.

The old man tucked the crutch under an arm while he held the pannikin. Slurp, slurp. He licked his lips. He smiled – the first sign of positive reaction Larry had ever seen in him except the time when he had struck the dog Kuri.

Slurp slurp. He held the pannikin out for a refill.

'Well, I'll be damned!' Larry said. 'Did you see that?' Then, 'No more, Percy.'

Percy shuffled determinedly inside, holding the pannikin out.

'Just a small one then,' Larry conceded.

Rangi arrived with Ngaire and Rita, chorusing, 'Happy New Year.' Ngaire saw Larry fill Percy's mug.

'Larry! Is it wise to give him beer?'

'A couple of small ones shouldn't hurt him,' he answered, not so sure now.

'That's the last one, Percy,' he said.

John Arrf lurched into the room on unsteady feet, wishing everyone the compliments of the season. He followed the wishes with a lengthy speech about friends and friendships, and conviviality. He smelled strongly of gin.

'Happy New Year,' Larry said when John was done. 'Help yourself to the booze, John.'

John checked out the supply arranged along the old kneading bench. He looked at Larry. 'In the usual place,' Larry said.

'Tricky!' John laughed. He opened the number one oven. He opened the number two.

'You'd make a bloody fine lawyer,' he said, reaching for the bread paddle.

Mac came with the Lady Loomis. His look was apologetic. She

favoured the assembly with a haughty expression.

She saw John. 'Oh dee-ah...!' she said.

John wiped his lips. 'My boy, I confess, I'd have had second thoughts about joining you on this festive eve had I known you were inviting that dried up old trout.'

Mac said, 'Now you look 'ere!'

Larry put a mug in Mac's hand.

'Miss Loomis,' he said, 'would you like a little port wine?'

Miss Loomis saw Percy.

'Him too!'

Percy had helped himself to Larry's beer.

'Oh hip!' he told them.

Larry said, 'Oh, what the hell! It's New Year!'

Larry heard the Harley.

'The party's about to start,' he prophesied.

A bevy of giggling women stumbled through the doorway, followed by Speed and Grunter. In tow was a pack of boisterous males toting a crate of beer.

'Me mates,' Speed apologised. 'Happy New Year!'

'Oh hip!' Percy yelled, and fell down. His crutch knocked a bottle of wine to the floor.

'Help him, someone,' Suzie said. 'Watch the glass.'

Ngaire said, 'If you'll excuse me, I'll take Rita home.'

Old Percy attempted to climb up his crutch.

Rangi said, 'Here, sport. Let me help you.' He pulled Percy upright. 'Bring the box over,' he ordered Grunter.

'Here, sit on this, sport.'

Percy pointed to the pannikin under the bench. 'Oh hip!' he said.

Grunter retrieved the mug and filled it.

'Have one on me, mate,' he said.

Percy swung the crutch at Grunter.

Grunter ducked, laughed, and gave him the pannikin.

'He shouldn't have more – he's fonged as it is,' Suzie said. Lady Loomis said, 'I say!'

Speed said, 'Get stuffed, lady!'

Larry apologised that they had run out of glasses.

'We'll nip it out of the bottle, mate,' a pack member answered.

Old Mac said, 'Did I tell ye aboot the wee Scots lass...'

'Over and over!' Speed said.

The dog Kuri peed on a visitor's leg.

The lawyer began a speech about the rights of the common man.

'What the hell's he talkin' about?' asked one of the Orewa girls.

'He's had a few,' Larry answered. Grunter poured vodka into Lady Loomis's wine, then he stood behind Old Percy, reached over, and topped his pannikin off.

'Merry Christmas, all,' he toasted.

Speed strummed the guitar.

Rangi said, 'I'll be back in a mo'. See what Ngaire's up to.'

Speed said, 'The poor bastard's in love. He'll never be normal again.'

Grunter played the uke. Suzie sang. *Going to take a sentimental journey...* Ngaire and Rangi returned. Rangi had brought his guitar. *Going to set my mind at ease...*

The lawyer applauded. 'Jolly good! Jolly good music, jolly fine company, and I must say, a jolly fine lot of young women you've brought to grace the premises this night.' Apparently, he had forgotten the Lady Loomis.

He poured gin. 'Happy New Year!' he said.

Rangi banged a bottle on the bench.

'Ladies and gentlemen...'

'Get rooted!' a visitor proposed.

Larry called out: 'Please!'

Rangi put an arm around Ngaire. He kissed her on the mouth. Someone whistled.

'We're getting married,' he said.

It took moments to register.

Mac said, 'You mean you're not coming back to the job?'

Speed said, 'Screw the job.' He turned to Rangi. 'Bloody quick, but bloody good deal, mate.'

'This calls for a special toast,' Larry said. He opened the door to number three oven and brought out the champagne.

The Lady Loomis put an arm around Ngaire.

'My dea-ah… I'm so happy for you.' She wiped her eyes and blew her nose. 'Alexander, isn't this wonderful?' She leaned on Mac's shoulder. Mac patted her hand.

Mac said, 'Yes, yes, me dear,' though he wondered how he would keep the job on schedule.

By eleven the champagne was gone and so was the lawyer. He had said that he was going outside for a spot of fresh air. He hadn't returned.

Old Percy had fallen off his box. Someone had shoved him under the dough-kneading bench and there he slept.

Old Mac had introduced Lady Loomis to Black and White. She didn't like the taste until he thinned it with lemonade. She claimed then that it was 'most delicious'. In record time she put away two pannikins of the mixture. To give her room for more, Mac took her into the weeds at the side of the building where she complained that her mouth was numb and her throat constricted. Mac took her home. They fell over the lawyer, asleep in the weeds.

At midnight, to the sound of church bells, they yelled and whistled. Arranging themselves into a circle, they joined hands and sang 'Auld Lang Syne' – those who could stand.

An Orewa girl placed herself in the centre. She danced with weird grace, with an imaginary partner, and a beat of her own, until she became dizzy and fell down.

Larry mounted Operation Rescue. Speed put Percy and John in the sidecar, facing each other.

The constable rode up on his bicycle. He inspected the cargo and gave them a clean bill of lading, though he wasn't happy about Percy.

'You could kill the old bugger, getting him drunk like that,' he admonished.

He inquired of Speed when they would be leaving Warkworth.

When Speed told him in a week, the constable advised him not to delay the departure.

The dog Kuri lifted his leg against the constable's bike wheel.

They delivered Percy to his cottage.

'Better hold your breath,' Larry suggested at the first whiff when he opened the door. His respect for Ngaire, who had nursed Old Percy through an illness, increased.

John's wife met them at his entrance.

'Don't bring the sod in here,' she ordered and slammed the door.

They took him back to the bakery.

'I don't have any more beds. Leave him in the sidecar,' Larry said.

He rolled a flour sack into a pillow and placed it under John's head, covering him with a second sack.

It was past Suzie's normal bedtime. She collapsed diagonally across the bed. Larry pulled her legs straight and lay beside her.

The dog Kuri settled between them.

LARRY'S INTEREST IN SINGLE sideband (s.s.b) suppressed carrier communications began in 1947 when he read an article written by an American radio amateur, one of the original developers of amateur s.s.b. mode of radio communication, and he was hooked.

Mary had complained that he thought more of his 'wireless' than he did of her and that was before he knew about s.s.b. Since then, he'd spent more and more time in the 'lab', as he called that corner of the old bakery where he studied and experimented, and now Suzie complained. But although she voiced the same message as Mary, there was a difference; Mary was easily huffed at his inattention, but not Suzie. Suzie bit his ear until he noticed her. Then she unbuckled his belt.

As summer turned into winter, scuba diving became her number two hobby. Larry hoped that her preference would reverse in the summer.

He was surprised that she came to see him so often. There was no shortage of obliging young males in Auckland now that the war was over and the servicemen back home, and he was, he knew, dull company, determined as he was to spend his out-of-bed time working, studying and experimenting. He had told her that one day he'd be leaving – going to America.

'What do you see in me, Poker?' he asked one evening. Poker had become a pet name for her.

'Not much,' she said. She ran her hand through the hair on his chest.

'I'm serious. What do you see in me?'

She twisted his hair into little ringlets.

'Maybe I like you,' she said, which, he realised, was as close to a declaration of love as he could ever expect to get from the pragmatic Suzie.

Since coming to Warkworth, Rangi had led a monastic life, for Ngaire had insisted that she needed time and refused to let Rangi into her bed until they were married. Finally she set a date. Speed, Grunter and Mac had promised that they would attend the wedding. Larry wasn't sure that he could stand another of their visits. Meanwhile, he visited the American Consulate in Auckland. They recognised him now. But their answer was the same: nothing yet.

'Just hang in there,' they said.

Hang in there! How long could he hang? America receded further and further. Only the over-the-air conversations with American amateurs kept it from dropping right off the horizon.

One day a postcard came from Mary, on it a picture of the Houses of Parliament in London. She wrote:

Here I am, sweetie, in London at last! I wish you were here. We could have so much fun together. I wish that every day. All my love, Mary.

Suzie was with him when he picked up the mail. He showed her the postcard.

'You had something going with that one, didn't you!' she responded. She was unusually quiet the rest of the afternoon.

Suzie was in Auckland the morning he picked up Moira's letter from the Warkworth post office. A sudden small thrill passed through him. But he waited until he was back in the cottage and settled on the bed before he opened it.

My dear Larry,

I have thought about you so much and I wonder how you are. It's presumptuous of me to write like this again, but I had to tell you: we're going to America! Ian is doing research on genetics. He applied to an American research institute for a fellowship. After a year of correspondence and waiting (and frayed tempers), he's been accepted, although from his demeanour, you would think that we were merely going to Glasgow. Yesterday when I asked him if he was excited, he said that he was excited about furthering his studies, but wished he could do them without going to America! My dear, we Scots are a dour lot.

But no matter how Ian feels, I am excited. My life here is so boring. I've wanted to get a job, but Ian believes that a wife shouldn't work. I want a baby. He doesn't - not until his studies are completed and goodness knows when that will be!

As I write I am making up my mind that I will have a surprise or two for the stolid Ian in America. The submissive wife turns!

Larry, my father died eighteen months ago. When Pam went nursing and I showed no interest in a commercial career he sold the businesses, and I think his heart with them, for he was never the same after that. My mother and I tried to get him to take a trip to Australia and New Zealand, but he wouldn't go. He had the conviction that they sent criminals to Australia and remittance men to New Zealand!

Larry put the letter down. He scratched the dog Kuri between the ears. Would he ever know women? Moira going to America. And possibly Mary, one day.

He wondered what Moira would think of him now. Would she consider him dour too? Probably. How could he be anything else when he had to work sixteen hours a day? He chased the dog Kuri off the bed and resumed reading.

Larry, please dear, write and tell me about yourself. I wonder, are you in America yet? I need to know about you. I'm sending this to the last address you gave me so I do hope it finds you. Wouldn't it be wonderful if we should meet in America...

THE MORNING OF RANGI and Ngaire's wedding opened cold and wet. In spite of the weather, Larry and Suzie had gone to Leigh to catch crayfish for the reception, but the seas were enormous. 'We could go back to the house and tear one off,' Suzie suggested, though they had already 'torn one off' early that morning. Larry didn't feel that he was yet sufficiently recovered.

'Tomorrow,' he temporised.

'Why is it that the men I meet are such weaklings?' Suzie countered.

Speed, Grunter and Mac had arrived the previous day. Speed

and Grunter had agreed to dig the hole for the hangi in the garden behind Ngaire's house. They had worked half-heartedly the previous evening, delayed by the rain and frequent trips to the old bakery for quenchers. When the quenchers ran out, they joined Rangi and Mac in the pub.

Grunter was in a baiting mood. He said to Mac, 'Old Hoity-Toity's bitch had pups, that right, boss?' 'Aye, five of them. And don't call her Hoity-Toity!'

'Sorry about that, boss. But it takes about nine weeks for a bitch to have pups, that right? And nine months for humans?'

Mac nodded, wondering where this was going.

'So... according to my reckonin', in three months Hoity-Toity should pop a litter. You better marry her quick!'

Speed added, 'And you dig your own bloody hole for the hangi.'

The rain beat on the tin roof. The minister yelled to be heard.

Rangi had asked Grunter to be the best man, but Grunter had refused. 'With these feet!' So Speed was the best man.

The two had primed Rangi all morning to build up his stamina. They over-primed him. When he was asked, would he take this woman to be his wife, and opened his mouth, nothing came out. The minister waited. Speed broke in. 'Hey! He wants to know if you want to marry the sheila.'

Rangi came out of his lethargy. 'Too right – you bet!'

The reception was at Ngaire's. To be certain that the hangi would be ready, Ngaire had collected the diggers from the pub and put them back to work digging the hole and building the fire the previous evening. She wrapped the food in tea towels and clean flour sacks. Larry wrapped the bundles in ponga fronds, placed them on the hot stones, covered them with sacks, and refilled the hole with soil.

The wedding over, Grunter dug away the dirt. He carried tea towel-wrapped food to the kitchen door. Mindful of not tramping mud into the kitchen, he put the bundles on the doorstep and returned for a second load. The dog Kuri smelled the meat. He dragged the parcel containing the two legs of lamb – the hangi's major meat course – down the steps and into the mud, biting and tearing at the tea towels until he got to the meat.

Grunter was famous for his swear words. The dog Kuri, however, because of his long previous relationship with Grunter mistook them for words of endearment; he wagged his tail and continued to attack the meat. Grunter's broadside boot landed with precision and lifted the dog ten feet or more into the air.

Grunter called through the door to Speed: 'You better hose the lamb off. The bloody kuri got into it!'

'Shit, they won't know no bloody difference,' Speed answered. Later, at the table, Lady Loomis said, 'Ngaire, you prepare the best hangi lamb I've ever eaten. You must give me the recipe.'

'I didn't prepare it,' Ngaire answered, 'the boys did. You'll have to ask them.'

'Nothing doing – old Maori secret!' Grunter said.

After they'd eaten and before the speeches began, Grunter wheeled in a perambulator. 'From me and Speed,' he said.

Ngaire said, 'You two!'

Rangi said, 'Pae kare! Jumping the gun a bit, aren't you, sport?'

'You're the one with the gun, mate,' Speed answered. John the lawyer said, 'I have a little token... If one of you men will help me...'

Speed and Larry brought in the boxes.

High quality dinnerware was in short supply after the war, and Ngaire knew how lucky she was, but she'd always found it hard to like John. Now she found it hard to find the right words to thank him. John mistook her hesitation.

'That's all right, my dear,' he soothed. He patted her hand.

'You're a bloody good sport,' Rangi said.

Larry said, 'On behalf of Suzie and me...' and put their present on the table.

Mac said, 'From Elizabeth and me...'

Lady Loomis said, 'It's only a paltry few things my de-ah. But I thought you'd like some new bed linen now that... well, you know what I mean, my de-ah...'

Larry had loaned Rangi the van. He had tightened the wood screws and refitted the headlamp – which had fallen off again – and mopped up the flour that had not stopped coming from the cracks. He washed the seat covers and put a whoopee cushion on the driver's seat. He locked the van in Joe Montini's garage against marauding Plenkovich kids.

'I'll bring the limousine to the door,' Speed volunteered. 'I wouldn't want the rain to put the new hubby's fire out!'

He brought the Essex to the front of the cottage, tied tin cans to the rear bumper and a rope from the bumper to a fence strainer post. They gathered on the porch. Speed played the accordion and Grunter the uke. They sang 'Haere Ra; Now is the Hour', in English and in Maori, and Ngaire cried and Suzie cried and Lady Loomis dabbed at her eyes and 'Oh dea-ahed' until Rangi said, 'Hey! We gotta go!'

Rangi fought the gear shift. He let the clutch out. The rope tightened, the rear bumper pulled into a V-shape, the strainer post tilted and pulled free from the wet ground. And as the fence ran from Ngaire's gate post to Lady Loomis's gate post, Lady Loomis's gate was the last to leave. The ensemble disappeared in tow around the corner.

Mac said, 'Stone the bloody crows!'

Lady Loomis said, 'Look what they did to my fence!'

The lawyer said, 'They could be sued if someone gets hurt!'

Grunter said, 'The posts were rotten anyhow.'

Larry wondered what damage was done to the Essex.

DEAR *MOIRA*, L ARRY WROTE, and then he ran out of words. So much to say, but how to say it to another's wife?

He liked it that she wanted to hear from him and about him. But where to start? Would she want to read about his friends? Would she understand them? What could he tell her about himself? That he worked sixteen hours a day and had little time for anything else? She had said that her husband was dour. Am I any different, he asked himself.

He'd describe Warkworth. Keep it impersonal. Warkworth had to be as different from Dundee as day from night. Warkworth in its setting of ferns and green hills against the gray brick and pavement of Dundee; balmy southern nights against harsh northern chills – could he do the town justice?

But he could tell her about Grunter and Speed and the lawyer John, he supposed. Lady Loomis even, and Mac. And Rangi and Ngaire's wedding.

He sat at the work bench, the dog Kuri at his feet. Percy shuffled to the door reminding him that it was *that* time. Larry plugged the electric kettle in. Tea helped him think. He took the lid off the tea caddy. One spoonful for Percy, one for himself, one for the pot, and three for the extra cups he'd probably drink while writing the letter.

Percy ate the crackers and slurped his tea down before Larry had poured his own. Almost as quickly though, Larry downed a cupful. Then he started writing, slowly at first then with fluency. He told Moira that his friends, without their knowing it, had assisted his difficult transition back into civilian life though, as he wrote the words, he realised that, in no small measure, so had Mary.

He described his work and how it absorbed his time. He told her about John and his bouts with the bottle.

He didn't tell her about Suzie or Beverley, although Beverley was on his mind; he had heard that she had become engaged.

He told her about Rangi and Ngaire.

...they're going to have a baby. They're so happy.

Mac, my former boss, has also found a lady friend in Warkworth, though he doesn't appear to have attained Rangi's degree of contentment. Mac's work is about four hundred miles south of here which probably doesn't help his situation. Neither has been married before, although they're both near fifty. When he's here he stays at her house, and if that hasn't caused the tongues to wag!

When I read that you were going to America I confess I was envious – jealous! But really, I'm happy for you.

I well remember, when I was stationed in Algeria during the war, so many airmen wretchedly pining for home, on their days off hating to leave their tents lest they breathe the foreign air. But there were those of us to whom it was an adventure to ride the ancient tram cars into Algiers squeezed between fierce-looking Arab men, their purdahed wives, their live, scrawny chickens they took to market in string baskets (and once a live pig). And practise our terrible French on those who would put up with it, try to date the mademoiselles (without much success – they were an aloof lot), but generally have a wonderful time. Reading your letter, and your plans to enjoy yourself in America, I say go to it. Don't be afraid to breathe the foreign air.

Her husband, Larry decided, would stay in his tent.

Larry wrote that his prospects for going to America had not improved.

...and the trouble is, I'm putting down roots. I've already picked out the land on which, one day, I'd like to build my house! It bothers me that I pay out rent money that should be contributing toward the purchase of my own place.

He finished the letter and sealed the envelope. He would have written a short note to Mary too, but her postcard had not given a return address. So be it, he thought.

He called the dog Kuri, put him in the apple box.

'You miserable fleabag, let's catch a couple of crays, eh?' As he turned out of Bakery Lane, he saw Beverley sweeping the footpath in front of the depot. He was sorely tempted to ask her to ride with him to Leigh, but he feared her rebuff.

As he rode he thought that in spite of Suzie, and busy as he was, he was lonely. A sorry state of affairs that his only regular company was a flea-bitten mongrel – not even an apology for a dog.

'Hey... you're all right!' he yelled over his shoulder.

The dog Kuri stood. With no new intelligence forthcoming, he sat back down.

LARRY HAD COMPLETED THE first radio transceiver of his own design. It hadn't been easy. Bernie Steinmetz's supply of war surplus materials had tapered off. Although Bernie had started importing components, what he ordered had nothing to do with his customers' requirements, but more to do with what items he'd got a good deal on, so Larry suspected. Tired of arguing over the telephone, Larry rode to Auckland to see Bernie.

As he squeezed between the piles of what seemed like mostly junk he could hear Bernie in his office screaming into the telephone. From the sound of Bernie's end of the conversation, he was having a bad day. As Larry reached the office, Bernie snorted, slammed the phone down, looked up as Larry entered, and snarled, 'And what do *you* want?'

For once Bernie's waistcoat buttons actually matched the buttonholes, but his skill with the razor had taken a turn for the worse. Tufts of salt and pepper whiskers sprouted where his razor had missed them, and he'd cut one sideburn a good inch shorter than the other. Larry explained his needs, finishing: 'Bernie, here's the list of components I need. I've designed the radio around them, so it's these or nothing. None of your substitutes.'

Bernie leaned back, tilting his chair, and scanned the list. Then, peering over the rims of his glasses, he stared at Larry before he spoke.

'And what have you done with your little negotiator? She still with you?'

So now the time had come to tell him about Mary.

'Mary's in England.'

'England! What's she doing in England?'

'Travelling.'

Bernie shook his head.

'And you're running the business?'

'Anything wrong with that, Bernie?'

'She's got the brains.'

'I seem to be managing all right.'

'You think so? I would say that that remains to be seen. From what I...'

That remains to be seen – a favourite expression of Johnny from Christchurch. (That remains to be seen said the monkey when he shit in the sugar and covered it up.) Larry laughed to himself, forgetting for the moment he'd ridden to Auckland to do battle with Bernie.

'...all this special stuff! You think import licences grow on trees or something? If you don't like what I got...'

It occurred to Larry that he could tell Bernie Steinmetz to shove his parts, close up shop, and get out from underneath. He was going to be a radio engineer; he would not haggle and argue like a Kasbah Arab selling brass geegaws and hookahs. But a moment's reflection and he realised that that was the short-term view. The long-term view was that he'd have to hang in there (to borrow the words of the American Consulate's secretary) until he was an engineer, for at least the manufacturing afforded him a living, a better than usual living if he considered the accounts receivable as cash, something he'd had a problem with in spite of Suzie's efforts to educate him to the contrary.

But the short-term view prevailed. He stood.

'Bernie, you're a stupid bastard.'

He called to the dog Kuri, in the process of wetting down a stack of used Jeep tyres. They edged through the heaps to the outside, Bernie following as quickly as his weight and size would allow. He caught up with them at the Velocette.

'No occasion to get mad, my boy. We can work something out,' he pleaded, unusually humble all of a sudden.

Larry plonked the dog Kuri in the apple box.

'Yeah! You'll give me what I want, I suppose. Seems to me I've heard that song before – right here, in fact.'

Larry started the motor and drove away. By the time he'd reached Khyber Pass he'd cooled. He pulled into the kerb and sat. And now what would he do for components? He turned to the dog. 'Hey, fleabag. You got any bright ideas?'

The answer came in the Tip Top over lunch. He had tied the dog Kuri to the bike at the kerb, had ordered tea and toast and a meat pie for the dog. While he stirred his tea he studied the possibilities – really only one: Willard Electric in Wellington. He'd write. Better, he'd telephone. Better yet…

He ate the toast and gulped down the tea. The dog Kuri demolished the meat pie in two gulps. He expected more.

'That's it, fleabag. In the box. Glasses on.'

Hours later, in Paekakariki, he stopped at a café. It was six o'clock; too late to ride on to Wellington. After a bite to eat he asked the way to the New Zealand Hydroelectric Line Camp, number five.

Tomorrow was Guy Fawkes Day. Larry bought a cherry bomb.

It was eight o'clock when he coasted the bike into the camp. He walked between the two rows of huts. Through an open door he saw Grunter and Speed playing cards at a cable-spool table. He held the dog Kuri by the collar while he lit the cherry bomb and rolled it into the hut. Grunter pulled his chair back to see what had hit his foot. The bomb exploded.

The dog Kuri broke from Larry's grasp and departed the area. Grunter and Speed emerged moments later followed by a swirling volume of acrid smoke.

The explosion provoked a turnout from the other huts. One inmate, on seeing the smoke, struck the length of railway line that hung at the cookhouse door.

Grunter reconnoitred the area. He found the Velocette.

'Pae kare! Wait till I get me hands on that bastard!'

He found the bastard leaning nonchalantly against a door post. Larry lifted a hand in salutation. 'Happy Guy Fawkes Day,' he said.

'Ever entered a dunny head first?' Grunter asked, quickly closing the gap between them.

'A fellow comes 400 miles to see you and you threaten to dunk him in the dunny. What sort of hospitality is that?'

'Got any grog?' Grunter moderated.

'I may have.'

'You better produce it bloody quick.'

In Speed's hut Larry filled the glasses. He lifted his own high. 'Kia ora,' he saluted.

155

'Cheers,' from Speed.

'You bastard,' toasted Grunter.

'Rangi's going to be a poppa!' Larry said.

'Must have shot his bolt the first night,' Grunter opined. 'How's his missus feel about it?'

'Thinks it's great.'

'Lucky bastard,' Grunter said.

Meanwhile, in his hut, Mac nursed a pannikin of Black and White on his chest. It wasn't the first full pannikin to have been so placed that evening, it was perhaps the fourth or fifth. Over the years Mac had come to believe that a drink or two after dinner improved his thinking. After three or four he had brilliant ideas. Like the time he'd thought to use radios to help the stringing of the cables. But others took the credit. A song went around in his head: *It's the rich what gets the credit, it's the poor what gets the blame!*

He had dedicated this evening to a decision about Elizabeth. He took a long swig. He heard the noises outside.

'Stop the bloody racket!' he called out. *It's the rich what gets the pleasure...* He stopped. Elizabeth was the rich. He was the poor. *It's the poor what gets the blame!* He talked to the pannikin.

'And don't she let me know it. Calling me a good-for-nothing – the bitch! Pretending one minute she likes me, the next minute calling me a good-for-nothing! She wants me pension, that's what she wants!'

The pannikin sat half full on his chest. He gazed over it at a picture of Elizabeth he'd hung over the fireplace. The picture was twenty years old.

'I had it taken especially for you, Alexander, so you won't forget me,' she'd lied. 'But I still can't see why you can't get a job up here. Ngaire's husband did. You're a foreman! Why can't you get one?'

'I'll think about it, my dear,' Mac had said, knowing full well that it could be years before the department built a new line through the area.

'I could retire,' he suggested.

'What? And how much would that pay? A fraction of what you earn now, I'll warrant! Don't you think for one minute that I'm going to support you on the little I have, the way you drink!'

Far from her now, Mac lifted the pannikin. 'To you, my dear,' he toasted, 'you tight-arsed bitch!' *It's the rich what gets the pleasure…* The pannikin fell to the floor.

Larry said, 'How's old Mac?'

Grunter rubbed his nose with the back of his hand. 'Aue! Every night he gets pissy-eyed – ever since he met that bitch in Warkworth. He's even nipping on the job now.'

'Yi, yi! Which is his hut? Least I can do is say hello to him,' Larry answered, appalled that Mac was drinking on the job. 'Stay put, e hoa,' from Speed. He reached for his old pig-hunting rifle, aimed at the top of Mac's door, and pulled the trigger.

The dog Kuri, fast becoming a veteran at rapid departures, left again. Larry said, 'Holy shit!' Even in the dim light of the pole lamp he saw that Mac's door had grown a neat, round hole.

The door opened.

'Stone the bloody crows! What the hell you think you're doing?' Mac yelled to the air at large.

Speed called across the space between the huts: 'Hey, boss, come and meet the visitor.'

'You bastard. You shot a bloody hole in Elizabeth's picture!'

'Should have been the bitch herself,' from Grunter.

'Now, you look 'ere!'

'Larry's here,' Speed said. 'Larry?'

'Hey Mac, you forgotten me already?'

'Larry! Stone the bloody crows! Whatcha doin' here, lad? Good to see you.'

ALLAN WILLARD PROVED TO be courteous and obliging, his place of business neat and orderly. He said that yes, he'd do his best to provide Larry with the components he needed. It wouldn't be easy – not with the present-day import restrictions – but he did have a couple of friends in the right places. His prices were better than Bernie's, too, by far.

Returning to the outskirts of Auckland, Larry remembered with a start that Suzie had said she was coming to Warkworth to celebrate the anniversary of their first meeting – and that was yesterday. Yi, yi! He wondered if she had returned to Auckland when she had found him gone. Deciding that he'd be in double trouble if he didn't check to see, he drove to her father's timber yard, nearly colliding with a city bus in his rush to determine his fate.

Suzie was at her desk. When she heard the door open she looked up from her typewriter, and looked right back again, only now she banged away at it with renewed emphasis.

Well, now the pig's in the puha, Larry thought, wondering what to do next – not a new feeling. Again he was out of his depth with a woman. Mary, and now Suzie.

'Princess, I'm sorry… something came up…'

Suzie stood quickly and, without as much as a glance in Larry's direction, left the room, slamming the door shut with such force a picture fell from the wall. The gun-shy dog Kuri sought escape. Larry hefted him into his arms and soothed him with words. So the unflappable Suzie was flappable! But why such a bloody great fuss? After all, something had come up.

Riding home, he mulled over what he thought was Suzie's totally unreasonable conduct. The least she could have done was let him explain, but no, she'd stamped out of the room – and, he suspected, out of his life. He wondered if he'd miss her. At least he'd get more work done with her not taking up so much of his time. Then he thought about their lovemaking. It was good, Suzie was an avid partner, but it had become mechanical. Bang, bang, and Suzie slept. Actually, when he thought about it, it had always been bang, bang. There she differed most from Mary. After sex, Mary and he, legs intertwined, had talked, often into the small hours, until one or the other had fallen asleep.

Back at the cottage he showered, changed clothes, and headed for the old bakery and work, but at the door changed his mind and walked on to the pub. Since leaving Suzie's place of work he'd carried a sadness which was eating away at him. Perhaps a drink would raise his spirits.

John Arrf sat alone in the after-hours bar talking to the proprietor. Larry took the stool beside him, noticing as he did so that John's face had been quite badly clawed.

'And what's the other chap like?' he said in jest.

John laughed wryly, drained his glass, downed a refill, then explained how he came to be clawed.

The story involved a squabble with his wife over his shooting possums in their fruit trees. His wife, the larger of the couple, had attacked him, wrested the .22 calibre rifle from his hands and, holding it by its barrel, smashed it against a tree.

Because of the quiet way John told his story, Larry found it hard not to laugh, but he sensed that to John the whole thing was anything but a joke. Larry shuddered to think about life bound to such a woman. A bull elephant, according to Joe Montini.

John took to morosely studying his drink, and Larry's sadness returned. First Mary and now Suzie had passed him up. But one comfort, Moira hadn't given up on him – a small consolation though, since she belonged to someone else.

Larry slid his glass across the bar for a refill, but instead of filling it, the proprietor dropped it into the sink. 'Gentlemen, please, let's wind it up,' he said. 'Let at least one of us get some sleep tonight, eh?'

Although his eyes remained open, John seemed to have removed himself to somewhere else. Larry gently shook his shoulder. 'John! It's time to go home,' he said.

John blinked his eyes a couple of times. 'Ah yes... time to go home.' He reached for the glass to finish his drink, but the proprietor had dropped it into the sink, too.

'That glass was two-thirds full,' John said, sliding off the stool. 'You owe me a drink.'

The bartender rolled his eyes. 'John, John, John!' He swiped at the bar with a wet rag where the drinks had sat. 'Only a bloody lawyer...'

Larry grinned at that and wondered at John's ability to put liquor away. Out on the street John tenderly stepped around obstacles that didn't exist, and a couple of times bumped into the wall, but he made it to the footpath in front of the hotel, where he looked across the road to the butcher shop. He waved his hand in its general direction. 'Look yonder, my boy – I used to see Old Fritz's eyes in that bloody Holstein, and now, bugger my days if I don't see his friggin' daughter's!'

Larry followed John's gaze across the road to the bull, but nothing had changed since he'd last looked; he saw a wooden animal with painted eyes, and that was it. Yet Mary had seen something. 'Its eyes follow you,' she'd said.

At the entrance to Bakery Lane, John stopped again. 'My boy, do you think there's a bottle left in one of those ovens?'

Larry looked at John with amazement. How did he do it? And he was a small man!

'There should be something there,' Larry answered, thinking, well, there goes work tomorrow.

'Thank you, my boy – whatever you have will be fine. Anything is better than having to face my wife's hot tongue and frozen arse this night.' Larry laughed. But why didn't John pull up stakes and head out? And then Larry remembered being told that if John left his wife, the money stayed with the trust.

The locals said that no one had ever held a candle to Old Fritz

160

when it came to hanging on to money. From what Larry could see it went well beyond that – the old boy controlled his money even from the grave.

They arrived at the bakery. Larry poked the bread paddle into the number two oven and brought forth a bottle of Black and White – booze he'd bought for Mac. Already feeling somewhat fuzzy, he wasn't sure that he was up to getting involved in a session, but he poured himself a drink anyway.

Part way through the bottle, John said, 'My boy, I detect a sorrow in you this night, and that's not like you at all, not at all. Should you need a sympathetic shoulder, please consider me your dear friend, as I consider you. Isn't that what friends are for – to succour each other in times of distress? And now, that said, I ask you, am I correct in assuming that your sadness has something to do with a woman?'

Remind me not to battle John in a court of law, Larry warned himself before telling him about Suzie.

'The plain truth is, John, I was so concerned about getting components for my radios I forgot all about Suzie. If she'd have just let me explain...'

John swirled the neat Black and White around in his glass and studied it intently before he spoke. 'My boy, I believe that your Suzie is an uncommonly sensible girl, perhaps a little rough around the edges, and headstrong, but decidedly forthright and honest. When she puts her pride behind her, she'll realise that she's treated you in a rather dastardly fashion and will wish to make amends – of that I'm quite certain. Would that my old lady was of like disposition. But now, to change the subject, I see a .22 on the wall there. I wish to borrow it for a few minutes, if you'll be so good as to accommodate me.'

Larry was startled. Yi, yi! But before he could speculate, John said, 'Rest assured, my boy, I have nothing nefarious in mind, unless you consider shooting a symbol of repression a crime. I refer to the bull on the butcher shop, put there by my late father-in-law, I believe, to keep a painted eye on me. Realise, it's directly opposite my office.'

Larry lifted the rifle from its nails and handed it over.

'Okay, John, but I'm coming with you.' The truth was that Larry felt like shooting at something himself for he did not believe that Suzie would return. When Suzie made up her mind to something it stayed made up. He thought then about what John had said, that Suzie was rough around the edges, and he had to acknowledge the truth of the observation. Compared with Moira, or even Mary, Suzie was rough around the edges, but also, as John had said, she was forthright, and patently honest. He would miss her greatly – he already did.

A telephone pole stood in front of John's building. John put the bottle of Black and White – which he had thoughtfully brought along – on the footpath, steadied the rifle against the pole and aimed at the Holstein's head. Before he pulled the trigger, however, he said, 'My boy, I view what that animal represents with the same abhorrence I did the Nazi swastika. I shall demolish it.' He pulled the trigger. The shot echoed and re-echoed along Queen Street; the dog Kuri hightailed it back to the bakery, but as far as Larry could see nothing else happened. The rifle was a bolt-action, single shot Remington. John reloaded and fired again, and when that too missed, he nipped at the bottle of Black and White, which did improve his aim, for the next bullet glanced off something before it sang into the night. Then came Larry's turn. His aim was no better than John's, but the light was difficult.

'We should have a shotgun, my boy. But give me another crack at it. Perhaps if I aim between the eyes…' John steadied the rifle against the pole once more, and missed again. At this point, Constable Weatherspoon rode up on his bicycle.

'For Christ's sake – two of you at it now! Look at the time, man! It's two o'clock in the bloody morning! Now give me that rifle. Your old lady is insisting that I have you committed, and so help me God, I think I will. But we'll talk about that in the morning. Now go home, the two of you, before I lock you both up!'

Larry pumped up the air mattress and placed it on the floor

behind the ovens. When John lay down on it, looking for all the world like a happy, cherubic babe holding its bottle, it seemed that the wifely demon that had possessed him earlier had been vanquished. John began a nonsensical song:

> The elephant is a wonderful bird
> It flits from bough to bough
> It builds its nest in a rhubarb tree
> It whistles like a cow...

Will I ever know human beings, Larry wondered.

I T WAS CHRISTMAS DAY. Larry had been scuba diving. He lay on his back by the Velocette under a pohutukawa, his hands clasped under his head. A bellbird tinkled in the distance. The dog Kuri barked.

'You stupid fleabag! Why'd you do that?'

The dog put his head under Larry's arm, licked at his face. Larry sat up quickly and pushed the dog away.

'I've told you before, don't do that!'

He opened a Waitemata, leaned on an elbow, and drank from the bottle. He missed Suzie.

A car came bumping down the dirt tracks. He was annoyed. True, he was lonely, but he wasn't lonely for just anyone. He was relieved when they bumped their way to the other side of the cove. Even then he could hear their voices yelling back and forth. He hoped they'd quieten when they settled down.

He wondered about his life and where it was going. He worked and studied, but for what purpose? Most people had a goal, something to aim for. They wanted to get married, buy a house or a new car, or take a trip somewhere, have children. Yes, he had a goal, but was it a real goal, something actually attainable? It was three years since he'd first filled in the papers applying for admission to America. Now even his hope was tired.

A shadow fell over him. The dog Kuri jumped up, wagging his tail.

'Hello, you bloody turd,' Suzie greeted him.

'Suzie!' He scrambled to his feet.

'Well! Are you just going to stand there!'

'Oh, Poker…' He wrapped his arms around her.

She nuzzled his neck. 'You bloody stink bag. I should cut your dingle dangle off!'

They kissed.

'Talking of dingle dangles…'

Back at the Velocette, he said, 'Poker, before you came I was the most miserable bloke on earth.'

'That makes two of us,' she answered. 'I missed you awfully.'

They lay back on the grass. She held his hand in the two of hers.

'I missed you too,' he said.

'That was obvious – it was barely worth coming all this way for,' she said.

But for now they were content with holding each other. How great it feels to have someone, he thought. Through the leaves Larry saw the olive-green and yellow of a bellbird.

'Ssshhh,' he cautioned. 'Look!'

She whispered, 'What?'

'A bellbird.'

A faint *ding-dong* came from afar.

'Listen!' he whispered.

The bird above them lifted its head. *Ding-dong*, it answered.

The dog Kuri stood and looked up.

'No!' Larry ordered him.

'Oh, honey!' Suzie squeezed his hand. He answered her squeeze and leaned to kiss her lightly. There were tears in her eyes.

'That's the most beautiful sound I've ever heard,' she whispered.

They heard it again. Faintly. *Ding-dong*. The bird above answered and took flight.

Suzie was quiet after that. She didn't even bite him.

He eased his position on the grass.

'We could go scuba diving,' he said.

'Oh, honey. Not now. Just hold me.'

At the house she cooked a crayfish he'd caught that morning. Now she was chatter chatter as she moved between the sink, the stove and the table. Her chatter had irritated him in the past because it was empty, and it didn't stop, but tonight it was music. It had surprised him that she had been so affected by the bellbirds. The remainder of the day she had stayed quiet and alert for the sound of them. Once she'd grabbed his knee.

'Hear it?'

He heard it. 'I think it's a tui.'

'It's a bellbird – I know.'

Now he watched her bustle about the small kitchen. Actually, this evening, he wouldn't have minded had they gone to bed *before* they ate – it had been a long seven weeks. But as things turned out, it was worth it. The crayfish was good, the vegetables were perfect, and afterwards, so was Suzie.

A week later, Larry opened a letter from *CQ Magazine*. The editor asked if Larry could supply a monthly article. Before Christmas he would have thought, how can I? But now, his depression gone, he thought, of course I can. He began an outline and then the article. After several hours, thirsty, barely aware of what he was doing, he went to the tap to fill the electric kettle, and was startled to see old Percy leaning on his crutch in the doorway. How long had he been there, Larry wondered.

'Percy! What the hell are you doing here at this time of the night?' he said. Then he realised that it was early morning – the sky had already lightened to the east. 'Why are you up so early?'

Percy ignored the question. He had seen the teapot in Larry's hand; he waited for his tea. This morning he munched at something. It turned out to be spittle, which he dumped on the concrete when Larry brought his mug of tea.

'Percy! Not in the bloody doorway!'

Larry hosed the mess into the weeds. The old man backed away. Larry felt strongly tempted to hose him down, to teach him not to spit in the doorway, except that he doubted that the poor old bugger would make the connection – unlike the dog Kuri, who made himself scarce if Larry so much as bent to pick up a hose. Larry softened and gave Percy his tea.

Percy's hands shook so much he spilled the tea on the concrete, decidedly not his usual performance. Usually, slurp, slurp, and the tea was gone. None spilled.

'What in the hell's the matter with you this morning?' Larry said, looking Percy over. He seemed normal enough. Or did he lean heavily on his crutch this morning – more than usual.

Larry said, 'Percy, give me the mug. I'll refill it. But this time try not to spill it, eh?' He took the mug.

Larry had been up all night, yet he felt fully awake. Soon he'd have the article finished. Then he had a new fishing boat installation to make at Leigh. He wondered if he would have time to go on up to Waipu to see about another installation. He was filling the cup when something banged against the bakery wall and Percy's crutch clattered into the quiet room.

'Percy!' Larry ran to the door.

Percy lay on the concrete over the place he had spilled his tea. From his open mouth came desperate, rasping respiration. Larry panicked, until he remembered that he should check Percy's tongue – see that he didn't choke on it. He peered into the old man's mouth. When his tongue seemed to be roughly where it should be, Larry lifted his head on to a folded flour sack, then ran for Ngaire.

Ngaire felt Percy's pulse. She lifted his eyelids, listened with her stethoscope. 'Probably he's had a stroke,' she said at last, 'but phone Doctor Shaw.'

And a stroke Percy had had. Rangi and Larry loaded him on the air mattress in the back of the Essex, where Ngaire attended him, for the trip to the hospital. Given the urgency of the trip, driving across Auckland in the early morning traffic proved a challenge, particularly when an intrepid brewery truck driver defied Larry his right to a lane.

'Larry! Don't put us all in hospital,' an alarmed Ngaire called from the back.

Suzie had developed a soft spot for Percy though she pretended otherwise. But Larry was taken aback by her response when he drove out to her father's place of business to tell her about Percy.

'Larry, won't it be for the best if he dies? I mean... well... what sort of a life does he have?' she said. 'And if he's bedridden, who's going to look after him?'

The ever pragmatic Suzie, Larry thought, irritated by her logic, irrefutable though it was. But that was Suzie, like everything else about her, bang, bang.

'Hey! How do you know that he doesn't enjoy his life?' he protested. 'And how do we know that he'll be bedridden?' His voice had taken on a sharp tone and he knew it, but he couldn't stop himself. A word Suzie didn't understand was delicacy.

Suzie answered his protest with profound philosophy: 'You old softy,' she said. 'You've got to realise, we've all got to go sometime. When your time's up, it's up and when it isn't, it isn't!'

'Let's hope that his isn't!' Ngaire said, defusing the moment and making Larry pleased with her. He was sorry that he'd spoken sharply to Suzie who, after all, had made little pies for Percy and often given him part of her dinner.

Then Suzie decided to return to Warkworth with them. She insisted that Ngaire take the front seat while she climbed into the back. The mattress had to be in the back for something, she said.

'Yes, you'll probably go to sleep,' Larry answered.

The whine of the differential made further talking difficult. At Silverdale Suzie tapped Larry on the shoulder.

'Let's stop,' she shouted.

Larry pulled into the kerb. Suzie climbed out of the vehicle. Making an elaborate show of dusting off her clothes, she said, 'If the old man does kick the bucket it'll be because he was suffocated from the shit that floats around in the back of this contraption!'

Larry said, 'I've got a mangy old dog that doesn't have enough sense to come in out of the rain; a friend who shoots up the town when he's had a few; another with cross-eyed feet and a mind to match, *his* friend no better; and now a girlfriend who wishes the sane one among us dead! I am blessed.'

Suzie responded with more philosophy. 'You just don't know when you're well off!' she said.

THE WOODEN RIM OF the Essex's steering wheel was held to the boss by three iron spokes. Coming back from Waipu, while turning a sharp bend in the road, the rim broke apart in Larry's hands. He grabbed frantically at the boss and barely avoided a trip down a hundred-foot slope. He wrestled the van to a stop and sat there without moving until his shaking subsided. Then he gave the dog Kuri his opinion of Essex vans, and this one in particular. Thinking he was being lovingly addressed, the dog barked approval and stuck his head under Larry's arm.

Larry carved a new rim. He tightened the body screws; he fixed the headlamp which now regularly parted company with the mudguard; he tightened the other headlamp. Mindful of Suzie's complaints about flour and other material floating about the cabin, he washed out the vehicle's interior. He put the air mattress in the back and drove to Auckland to get Percy.

Larry helped the orderly manhandle Percy through the rear doors. When the dog Kuri saw who was being loaded, he left through the driver's side window. It was a while before they could find and catch him. Only when Suzie, sitting in the front seat, covered his eyes and held him tightly did he consent to ride with them, but he was not gracious about it.

Percy was decidedly different. One eye and one side of his mouth drooped. The arm that had managed his crutch was bent, as if held in an invisible sling. His eyes, though, were vacant as ever.

They stopped at Silverdale. Suzie held Percy's head and gave him water, holding the mug to his lips.

'I wish I knew if he understood me, the poor old bugger!' she said. 'How's he going to look after himself?'

'The district nurse will call in on Mondays and Thursdays. Also, I've arranged for a woman to take care of him part-time. Ngaire and I'll look in on him as we can,' Larry said.

'Oh Larry! You can't take on more work! You don't get enough sleep as it is.'

'But it's Percy.' He grinned. 'And it's only when you're around that I don't get enough sleep!' He squeezed her knee.

'Then you're going to have to give me up,' she said.

He pecked her on the cheek.

'Nothing doing, old girl, you're stuck with me now.'

Ngaire, Suzie and Larry had cleaned Percy's cottage. They burned a mountain of odorous socks and long johns; two years of them, Ngaire said, accumulated since his last sickness. They put the mattress outside to air and washed the bed covers.

Cleaning the bath was the worst. The old man had the habit of emptying the teapot into it, and by the look and smell of the garden in the bottom, everything else as well. They scrubbed the cottage with Jeyes Fluid. The disinfectant started them coughing and their eyes watering. When they had finished, Suzie complained that her clothes stank, and Larry, sniffing his, agreed.

They supported Percy into the cottage. The doctors had directed that he should walk a little each day, and now that they carried the weight of him Larry wondered how he would manage when Suzie went back to Auckland.

Inside, the old man made to spit on the floor, but Suzie scolded him. He retained it until Suzie held out a can.

'See, he knows!' she said.

Ngaire said, 'He knows the basic things. He's managed for years on his own – except when he was sick.'

Percy looked about the room.

'Syrup!' he said, or that's what they thought he said.

'What about syrup, honey?' Suzie asked, surprised and pleased at his new vocabulary. But that was it. They put him in bed and covered him up, and in moments he was asleep.

Larry was learning that there was a profound goodness and a sweet softness to Suzie that she didn't want people to know about. She hid it with a blustering bravado that didn't always work. She was close to tears now, Larry saw. He took her arm.

'We'll look in on him later, Poker, and again in the morning before Mrs Sturman gets here.' Mrs Sturman was the lady who had offered to help with him.

That night, while Suzie slept, Larry remembered how Suzie had been close to tears when Percy had spoken. Would Mary have been so moved? He decided that no, she wouldn't. And then he remembered how the song of the bellbirds had moved Suzie to sympathetic behaviour for an entire afternoon. He turned on his side, facing her, and slid an arm under and around her body. He waited for the change in her breathing to indicate that she was aware of him, but there was no change. None the less he felt a new and sudden closeness, and he kept his arm there until it went to sleep. Later, he went to the kitchen and brought back his homework. He studied until his eyes watered. When he closed them for a moment he slept, and when Suzie awoke, he lay as he had been when the book had fallen.

It was ritual that Suzie awakened him with a savage bite, but this morning she slid out of bed and dressed. She walked to Percy's, the dog Kuri following, and helped Percy to the toilet. She washed his face and hands and made him tea. He was slurping it down when Mrs Sturman arrived.

When Suzie returned to the cottage, Larry was half awake. She undressed and climbed into his bed. He sat up.

'God! You're cold! What've you been doing?'

'Waiting for you to wake up,' she answered. She took his hand, put three fingers into her mouth and bit down.

He pulled away. 'Hey! That hurts!'

'How else do I get your attention?'

My dear Larry,

I am writing to tell you that finally we are in America, living in a nice wee town, and it's so wonderful and so exciting, I hardly know where to begin to tell you about it. The town is Georgetown, which is in Connecticut, not very far from New York city. We've rented a flat — an apartment they call it here. The real estate man says it's tiny by American standards, but by ours it's huge — almost the size of my parents' home in Dundee!

Ian's work is a long way from here, but Americans seem to think nothing of travelling hours to work. Ian grumbles about it but I suspect that, really, he doesn't mind. In the train he is able to read and study. He does have a lot of homework to do and he is very conscientious about it.

I think he is surprised at how neat and tidy everything is in America, and that no one has robbed us yet! Of course he wouldn't admit that America is nicer than he thought it would be, not even to me.

It's my intention to ride into New York as soon as I can marshal the courage. I wish to see the famous Times Square, the Empire State Building, Macy's, and the other places I've *heard and read so much about most of my life, although I shall have to go alone, for Ian has not the time, nor, I think, the inclination. With him away from morning to night, and studying evenings and weekends, I do get awfully lonely. Thank goodness for the wonderful shops! I've even dared to eat alone in a small diner and strike up a conversation with the owner, a dear little Italian man – bold bird that I am...*

Larry stopped reading. He thought, they're in America and the husband cannot find the time to take his wife into New York. What sort of a man is he, for crissake! But what surprised him most was Moira's boldness, when before she'd been reserved, forceful only when he'd tried to go beyond light necking.

Once, when he'd started to storm away in frustration, she'd taken his hand and put it to her cheek, a cheek wet with tears.

'Larr-ee, can ye no understand? Would ye hae me behave like a strumpet? Would ye hae me shame my parents?'

She'd been only eighteen, he reminded himself now; cloistered, Presbyterian. Since that time she'd been in the air force, lived in London, married, gone to America...

He read on.

...I feel for you, the difficulties you are experiencing keeping your goal of coming to America in sight. All I can say to that is, when you feel like giving up, mind our legend about Robert Bruce and the spider. Remember, because of his endurance, he became king of Scotland!

Thinking that it might be easier to become king of Scotland than to get to America, Larry rose from the kitchen chair and filled the electric kettle. He put tea into the teapot, and bread into the toaster. Meanwhile, the hungry dog Kuri haunted his feet. Between them they'd cleaned out the mice in the old bakery. Larry fed him the remains of his last night's dinner that would have been his tonight's dinner.

He wondered at Moira, married, and yet writing to him. He wondered about the husband who must know that she was writing. In like circumstances, would he be as tolerant? He doubted it. Inexplicably, he felt drawn to this new Moira.

But it was time to take care of Percy. When Larry entered his kitchen Percy was standing precariously against the wall, straining hard to manoeuvre his crutch into position while retaining his balance.

'Percy! Wait. I'll help you.'

Larry got the crutch under Percy's arm and guided his fingers to the grip. The old man tested his weight.

'I'm holding you!' Larry assured him, unsure as usual, though, that Percy comprehended. 'Now, let's see if you can walk.'

Percy dragged his left foot a step. Then the right. His left. At his door, he looked into the night.

'Shhyrup!' he said.

Percy's face was away from the light, but Larry could have sworn that for a moment, it had lost its placid look. Was the 'Shhyrup!' an exultation, a hurrah?

Larry helped him back to his bed, brought the chamber pot, a chipped, enamelled antique, similar to the one Larry had used as a boy before his parents had installed an inside toilet, and waited while Percy, sitting on the edge of the bed, used it. Larry emptied it into the commode.

Riding home, it came to him that the 'Shhyrup!' was Percy's previous 'Oh hip!' The discovery pleased him.

Won't Suzie be pleased that he's walking again, he thought.

Then he rolled a sheet of paper into the typewriter and started the next month's article for the American magazine.

WARTIME FURLOUGHS IN CAIRO had developed Rangi's ability to absorb whopping quantities of ale. Working with Grunter and Speed had fine-tuned his ability. But since marriage his prowess had deteriorated.

This day, however, he had been getting back into form, drinking since the bar had opened, for at three o'clock that morning Ngaire had given him a son. He had been joined at the bar by the lawyer John Arrf who, because he'd won a case that day, also celebrated. And for no good reason that anyone knew about, the baker Joe Montini had joined them. All were in fine fettle when Larry came into the bar at the end of his workday, although Rangi's capacity to remain pedestrian or perpendicular for much longer seemed in doubt. However, his eyesight was fine. Through the rush-hour crowd he saw Larry enter. He greeted him with a yell and a robust handshake.

'Me old mate! Kei te pehea koe, e hoa? You hear about it? I got me a kid – with a spout. Ka pai, eh?'

'I heard about it,' said Larry. 'You borrowed the Essex to take her to the hospital this morning, remember? But congratulations. And ease up on the booze. You got a date with the hospital at seven.'

'Hey… not to worry, sport. *No problema.*' Rangi ordered a new round.

Contrary to Rangi's optimistic summary, Larry saw that there was a problem – the problem of getting Rangi to the hospital by seven, for if he didn't make it, the blame would likely fall on his mates.

Rangi called for another round, but Larry took his arm. 'Save it until we've been to the hospital. Meanwhile, let's meet Suzie at the bus and give her the news. Then we'll all have something to eat. You eaten anything today?'

Rangi acknowledged that he hadn't.

Rangi greeted Suzie with a beery kiss and a hug that squeezed the breath out of her. 'I'm a father!' he explained.

Beverley came through the depot doorway.

'Congratulations, Rangi,' she said from a safe distance.

'Thanks, pretty one. Got a kiss for the proud papa?' Rangi made to walk toward her, but when he let go of Suzie, his feet ran in the other direction. He over-corrected and would have run the opposite way had Larry not grabbed him.

Suzie said, 'Why aren't you with your wife?'

'Not to worry so much, e hine,' Rangi said, grinning wickedly at Suzie. He tried to reward her with a second kiss but she skipped away.

'Visiting hour's not till seven. Let's get some tucker into him,' Larry said, steering Rangi toward the fish and chip shop.'

They were in bed. Out of the blue, Suzie said, 'Let's have a baby!'

Larry sat up abruptly and, just as abruptly, lost his intention to perform what he'd been about to perform.

'That'll be the bloody day!'

Suzie had shown little previous nesting instinct. Ngaire's baby must have brought it on, he thought. He wondered if he should fill the bathtub with cold water and dump her into it. Or perhaps the greater punishment would be to deprive her of the pleasure she'd just talked herself out of, at least until her urge had waned.

'I'm going to make tea,' he said, getting out of bed.

'I was kidding,' she said.

He made the tea.

In spite of last night's rejection, Suzie was filled with munificence the next day and said that she would bake him a pie. Later, taking stock of the culinary ingredients, she spotted the letters tucked between a jar of sago and a tin of flour. She told herself that she wouldn't be curious, but before long she found herself reaching for them. In for one, in for a dozen, she excused herself. She read them all, the letters with the English stamps first.

When Larry came home, he knew there was something. Suzie radiated it. 'Okay. What's up?'

'I read your letters.'

'What let...? Oh! Those.'

'Who is she?'

'Moira? I met her during the war.'

'She's married to that Ian chap?'

'Yes.'

'And yet she writes to you!'

'Why not? We're friends!'

'Yeah!' She changed the subject. 'I baked you a pie.'

'Remind me to reward you some time,' he said, piqued that she had read his letters, yet really not giving a damn.

She put her arm around his shoulders. 'You can reward me now,' she said.

'Poker! I haven't had anything to eat all day.'

'You poor boy,' she said, but she served the meal and then the pie.

Later that night, cuddled into Larry's back, she remembered something.

'That Moira has the hots for you,' she said.

JAKE TESTED AND OPERATED the first two new radios, found them satisfactory, and gave Larry a purchase order for eight. The Waipu company ordered seven.

The time had come to name the new radio. How did people arrive at titles? There was a locally made broadcast radio, the Columbus – named after the great explorer, no doubt. Larry's motorcycle was named the Velocette. Where did that name come from? Velocipede? Velocity? Then there was Kiwi shoe polish – but what was the connection between kiwis and shoes?

A Greek name… Icarus perhaps. But no, not Icarus – his wings fell off.

A Maori name. Tui? But the tui mimics other birds. His was an original radio.

Korimako, the bellbird? Korimako – *The Radio With the Melodious Voice!*

It was Suzie who said it: 'What's wrong with bellbird?'

And indeed, what was wrong with bellbird? *The Radio with the Bellbird Voice.* 'Suzie! You're a doll!' He kissed her.

She had come to Warkworth on the Friday evening bus. The next morning, at breakfast, she said, 'Larry, you're working too hard. Take the day off. I want to hear bellbirds.'

But the pohutukawa blossoms were gone and so were the bellbirds. They sunbathed, slept and talked.

Back at the cottage Larry took Suzie by the shoulders.

'Thank you for a wonderful time, Poker. God! I needed it.' He kissed her forehead. She unbuckled his belt.

'Hey! I'm tired!'

'Didn't I leave you alone all day?'

The days Suzie came to Warkworth, she cooked Percy's meals and washed his clothes. She called him a stupid and cranky old bastard – to his face and to his back – and she ordered him about. When he spat on the floor, she threatened to rub his nose in it; and he loved her.

Percy had not liked Mrs Sturman. One day, as she was setting the table, her arms full of dishes, he stuck his crutch between her legs. The bewildered woman came to Larry.

'I know you have your hands full, but you'll have to get

someone else. I can't take any more of that old man,' she said. 'I'm sorry.'

Suzie and Larry, and Ngaire when she could manage the time, took over Mrs Sturman's duties.

The dog Kuri discovered the old man's reduced offensive capability. He scuttled past him with greater and greater boldness, daring even to enter his house.

The orders for new radios came in faster than Larry could build them. Building the radios, installing them, repairing the zc1s, writing the monthly *CQ Magazine* articles, tending Percy; there weren't enough hours in the day. He hired a girl part-time to help with the assembly.

Then a letter came from a Fijian fishing company; they sought information on the Bellbird radios. Larry thought, how can I do it all? And with money now a problem!

The Essex ran rough. When he drove to Waipu, over a hill the locals called The Dome, the radiator boiled. He needed a newer vehicle, and even more so, a larger inventory. But where to get the money? Running a business, he realised more and more, took a lot of effort and precious time from his real work – which was designing electronic equipment. Manufacturing should be done by someone else, he concluded. How had he let himself get trapped into such a circle?

He threw the soldering iron down and headed for the pub. The private bar was about a third full. John Arrf sat talking to Joe Montini. John looked up when Larry came in and turned on his stool to greet him.

'Larry… jolly good to see you, old chap. We see less and less of you.' John effused a glow that told Larry that he had been keeping the stool warm for more than a few minutes while Joe's red cheeks and profuse sweat indicated that he'd been there a while, too.

Joe said, 'Larry… funny, we were just talking about you. We were wondering when you're going to give all that work a spell.'

Larry shook his head sadly, as if to suggest that life was a penance. 'I wish I could. It seems that the harder I work, the harder I have to work. I never thought I'd envy the eight-to-fivers. And all I want is to become an engineer!'

John was in a philosophical mood.

'But work is good for you, my boy. Did you know that the suicide rate is higher among the rich? They kill themselves out of boredom!'

'So the answer to my problems is poverty and more work – is that what you're saying, John?' Larry countered with a wry grin. But John hadn't finished. 'In simpler societies,' he continued, as if Larry hadn't spoken at all, 'where people have little recreational time, they have no psychiatrists, no mental institutions – and no need of them, even. What a blessing, if you come to think about it.'

'And no bloody lawyers,' Joe Montini added, for although he drank with John he despised his occupation, having once been bitten by it.

John cast a disdainful look over the rims of his glasses at Joe. 'Yes, Joe, you're right, and no bloody lawyers. However, all but the most primitive societies have bakers, so you'll not have to worry should the immigration authorities decide to export you back to Italy.'

'But, my boy,' he said, directing his gaze back at Larry, 'there's work and work. I see you actually building radios yourself. Now there's a truism that says the head makes better coin than the hands, and another that says one should be happy with what one does. Have you considered using less enterprising people to do the menial work so that you can spend more of your time with your engineering?'

'Yes John, I have, but there's the problem of money. I had anticipated that I only had to get into business and the money would come rolling in, which, unfortunately, hasn't come about.'

'My boy, anticipation might be described as a bird sitting on a horse's posterior waiting for its hot breakfast – fine if the horse has eaten. Not that there's anything wrong with anticipation – quite to the contrary – anticipation is often the carrot that keeps

179

the horse moving ahead – a mixed metaphor, I know, but we were talking about horses, I believe. But in business, anticipation should be merged with planning – both long and short term – and other people's money. A smart businessman will use borrowed money, but to obtain it you need to have good bookkeeping, realistic well-planned forecasts, show good planning, and have unbounded faith in God Almighty. Therein, in my opinion, lies the path to monetary success. Would that marital success could be as easily obtained,' he concluded, falling into a brooding mood again until another subject occurred to him about which he felt wont to philosophise.

Come six o'clock, the proprietor closed the public bar and the front doors, but continued serving in the private bar. His wife brought his dinner, which he picked at between serving drinks, most of them to John. 'It's no bloody wonder I got a bloody ulcer,' he complained, putting a half eaten lamb chop back on the plate to serve another round. Meanwhile John continued to expound on his favorite theories and subjects, until his ability to turn his thoughts into coherent words confounded him.

'John, you're talking a lot of bullshit,' said Joe, who had difficulty following John at any time, much less when they'd spent the night, and God knows how much of the afternoon, drinking. 'I'm going home,' he said. 'You can talk Larry's ear off for a change. So cheerio.' He abruptly downed his beer and left.

John sighed and said, 'Not a bad chap, Joe, but of limited intellect, I'm afraid. Just the other day, in a discussion about politics, I mentioned the word dogma. Joe thought I was talking about a female dog.'

'We can't all be geniuses, John,' put in the proprietor.

'I would have to agree with that,' John answered slyly.

But from there on out it was all downhill. John meandered from subject to increasingly incoherent subject. He stopped finally to say to Larry, 'You understand me, my boy?'

'No problem, John,' Larry answered untruthfully, for he had been thinking about business and money, and Moira in America. Moira going to New York! Moira going to Times Square. Moira going to the Empire State Building. And he thought about her drongo husband who couldn't find the time to take her to those places.

'…I'll kill the bitch,' John said, or so Larry thought he heard him say. Larry sobered.

'John! What the hell are you talking about? Who are you going to kill?'

'What's that, my boy? What did you say?'

'I asked you, who you are going to kill?'

'Kill?' John made an effort to look at Larry. He took his glasses off. He cleaned them with his handkerchief. 'Was I wandering, my boy? Deary me!' He finished his drink and climbed down from the stool.

'I have a case in the morning,' he said.

He zigzagged to the door. 'G'night,' he called.

'Now you take it easy, John,' the proprietor called after him. He turned to Larry. 'What was all that about?'

'God knows. You know how he rambles.'

'I hope he's not thinking of knocking his old lady off – even if she is the bitch I hear she is. Well… drink her down and let's close her up. I could do with a good night's sleep meself for once.'

Yes, and you should sleep well tonight, Larry thought, roughly totting up what he alone had spent.

Glancing across the road to the butcher's shop, Larry was surprised to see two Holsteins gazing down from the parapet. He closed an eye. One disappeared. He'd drunk more than he had realised. He wished he didn't have to drive to Waipu in the morning.

There were two telephone poles at the entrance to Bakery Lane where there used to be one, and two porch lights. And when he climbed into bed, the bed moved in circles. He fluffed up Suzie's pillow and put it on his own so that his head was higher. The spinning stopped. He slept, waking once to pee. While he peed he tried to remember what John had said about knocking off his old lady – or whoever – but he couldn't remember, and as soon as he was back in bed, John forgotten, he slept.

181

THE ESSEX BOUNCED ACROSS the railway line. The front left rim and wooden spokes broke away from the hub. The vehicle dropped its corner on to the pavement. The tyre continued along the highway until, at a bend, it veered off the road and plunged into a deep gully.

The ensuing litany about Essex motor vehicles so alarmed the dog Kuri, already jittery at the abrupt loss of forward movement, that he bounded out the window and took the direction the tyre had taken.

The vehicle was dug firmly into the pavement, otherwise Larry would have compelled it to follow the wheel. It took the local wrecker half the morning to haul it to the back of the garage, where he parked it with the other derelicts.

Essex wheels were in shorter supply than Essex vehicles. Until he found a wheel, Larry shipped his equipment by bus.

Next, the muffler fell off. His exits from Warkworth, until he found a replacement, rivalled a squadron of Spitfires on climb-out, and until they became inured to it the shopkeepers came running from their shops.

An afternoon later, Larry worked on a logo for the new radio's front panel. He'd drawn a bird perched on a bell, a bird alongside a bell, and a bird on a pohutukawa branch. His bird didn't look like a bird and his pohutukawa didn't look like a pohutukawa.

A scraping sound coming from outside drew his attention. The dog Kuri slunk under the bench, his mangy tail planted between his legs. Old Percy loomed into the doorway.

'Shhyrup!' he said.

Larry jumped up from his stool. 'Percy! For God's sake! Wait! I'll bring you a chair. It's great to see you! Here, sit on this. Give me your crutch. Sit there and rest. I'll make tea.'

Last night, right out of the blue, Mac had shown up. He'd stayed only a few minutes before going to Lady Loomis's. And now Percy!

Percy had trouble holding the pannikin of tea. Larry helped him.

Through the window he saw Rita skipping down the lane.

'Rita! Tell your mother old Percy's here!' he called out.

Percy's coming somehow brightened his day. Before his coming, Larry's spirit had tired, his problems pressed: a falling-apart Essex, not enough money, the Fijians wanting him to come to Suva, a Whangarei company wanting to know how soon they could get radios. Not enough money.

Allan Willard had extended his credit, but it was not enough. Bernie Steinmetz had come to him with a deal. He was tempted until he remembered what John the lawyer had once said: 'You don't get back into bed with a woman if she's given you the clap.'

His mother's bookkeeping system had been simple. She had put the money to pay the bills in separate tobacco tins: a tin for the land payment, a tin for the rates, a tin for their school clothes. His method was similar. Although his money was in the Bank of New Zealand, he imagined various compartments. Money to pay Allan Willard, money to pay the company that made the chassis, money for the rent. Also, he imagined a compartment labelled 'profit', but to date it was empty. He had no idea whether he was making money or not.

He asked Suzie for help. She had offered help in the past but he had not seen the need for it. She had predicted problems. To her credit she didn't say, 'I told you so'. Instead she constructed a double-entry bookkeeping system and explained its operation.

'It's only as good as the information you put into it,' she said. 'No more notes on the backs of envelopes. No more half-arsed billing.'

She told him that he'd made a good deal of money.

'Where is it?' he asked, incredulous. The advantage of tobacco tins was that you could see the money.

'It's in inventory and it's in accounts receivable.'

She looked through his papers. 'When did you send bills out last?' He didn't know. He thought that it was about two months ago.

'Two months my foot! Five months.' Some bills had never been sent out.

'You turd! How do you bloody well expect to stay solvent if you don't send out bills?'

'I must have overlooked them.'

She went on and on. To silence her, he said, 'Listen, you most gorgeous of all God's creatures, how'd you like to be my live-in bookkeeper? I don't have much money to pay you, but I promise I'll make it up to you in other ways.'

'You don't have the fortitude!' she said.

He put his hands together in pretended supplication.

'Lord, give me strength.'

She came behind his chair and put a hand down his shirt. 'That's a good start,' she said, biting his ear.

'But let's talk about your business. First, you've got to get rid of the Essex. It's costing you a fortune. Do you know how much you're spending on that bloody rattletrap? No? I thought not. That used wheel you bought cost half as much as the whole shit-can cost originally! You've got to get something better.'

'And get it with what?'

'When there's a way there's a will,' she prophesied.

'It's, "If there's a will there's a way", Poker,' he corrected her, and he wondered how to convert wills to folding stuff.

The way came through the door a week later in the form of John the lawyer.

'My boy, I had a little chat with that girl of yours last week. You know, you have the damnedest ability to select your women not only for their physical attributes but for their down-to-earth common sense. Now this Suzie, she knows what she's doing.'

Larry remembered that he hadn't selected his women. They'd selected him.

'The young lady has described to me the state of your business affairs – in the strictest confidence, of course – and it seems to me that had you received earlier and proper fiscal guidance you could have had quite a business by now. A lesson you have yet to learn, my boy, is that while you may have the best product in the world, if you don't have the cash to support it, the best product in the world is worth nothing. And, of course, cash turnover is vitally important to cash position. I agree with your young lady's prognosis, you need help.

'Your major obstacle, it seems to me, is lack of capital. With an infusion of capital and proper management, I believe that you will have a viable business. I like to see a man get ahead – to the extent that I'm prepared to guarantee you a loan from the Bank of New Zealand. Note now that I won't be lending you money, the bank will be lending it, but if you don't repay it I will have to, and you may believe me, I'm going to make quite sure that I don't!' He paused to let the threat sink in.

This was the longest sermon Larry had ever heard from a sober John. He was too stunned to answer. He'd heard that John was a sharpy, to watch him, yet he could see nothing but goodwill in his proposition. What could John gain from this?

John saw Larry's hesitation. 'Well, think about it, my boy.'

'John, I just can't believe that you can be so generous – that you'd do this for me!'

'That's all right, my boy. Think nothing of it. Now let me have the books your young lady has prepared so that I can get a better idea of what you'll need. I'll talk to you tomorrow or the next day.'

The more he thought about John's offer, the more Larry was filled with the marvel of it. That Suzie! How could he thank her? He started to prepare dinner. He began by peeling potatoes to go with the lamb chops he'd bought.

Mac came into the kitchen.

'Stone the bloody crows! Peeling spuds is no man's job. Thought you had a flunky to do that kind of thing.'

185

'You're looking at him.'

'Huh!' Mac scorned. He looked around. When he found no flunkies hiding, he said, 'Aren't you gonna offer me a bloody drink?'

'I've only got gin.' Expecting John, not Mac, he had bought gin.

'Gnat's piss, but if that's all you've got, I suppose…' He spotted the dog Kuri smelling his legs.

'If that bloody mongrel pisses on me, I'll kill him!'

Mac was in a foul mood. Larry wondered why. 'Hey Mac! It's me, Larry!'

Mac took the gin.

'Oh aye,' he said. 'It's a sorry day.'

'What's a sorry day?'

Mac emptied the glass, held it out for a refill.

'It's a sorry day I ever came to this friggin' dump,' he said.

It took some probing. 'All she wants is me friggin' pension,' he explained, 'the bloody bitch!'

'Oh, come, Mac, she has money of her own. Why would she want your pension?'

'Because she does!' His tone dismissed rebuttal. Larry bedded him down on the air mattress, behind the ovens.

Larry was driving the Essex back over The Dome, after a day in Waipu, when the engine-head gasket blew. The radiator water ran into the oil sump. The water gone from the radiator, the engine overheated and the head warped. The mechanic realised that the head had warped only after he had replaced the gasket and the water continued to leak into the sump. He shellacked the gasket. Larry tried various concoctions guaranteed to stop leaks, but the water leaked into the sump. Not that there was a lot of water to leak into the sump, the steam pressure had holed the radiator. Larry bought preparations guaranteed to stop radiator leaks. He put oatmeal in it. But it leaked. He filled half a dozen American, war-surplus petrol cans with water, stowed them in the back, and frequently stopped to fill the radiator. At night he drained it.

There was little market for a used Essex van with a warped engine head, a leaky radiator, a headlamp that turned itself backwards prior to falling off, and wood screws that loosened. The dealer from whom he bought the Ford Thames refused to take it as a trade.

'I've enough junk around the place as it is,' he said.

The two oldest Plenkovich boys bought it for five pounds.

It took two months to get delivery of a Ford Thames. It would have taken eight months had John Arrf not used his influence. As it was he paid full list price. Dealers didn't bargain when vehicles were in short supply.

When he was granted the bank loan, Larry ordered components for twenty-five radios and a ticket to Suva. He determined the Fijian fishing fleet's requirements, gave the owners a quote they accepted, and returned to New Zealand. Now he increased his order to fifty sets of components. A month later, he hired Maria to help with the assembly of radios. Suzie spent most of her time now in Warkworth. She said that the increased business required more of her time on the books, but Larry had noted that the need for more of her time arose after he'd hired Maria.

When he hired Maria, Larry had noted her beautiful body, long, blonde hair, full breasts, and attractive lisp. Suzie saw a so-so body, mousy hair, and over-sized breasts. She didn't hear the lisp until she came in from the cottage on Maria's first morning. Maria stood on a stool holding her skirt tight about her legs.

Suzie said, 'What's going on?'

'A mouth!' Maria answered, pointing under the dough-kneading bench.

Suzie called the dog Kuri. She pointed under the bench.

'Catch the mouth,' she ordered him.

Not understanding the libertine nature of men, Suzie believed the only way to make sure that Larry stayed hers was to see to it that he never wanted. Her senses were totally assaulted, therefore, when she caught him stealthily watching Maria when she arched her shoulders, which ached from leaning over the bench. They ached mostly when Larry was around, Suzie noted. She moved to Warkworth. Now her father's business received her part-time help.

'I'm going to learn assembly work,' she said one day.

'But Suzie, you have enough to do with the bookkeeping. You told me yourself that it's taking more time now.'

That evening, Suzie served him oysters on the shell. She cooked his favourite dinner: lamb chops, potatoes, carrots and parsnips, and a walnut pie. When he pulled his chair back and told her how good the meal was, and how full he was, she would have filled his pipe had he smoked one. Instead, she sat on his knee, blew in his ear and played with the hair on his chest.

'Honey, did I tell you that my father knows exactly how many linear feet of framing a man can put together in a day, how many square feet of tongue and groove flooring he can lay; even the extra time it takes to secret nail it?'

Larry saw which way the conversation headed.

'So that's why you want to do assembly work?'

'Yes, that and because Maria needs close supervision. She does as she likes when you're not around.'

She would do it anyhow, Larry knew. When Suzie got an idea in her head, nothing would change her mind. 'Okay, but lay off the supervision until you know more about the work.' She kissed him. 'Let's go to bed,' she said.

He put his hand over his mouth to cover a polite little burp. 'On the meal you just fed me!'

'So much for the oysters!' Suzie said.

She learned fast. Soon she soldered three connections to Maria's two. She learned how to construct harnesses, and on her own she decided that it would be faster to pre-cut and pre-strip the wires before bundling them. She side-stepped the issue of who was the supervisor by becoming it. Maria didn't like it, but she could hardly argue with a woman who slept with the boss.

Old Percy came most days now. With frequent rests it usually took him about forty minutes to drag himself the distance.

Awaiting a small parcel from Willard Electric, Larry checked the mail. A letter from Moira was angled in the box between several bills.

Remembering that Suzie became unnaturally quiet after he heard from Moira, he drove the Velocette down to the park by the river instead of returning to the bakery.

...this is an imposing, exciting land, so different from tiny, dreary Scotland, but also so dreadfully lonely. Though sometimes I feel like Alice in Wonderland, more and more I'm wretched inside for the sight and touch of a sprig of heather, a barefoot run through the bracken. I want to climb the braes, wade the brooks. Of course, you know and I know that there's few of those things I could do in stark Dundee. The truth is, Larry, I'm desperately homesick.

While I write this I am mindful that you told me not to be afraid to breathe the foreign air. That is what I must do. Asserting myself will likely cause a rift between Ian and myself. As is the old Scottish way, he has appointed himself head of the household. He has forbidden me to 'traipse', as he calls it, around the American countryside, and he insists on controlling all the finances, even the money my father left me. But I will do what I have to do. I am determined. Poor Ian...

As a matter of course, Suzie checked the letters in the cupboard. When she saw their numbers had grown, she told herself, 'I mustn't', but she did. But this time, although it took supreme effort, she kept her guilt from showing.

A few days later a 'wish you were here' postcard came from Mary. It was written on the back of a picture of Edinburgh Castle. Larry wondered if she was living in Edinburgh or just visiting. When he put the postcard with the other letters he didn't notice that the order of their placement was different.

Suzie's father had become testy about the little time Suzie gave his business and, daughter or no daughter, if she didn't come to Auckland right away and catch up on his books, she was sacked.

'I have to keep the old bugger happy,' she apologised to Larry before she left.

Five days later Suzie arrived back, her arms full of groceries she had bought in Auckland. Larry was sitting on the bench talking to Maria. Without a word Suzie stamped back outside. Larry followed her to the cottage.

She faced him, eyes fiery. 'You bastard!'

'Poker!' He hadn't thought about Suzie getting jealous.

'She's got nice tits,' he said.

He dodged a can of pork and beans.

'A nice body.'

A can of peas.

'But I love you.'

'Stinker!'

'Let's go to bed.'

'What!'

'I said, let's go to bed.'

Afterwards she said, 'They'd choke an elephant.'

'What?'

'Maria's tits. And don't think for one minute that I haven't seen you peering down her neck.'

'Jealousy will get you everything,' he said.

B RIAN WINSLOW, A FORMER New Zealander and a lieutenant in the Suva Police, and Ray Patel, his assistant, visited the fishing boat *Gloria*. Down in the bilges, Larry ran an earth wire from the diesel engine block to the cabin where he had installed the first of the radios under the contract he had signed on his previous trip. Sweat dripped into his eyes. An hour earlier he had decided emphatically that there were better places to be than in the bilge of a fishing boat in the tropics.

He heard a voice. 'Hello, La Salle! Are you there?'

'Down here,' Larry answered, wondering who would know his name here in Fiji. It didn't sound like the *Gloria*'s owner, the only person he knew in Suva.

Winslow peered down at him.

'Sorry to bother you,' he said.

Larry brushed the sweat from his forehead and wiped an oily, fishy hand on his pants. He wondered if he should offer the hand in greeting and decided against it.

'G'day. I'm Brian Winslow, Fijian Police.' If he noticed the oil, he didn't show it. 'Ray Patel,' he added, nodding at his partner.

He asked Larry how he was enjoying Suva.

'Fine, but have I done something I shouldn't have?'

Brian laughed. 'Just a few questions I have to ask you, that's all. Would you mind coming to the station? Shouldn't take more than thirty minutes. I'll have someone bring you back.'

Was this how you were taken into custody, Larry wondered. He knew of nothing wrong with his papers, but there must be something.

At the station Brian asked, 'Do you know a gentleman named John... now let me see, A-R-R-F?' He spelled it out.

'John Arrf! Yes. Why?'

'Well, I don't know how much I may say about this.' He turned to Patel. 'Does it give any kind of direction in the wire?'

'No? Well, we'll play it by ear. It appears that this man Arrf – odd name – is in trouble of sorts and you are a potential witness. I must ask you, have you ever heard the said gentleman make any kind of threat against anyone?'

'John? You're kidding! He's the mildest bloke imaginable.'

'You've never heard him make threats against his wife?'

His wife! Larry didn't like it. He sensed that whatever he said could mean trouble for John. He wondered what the poor bastard had done. Surely he couldn't have harmed his wife.

'No… not really. They don't get along very well – that's common knowledge. From all I've heard she's a bit of a… well, you know, hard to get along with.'

'I see,' the lieutenant answered. 'The problem is that the New Zealand Police have a deposition from the proprietor of a drinking establishment.' He shuffled his papers. 'Ah yes, the Warkworth Hotel. The proprietor has sworn under oath that you and he were in the private bar of the pub when Arrf stated that he was going to kill his missus, or words to that effect. Do you remember that?'

Do I remember!

'But he didn't mention his wife! He didn't name anyone, in fact. I remember, I asked him…' He stopped. *Oh shit*! he thought.

'Look… he was rambling, he didn't know what he was saying. He gets that way when he's had a few.'

Brian Winslow proved to be a policeman first and possibly a bloody good bloke later. Larry never did meet the bloody good bloke. The thirty minutes at the station he had been promised turned into three and a half hours.

'John, you poor bastard!' He asked silently, 'What the hell have you done!'

He took a taxi to Cable and Wireless on the hill and waited the remainder of the day to get through to Joe Montini.

'Joe! For God's sake, what's going on there? The police have been asking me all sorts of questions about John! What's he done?'

When he put the telephone handset back on the hook he was pensive.

'Yi, yi! Poor old John!' he commiserated. 'Shit damn!'

The prosecutor told the jury that the defendant, John Arrf, who sat before them, was a cold-blooded murderer. He had killed an innocent woman, a loving and faithful wife who had had no aim in life other than to look after her husband.

'For fifteen years she had served him, waited on him hand and foot, and while she served him, he schemed to kill her. And why was he so determined to kill her? There's only one feasible explanation: money! He wanted to control the family's fortune. Not satisfied with partial control, he wanted the whole thing! Remember now, under the terms of the trust set up by his wife's father, they had joint control and the only way he could get complete control was to kill her!'

John Arrf's lawyer was eloquent and convincing, too. Obviously, though, he didn't see John Arrf in the same light as the prosecutor did. He described John as a good husband and provider, an excellent businessman who had very capably managed and improved the family's businesses. Why would he murder his wife and risk losing everything?

The lawyer made it plain that neither did he see his client's wife as she had been described by the prosecutor.

'It has been shown, over and over, by the testimony that's been given, that this was no loving woman. Faithful she may have been – her tart and nagging tongue saw to that! But loving! Well, yes… she did love something; she loved to harass her husband! She harassed him to such an extent that he dreaded to come home at night, which is why, on occasions, he could be found in the bar of the local, trying to find the solace and relaxation denied him at home. And when he did go home – we've heard from the witnesses – often as not she locked the door on him. Remember the evidence: "Don't bring the sod in here. I don't want him!" That's what this loving wife told his friends when they gave him a ride home one evening – remember? – before she slammed the door in their faces!'

The lawyer described his client's hobby, gardening. He told the jury of the damage that possums do to fruit.

'Now we know that it was the defendant's habit to wage war on the pests. He has been doing it for years, as have our counties and the government. We also know that my client's wife was strongly opposed to her husband killing the possums, so much so, in fact, that she would physically attack him if he refused to stop. Remember the evidence that on an earlier occasion when he was shooting possums she had attacked him, clawed his face, and smashed his rifle against a tree. We have also heard the evidence that she'd tried to have him committed. Does this sound like a loving wife?

'Now let's move on to the evening of the tragedy. After a very trying day in court, my client took two bottles of gin home. He put one in the cupboard and opened the other. He poured himself a small pick-me-up. And what did this loving wife do? Did she join him, ask him how his day went, as most wives would? Not this wife! She swept the bottle and the glass to the floor, she took the unopened bottle he'd put in the cupboard and tried to brain him with it! Imagine that now! And did her husband fight back? He stated that he didn't, and there is no evidence to support that he did. None at all! This mild man went to his garden, his place of sanctuary, while he waited for his wife to come to her senses.

'You've also heard from witnesses that my client, when he was in the private bar of the Warkworth Hotel, was stated to have said that he was going to kill the "bitch". Now, ladies and gentlemen, I ask you: to whom or what did he refer? His wife? A possum? The glass in his hand? And to whom was he talking? Was he addressing his companions? The proprietor?

'That night he was what might be called by some, tipsy – he'd had a difficult day, remember. And there's little question that he was not talking to his companions. The evidence is quite conclusive that he talking – mumbling – to himself. Both witnesses have stated that, and that most of what he said didn't make sense. How can it be said, therefore, that this man's incoherent speech showed intent to murder his wife?

'We've heard that when the defendant left the bar and went home, he went to the garden at the back of their property. There he heard the possums busy in his fruit trees. He looked for the .22 calibre rifle, but then he remembered that his wife had broken its stock and damaged its sights. There was the shotgun, but he had forgotten to buy shells for it. Then he remembered the old .303 from his pig hunting days. And so he used the .303 to shoot the possums that had been eating his fruit. An overkill perhaps, but the only weapon available to him.

'The defendant was engaged in this pursuit – it's not easy to hold a torch along the barrel of a rifle so that it shines into the possum's eyes and illuminates the rifle sights at the same time – and he didn't hear his wife. The first indication of her presence was when she blinded him with flyspray. Then she wrestled with him to get the rifle, only, when she grabbed the barrel, the defendant had his finger on the trigger!

'Well, there's no need for me to reiterate the rest. You've seen and heard the evidence.'

Soon after, the counsel for the defence rested its case.

I T DOESN'T LOOK TOO good when they take so long,' said Joe Montini.

Suzie was distraught. As she had got to know John better she had liked him more and more, and John had liked her. And he liked the way she did Larry's books.

'No frills, no nonsense. Straightforward and honest,' he had told Larry.

'Do you think they'll convict him?' Suzie had asked Larry at least half a dozen times during the trial. She asked again while they awaited the decision.

'I don't know,' Larry answered truthfully, the same answer he'd given the other times.

His had been the critical evidence, perhaps the deciding evidence, his and the hotel proprietor's. How would the jury interpret what John had said that evening in the bar? The evidence confirmed that John had told the truth – the flyspray, for example, on his wife's hands, on John's clothes and glasses, on the rifle. Her fingerprints on the flyspray gun, on the rifle. But you never knew with juries.

'Mr La Salle,' the prosecution lawyer had said, a cocky little fellow with a shrill voice, 'am I correct in stating that you were in the private bar of the Warkworth Hotel, from approximately five o'clock in the afternoon on the third day of March of this year, until approximately half past ten in the evening of the same day, in the company of the defendant John Vladimir Arrf? And that the two of you spent that time drinking alcoholic beverages, thereby breaking the law...'

'Objection, your Honour! Whether or not Mr La Salle broke the law is irrelevant.'

'Quite... quite. Confine your questioning to the pertinent.'

'Yes, your Honour,' from the lawyer, smugly.

'All right, Mr La Salle. Let's get something straight. You stated earlier that you heard the defendant say, "I'll kill the bitch!" Is that correct?'

'No, sir. I didn't say that. I said that I *thought* that's what I heard.'

'Yes or no, Mr La Salle!'

'I told you... I can't be certain.'

'Yes or no, Mr La Salle!'

'I told you...'

'Counsel! You're putting words in the witness's mouth.'

'Your Honour…'

'Get on with your examination.'

And so it had gone on and on – the usual lawyer mumbo-jumbo. But Larry had refused to change his qualifier. He did confirm, however, that John *could* have said that he would kill the bitch, and had felt bad about saying it ever since.

So now it was up to the jury.

He threw the tools down.

'Poker! Let's go to Leigh. We should hear it on the six o'clock news if the jury makes a decision.'

Suzie boiled eggs and took them with them. They drank a beer each, and sat by the water's edge, under the pohutukawas. The radio played quietly.

Suzie held a finger to her lips, 'Listen… bellbirds.' They listened, the faint pinging, poignant notes, the closer, answering bell-like tones. She squeezed his hand. But soon the birds were gone.

Larry had almost dozed off when he heard her sobs.

'Poker! What is it?' He put an arm behind her head and brought her to him.

'He may never hear them,' she said, her tears unchecked.

'I doubt that he's the type who listens to bellbirds. He's a city bloke,' he offered, in an effort to soothe her. Suzie surprised him sometimes, the softness that lurked in her, of which, afterwards, she was usually ashamed.

'I can't see how they can convict him,' he said, with considerably more assurance than he felt.

When they drove back into town, the butcher was closing his shop.

'What you think of it, by choves?' he called out. 'Good, eh?'

Larry braked to a stop. They got out of the vehicle. 'You mean… John?'

'They gave the werdict at tree o'clock. *Not guilty!* Good chob, eh?'

'Oh, Poker!' Suzie and Larry held each other. Suzie started crying again.

The dog Kuri, aware that something of considerable import had taken place, tried to climb Larry's leg. Larry ignored him. Suzie picked him up. She danced in a little circle.

'Oh you wonderful doggy, you!' The surprised dog rewarded her with a series of deafening barks.

'Let's see who's in the pub,' Larry said.

They were all there – those who had been cheering for John. Most were already well celebrated.

Rangi said, 'Good-oh, mate!'

The proprietor leaned across the bar to shake Larry's hand. 'On the house,' he said with rare magnanimity, filling the glasses, even topping up those not empty.

They rehashed the case.

The proprietor said, 'Gentlemen, it's six o'clock. I've got to close her down. There's been too much publicity and the bloody do-gooders are at it again. But I tell you what, we're having a private party tonight – on me. So drink 'em up and we'll move into the other room. I got scouts out looking for John. I don't know how he'll feel about joining us, but I thought I'd try.'

They brought John in at seven, but now that he was here, they didn't know what to say to him, and they fell silent.

'God save the King,' the proprietor said, hoisting a glass. 'The King,' a few replied.

Larry lifted his glass.

'John,' he said.

'John!' they acclaimed in unison. The silence was broken.

Later, Larry said, 'John, I'm sorry…'

'About what, my boy? You did your job. Your evidence was clear and unbiased. When you refused to let them badger you into stating things beyond what you had actually heard, they could do nought but find me not guilty. The way our justice system works, just as a woman cannot be a little bit pregnant, neither can a defendant be a little bit guilty. If there's an element of doubt, the jury must give the defendant the benefit of it.' He paused to sip his drink, beer tonight. 'And now, that's all I am going to say about this unfortunate business, ever, except to thank you all for your support. I mean that from the bottom of my heart.'

Suzie wiped her eyes then hugged him. They shook his hand. The proprietor sprung for oysters on the shell with bread and slabs of butter, and someone brought fish and chips and sausages and chips from Tony's.

John was properly welcomed home.

Larry had been showing Suzie the land he'd chosen on which to build a house – when he had the money. She was warm with him this afternoon, pleased that he included her in his plans.

'Look at the view, Poker! You can see all the way to the Mahurangi. It will get a lot of wind up here, but the view!

She put an arm through his.

'You'll need a fence to stop the kids from rolling down the hill,' she said.

The suggestion interrupted his dreaming.

'Kids!'

She laughed. 'That stopped him!' She hugged his arm tighter and leaned into him.

'It's wonderful!' she said.

Her father was unhappy but relieved that she had moved to Warkworth. Relieved because now he could employ a full-time bookkeeper, unhappy because his daughter had moved away to live in a state he didn't like to think about.

In bed that night Suzie said, 'You're wanting to build a house – what's happened to your dream of going to America?'

'Poker, it's an impossible dream. I should have known better.'

Suzie sat up. 'If it's impossible it's because you are convincing yourself that it is.'

'Hey, it'll be four years soon since I first applied and I'm no closer now than I was then. It's time to think about settling down.'

'Nothing's going to happen if you sit on your bloody arse. When was the last time you checked with the American Consulate?'

'Suzie, I told you, it's hopeless!'

'Then what's been the purpose of the evening classes, and studying, and all that bloody nattering on the bloody radio night after night?'

'Just because I can't go to America, I don't have to stop learning.'

At breakfast Suzie said, 'Honey, why don't you ask some of those American friends of yours, the ones you talk to on the radio, if they can help you? They live there; they must know ways.'

He was surprised that she still thought about it.

'Why are you trying to get rid of me? Who's the other fellow?' She put an arm through his.

'You're my other fellow. But I mean it about asking those men. You know what John says: "Strike while the stove's hot!" '

'I don't think he says that, Poker. But I'll think about it.'

'You darling! Let's go to bed so I can properly reward you.'

'Let's have another cup of tea and go to work.'

'Weakling!'

COMING TO NEW ZEALAND STOP ARRIVING *18TH STOP* said her cable.

Moira! Larry answered that he would meet the ship.

Seven years since he'd seen her. Why was she coming? How much had she changed? He tried to bring her to mind. Her hair: dark-brown with an auburn tint, glinting red in some lights. Her voice: lilting, rising at the end of a sentence. His name when she said it: 'Larr-ee?' Not 'Larry'. A roll on the rs. He had listened to her voice, not always what she said.

'Larr-ee? Do ye no' ken wha' it is I'm saying to ye? Do you no' hear me?' He would smile and apologise: 'I'm sorry...'

With a soft word, a soft movement, the careful way she smoothed her skirt before she sat, the dainty way she ate, he felt like an oaf beside her, although she hadn't known it.

What would the decisive, practical Suzie think of her, he wondered. Suzie who didn't give a hoot about clothes, who could swear like a navvy if given sufficient reason – would she too feel like an oaf? Probably not, he decided.

A small knot of excitement built up in him about her coming. He tried not to let Suzie know it. Suzie had been jealous of Maria; she had acted oddly about Moira's letters.

Standing on the wharf, twice he had said, 'I think that's her!' Finally, he saw her coming down the gangplank.

He pushed through the crowd.

But was it Moira? If it was Moira she was taller, slimmer, *splendid* in a regal way. She scanned the crowd and saw him.

'Larr-ee!' She hurried forward, hand outstretched. 'Larr- ee. It's so wonderful to see ye again!'

He had wondered how he would greet her. Seven years – nearly a third of his lifetime; and now she was married. He took her hand, shook it politely. It came to him that she was a stranger.

'Moira, this is Suzie Robinson, and Suzie – Moira MacDougall.'

Usually Suzie would have said, simply, 'G'day. Pleased to meecha,' but this afternoon she said, 'How do you do?'

Larry chuckled to himself. So... she *was* awed by Scottish gentility.

Suzie and he had argued about the van's seating arrangements. The van had two bucket seats. He had proposed that they should hire a taxi to take Moira to the hotel. Suzie had said, 'Why waste money? I'll sit in the back!' She had put a blanket and cushion on the floor.

The trunks and suitcases built up to a mountain. Suzie would have to sit on them. Larry mused that the baggage Moira had brought with her totalled more than all he and Suzie owned. He called a taxi, put both girls in it, and drove the baggage to the hotel.

In the hotel dining-room Moira discussed the wine with the steward. Larry saw Suzie's bewilderment. 'Two beers,' he said when the steward hovered by him expectantly. Suzie smiled a thank you.

The menu was in French. Suzie pointed to an item. 'What's this?'

Larry looked. 'Goose liver.'

'*Goose liver!*'

It may be fairly stated that the dinner was a disaster. When the *pomme de terre* turned out to be a boiled spud, and the *agneau* tough mutton, Suzie protested angrily. 'Dimitri's feeds you better tucker than this shit for quarter of the price!' she spluttered. Dimitri's, in Otahuhu, was known by the mostly freezing works customers as the Greasy Greek's. Larry looked at his plate in embarrassment. When he looked back up, Moira's eyes rested on his for a moment. An impish smile he had forgotten dimpled the corners of her mouth. She's close to laughing, he thought. Suzie's nose puckered and snorted as she stabbed at her meal. Oh Suzie, he sighed to himself.

On the way home, Suzie said, 'Well, I blew the shit out of that dinner, didn't I? *Pomme de terre*! A spud's a spud as a pig's arse is pork. And as for that bloody mutton!' She couldn't think of words to describe the mutton which, admittedly, was tough old mutton. Then her mind leapt to another indignity. 'And boy, does she scoff up the plonk!' 'Suzie, plonk is cheap wine. What Moira drank was most certainly not cheap wine. And she had only two glasses. I remind you that you put away two bottles of beer.'

'Plonk's plonk!' she snapped, not to be jibed from an opinion.

They drove in silence until Suzie said, 'Actually, she'd be quite nice if she wasn't such a bloody snob. But that la-de-da accent… Poof!'

'Come on, Poker,' Larry protested, increasingly annoyed with her.

'All that frog talk with the waiter about the plonk! Why couldn't she speak bloody English like the rest of us?'

'The waiter served the meal, Suzie. The steward served the wine.'

'Shit. What's the difference? A waiter's a waiter.'

After a while, Larry began to realise that not many years earlier he, in all probability, would have voiced opinions not unlike Suzie's. But since those days he'd been in England, Scotland, Algeria, Tunisia, Italy, America, New Caledonia.

'Moira understands wine,' he said.

Suzie was given to philosophical waxing: 'It must make her feel superior to show off like that. And all that bloody luggage she brought with her! Anyone would think she was coming here to live.'

In bed, too excited by the day's events to sleep, she leaned on an elbow. 'Honey, thank you for getting the taxi. You didn't have to do that, you know. I could have sat on the luggage.' 'Nothing but the best for a princess,' Larry answered, pleased with her all of a sudden.

'Oh, and I meant to ask,' she said, 'what was that poo-lay thing she ordered?'

'*Poulet*. Chicken – chook.'

'Chook! Why didn't they say it was bloody chook? I would have ordered that instead of that old mutton.'

'Suzie! It was covered with melted blue cheese. Remember, you didn't like blue cheese that time…'

'That stinky stuff! She likes that!'

'Suzie, a lot of people like blue cheese. I like blue cheese. Just because…'

But Suzie wasn't listening – she was asleep.

HE HAD BEEN BITTEN awake. He looked at his watch. Fifteen minutes past five. The roosters were on the perch still.

'Dear God in heaven, why can't you give me a woman who keeps normal hours instead of this over-sexed psycho?' he grumbled. 'And one who doesn't bite.'

'He has – Moira. She won't bite – or do anything else for that matter!'

She scrubbed at the hair on his chest as if she was scouring a frying pan.

'Hey! That hurts.'

'You poor little mouse!' She scrubbed harder.

'Let me up! I have to go to the toilet.'

'Excuses, excuses. Dear God in heaven, why did you send me such a weakling?'

He was to drive to Auckland today, to bring Moira back. Moira had been in Dunedin visiting distant relatives.

'You don't need me along,' Suzie had said the night before. 'I'm not sitting in the back while you ride in the front like Jackie with your girlfriend.'

'Girlfriend... She's married, remember?'

'Is she?'

Neither of them knew, really. The night they had met the ship and had dinner with Moira she had not mentioned her husband. They had wondered about that.

Coming back from the toilet, Larry said, 'Poker, I wish you'd come. You drive – I'll sit in the back. Don't you realise that she's a stranger to me now? I'm at loss what to say to her.'

'I don't recall that being a handicap when you met me. Now, shut up and come back to bed.'

204

'Did you enjoy Dunedin?' he said, trying to break an awkward-ness that had been with them since the railway station.

'Thank you, yes, 'twas very pleasant.'

He stole occasional glances at her. She was attentive to the scenery.

They coasted down the hill from Silverdale. Moira had wound her window down. The air was brisk yet. She leaned forward to see across Larry, to catch the expanse of the bay. They crossed a bridge spanning a tidal inlet, drove past the campground, and coasted into Orewa. She gasped with pleasure.

'Oh Larr-ee, how beautiful! Please, would ye stop?'

He drove across the grass verge, across crabgrass struggling to populate pure sand, and eased to a stop under a pohutukawa. When he opened his door, the dog Kuri bounded from the van, ran to the pohutukawa, sniffed and peed, barked a path down to the water, and retreated when a wave spread up the beach.

'He's a stupid dog,' he said for something to say, opening her door. She laid a hand lightly on his arm while she climbed down. He had held this girl – this woman – in his arms seven years ago; now her touch was that of a stranger, but electric.

She pushed her shoes off and skipped lithely down to the water. A wavelet spread itself up the sand. She waded into it. It foamed around her feet.

'It's so warm – no' like the sea at home,' she called back.

He pushed his own shoes off, pulled off his socks. The dog Kuri snatched a shoe and ran off with it.

'Leave it!' Larry ordered. The dog turned, stopped. His stance said, 'Hey! Let's play!'

Larry joined Moira. The wave had receded. Tiny crabs scuttled before their feet.

''Tis so very beautiful and peaceful. I'm saying to myself, this is no' real. My mother will have the plaid about her shoulders and complaining of the cold.'

Remembering the grey streets, the grey houses, the grey skies, Larry silently agreed.

'This is the Pacific Ocean,' he said. 'Beyond that point are the Americas. So close. So far. Sometimes I...'

She slowed her pace, placed a hand back on his arm.

'Larr-ee, are ye no' wondering why I came?'

Yes. He was wondering why she had come. Her last letter had described how she was homesick for Scotland. She was having problems with her husband. And then the cable; she was coming to New Zealand! What had happened to precipitate so sudden a visit?

'I thought that it might have something to do with your marriage. It was a surprise though – a wonderful surprise – but when you went to America, that was a surprise too.'

'Larr-ee, I went to America because my husband went. Poor, dear Ian. I've no' been right for him, nor fair to him. 'Twas very unsettling after the war with a part of me wanting to return to London, another part of me telling myself I am beyond the usual time to marry, and Ian proposing. When I wrote that first letter to ye, my heart was hoping that ye'd cable me, and perhaps tell me no' to marry him. Yet, I'll no' say that I wasna happy at the beginning. Ian was very attentive. But his work has absorbed him more and more, and now he has no' the time for much of anything else.'

She paused as the water splashed against her feet. Her face had been intent. Suddenly she smiled.

'Ye mind, ye told me in a letter no' to be afraid to breathe the foreign air? I was thinking of that one afternoon when Ian was gone to Chicago for five days. So I gathered my courage together, and I went alone to New York. I saw the Empire State Building and Times Square, and I stayed in a hotel! I rode the subway, I took the taxis. I breathed the foreign air. I came home the day after Ian was home and he was upset with me, but now I had the determination to deal with it. I have told him since that I must have my own life and I am going away for a while. He has his work; I think he'll no' miss me much.'

She withdrew her hand from Larry's arm. An unexpected imp

in her kicked water at the dog Kuri. The dog barked for further attention.

'He's a darling wee dog. What's his name?'

'We call him Kuri. It means dog in Maori.'

'Kuri sounds nicer.' She bent down, scratched him between the ears, until a wave sent him scurrying up the beach. She straightened, waded slowly through the ankle-deep water. Larry waded beside her.

'But I've no' told ye why I've come, have I now? Larr-ee, ye ken ye were my first beau, my only beau until I met Ian, and in my heart, ye're still my beau. I'll have ye know that. And I have come to New Zealand because I have to know, do I still have the feelings for ye.'

Bidding for time to collect his thoughts, Larry picked up a shell, threw it at the dog. Suzie's missing-nothing eyes not on him, he had been drinking in the soft melody of Moira's voice again, hearing her correctness, and feeling the old magnetism. And now, was she saying that perhaps she loved him still – after he had not written even one letter to her until hers had found him after the war?

'Mayhap I'll find that 'twas nothing but a wartime dalliance we had,' she said. She clutched his arm, turned her eyes up to his.

'Ye'll no' think badly of me because I've told ye of what 'tis in my heart?' Her gentle, Gaelic plea was almost lost in the roar of a wave that smashed around their legs, wetting them both. 'Ach! 'tis wet I am!'

He was grateful for the diversion. Was she asking him to state his own true feelings, about now, about then? About love confused at nineteen and a war full of adventures yet to live? He had a sudden single memory of her standing against a privet hedge the first time he had kissed her, her cheeks flushed and uncertain. It caused him to reach out, take her hand. A tingling moved up his arm. The war was over. He could love this new Moira without being confused. But suddenly he was. He let go her hand.

'Moira. Suzie and I – '

'Aye, I surmised. Suzie's in love with ye. And ye, Larr- ee?'

The dog Kuri brought Larry's shoe, and dropped it. It floated out with the receding wave. Before Larry could retrieve it a second larger wave drenched him. Then the shoe was gone. They hunted for it. He was soaked again. They walked back to the Ford Thames.

Nearing Warkworth, Larry realised that he hadn't answered Moira's question, and was pleased that he hadn't had to.

He slowed coming over the last hill. 'Warkworth!' he said, a measure of pride in his voice.

'Oh Larr-ee, how can ye want to leave such a beautiful country?'

'There's no future in electronics in New Zealand. The country's too small to sustain an industry.'

'Aye, I ken, but 'tis a sad shame ye have to leave here,' she said.

SUZIE SAW RIGHT OFF that Moira's expensive green frock was wet around the bottom, and that Larry was without his shoes. He, too, had been in water, she saw.

'What took you so bloody long?' she said.

Moira quickly intervened. 'I'm sorry, Suzie, I made him stop at the beach. I've never seen such a beautiful beach.'

'And then the stupid dog carried my shoe into the water,' Larry said, resentful that he found it necessary to explain.

'And pissed on your pants by the look of it,' Suzie said.

Moira put a hand on Suzie's arm.

'Dear Suzie, please don't be angry. I wanted to wade in the water. We've no' such a beautiful setting in Scotland. Your beaches here! Those glorious trees with the red blossoms... And I canna believe how warm the water is. My father's favourite saying was that Scottish waters gave the polar bears the croup – that's why there are no bears in Scotland.'

'Oh, I'm not really angry, but he's only got the one pair of good shoes,' Suzie said, seemingly mollified, but, as Larry knew, inside she wasn't; she had wanted to make a point of his poverty. And she was telling him, 'You're out of your depth, old boy.'

'Oh, and Jake Watkins wants you to call him right away,' she said, looking at Larry.

Larry excused himself to Moira for a moment and went over to the bench under the side window, the part of the bakery he used as an office, and picked up the phone. Glancing out the window he saw the Harley, without the sidecar, parked in the weeds. He was to learn later that after his mates had enjoyed an extended session in a Wellington pub, a power pole had run into the Harley and neatly clipped off Grunter. Fortunately for Grunter only the sidecar suffered serious damage. While Larry waited for Jake to come to the phone, he called across the room to Suzie, 'When did Speed get here?'

'After you left this morning. You must have passed each other,' she said tersely.

'And Grunter? Mac?'

'On the noon bus.'

The works! Well, Moira said she'd like to meet my friends, he thought, suppressing a grin.

Before she met them, however, Larry gave her a glimpse through the pub doorway of the six o'clock swill at its majestic peak. A far cry from anything she would have known, or even remotely imagined. Above the centre of the crowd poked Grunter's head-hunter coiffure and the back of Speed's head, both men well lubricated judging by their movements. Larry opted to check Moira into the hotel before settling for the serenity of the private bar. She would meet them soon enough.

In the private bar, Rangi and Mac sat at the rail. When Larry brought Moira into the room, Mac's eyes bobbed excitedly. He removed his hat – an extraordinary concession – flourished it, and bowed.

'Alexander, MacAllister, McKenzie, miss. At your service.'

'Good afternoon, Mr McKenzie. I'm Moira MacDougall.'

'Aye, from the ole country, I hear, and 'tis like music from heaven tae hear the tinkle of ye voice. And those bonnie cheeks!' He reached out, pinched one between his fingers. The constable spoke from behind them. 'Pardon me, La Salle... I see those friends of yours are in town again. I trust their stay will be a short one.'

'I'll mention it to them, constable.'

'Good-oh, lad. Grateful to you. Good evening then.' He nodded at Moira. 'Good evening to you too, miss.' He nodded at Suzie.

'Nosey bugger,' Mac said when the constable had gone. 'Don't know why you don't tell him to fart up a rope.'

'He's just doing his job,' Larry said, enough distance in his tone to show that he didn't one hundred per cent believe what he preached. Moira, he noted, if she was offended by Mac's profanity, hid it well.

When the swill began to spill into the private bar, Larry collected Grunter and Speed and led them to the Bridge House, where he had made dinner reservations. The waiter twitched his nose at Grunter, but stopped twitching when John Arrf sat on one side of Grunter and Moira the other.

Ngaire and Rangi came, apologising that they were late (ten minutes). The baby had fussed, they said. Larry had invited Lady Loomis through Mac, but Mac refused to bring her. 'We don't want to spoil the bloody evening now, do we, laddie?'

Somehow, Old Percy had realised that something was going on. Though he was not around when they walked to the Bridge House, he showed up as the main course arrived. They heard his 'Shhyrup!' through the open window. Larry moved the curtain to one side. Percy leaned on his crutch in the centre of the road, at the edge of the street lamp's field of light. Larry sprang from his chair, rushed outside.

'Percy! You trying to get yourself run over!' He led Percy to a seat at the side of the building's main entrance. Since his stroke, Percy had taken to walking on the road to avoid climbing up and down the kerbs.

'Wait here, Percy. I'll get you something to eat.'

He transferred pieces of his chicken – not poulet, Suzie had been quick to point out with relish – and a bread roll to his bread and butter plate. He took it out to Percy.

'Here you are, old fellow. Stay on the footpath when you leave.'

When he returned, Suzie squeezed his hand. 'You old softie!' Over his protests, she forked a piece of her roast beef on to his plate, and with it a truce of sorts.

To Larry and Suzie's amusement, John and Mac vied for Moira's attention. Mac tried to outdo John with his joke about 'the wee Scottish lass', but Suzie quickly shut him down with a 'Shove it, buster!' Moira handled their attention skilfully and Larry couldn't help comparing Suzie's spirited ways with Moira's quiet finesse. He was immediately ashamed that he had made the comparison. He placed his hand over Suzie's and squeezed lightly. Moira briefly touched him with her eyes and smiled, sadly he thought.

The next morning, the Harley refused to start. Speed pushed it back into the weeds and boarded the bus with Grunter and Mac. Larry watched them leave, pleased to see them go, but sorry. They had become a part of his life. They would remain so.

On Saturday, Suzie said she had things to do in Auckland. Was she trusting them or giving them the rope to hang themselves with, Larry wondered, before deciding that good Suzie was giving them a chance for privacy; she had started to like Moira. He drove Moira sightseeing around the area. When Suzie was with them they conversed freely, but an uneasy prohibition held them silent when she wasn't with them. Yet he felt the magnetism between them. Had he felt the same attraction seven years ago? But then he had belonged to a group of young men who lived each day at full steam ahead in case there was no tomorrow. For Bob Harper, for Tiny Jones, for Jock Campbell, for Bo Elliot, Larry's close friends, there had been no tomorrows. They had 'bought the farm' according to the terminology of the day. Ironic that Jones and Campbell had come off farms that one day would have been theirs.

Without thinking of where he was going, Larry turned into Hepburn Creek Road. He stopped in front of the piece of land he had shown Mary and Beverley, then Suzie. Knee-high in fern, he and Moira walked up the hill to stand beneath a canopy of pongas. Larry swept the great expanse of the Mahurangi with his arm. 'Why would I want to live in the town when I could live up here?' he said.

Moira touched his arm. He felt her touch hot on his skin.

'Larr-ee, but what of America?'

'Moira, I have to start believing that it isn't going to happen. It's more than four years since I first made application and, as far as I know, I'm no closer.' He couldn't keep resignation from his voice.

''Tis the beauty of heaven ye have in this country. Heaven or money, is that no' the choice facing ye, Larry?'

'No… it's not the money. There's my work. I…'

'Aye. I ken about the work, Larr-ee. Ian has his work. Do ye no' think there can be a balance?' Then, somehow it happened; she was in his arms. She sobbed quietly into his shoulder. He stroked her hair.

'Moira,' he said, when he could find the voice to speak, for he had sobbed with her, 'tell me you forgive me.'

She kissed his lips, held him away, kissed him again. She dug her fingers into his shoulder. 'Larr-ee… why would I no' forgive you? I love you. I've always loved you. Oh…' She clung to him, smothered him with more kisses.

The blood pounded furiously in his head. He wrapped her close. 'Oh, Moira, such a fool I've been. I…'

'Hush. 'Twas war took ye away, and we were but bairns, no' yet given to knowing our wishes.'

'I could have written. I always meant to. But I seemed to get caught up in the war, and…'

'Oh, my heart, if there's blame ye're to be disbursing, a share has to be given to this silly person who was so scared of wrong-doing, scared of shaming her parents, scared of her upbringing. I… Oh, Larr-ee, say ye'll no' leave me again.'

'I promise. I promise I will never leave you again,' Larry said, lowering her to the fern, meaning it with his whole being, while sinking beside her.

An uneasy afternoon sky darkened the east. Dark, boiling clouds scudded above them. The air hinted at rain. They lay, legs inter-twined, flesh to flesh, mouth to mouth. Suddenly, a salvo of cold, shilling-sized drops splashed on their bodies. They pulled away, laughed, hugged, let the rain wash over them. Then, the clouds gone, the sun warming, they looked into each other's eyes and vowed never, ever again, to part.

The air chilled into evening. A cold reality released a sadness in each of them that neither wanted to talk about. They dressed in damp clothes and shivered.

'Suzie will be wondering what has happened to us,' Larry said.

'Aye,' Moira whispered. 'That she will.'

A subdued Larry slowed to turn into Bakery Lane, then pushed the accelerator and continued on. Moira formed her eyes into a question before she put a hand on his arm. Larry crossed the bridge, turned right to Matakana Road, and took the road to Leigh.

'We're no' going home?' she dared to hope.

Larry shook his head and drove on.

Moira snuggled her agreement into his shoulder.

A little later: 'Larr-ee?'

'My precious?'

'Whatever happens, I shall always love you.'

Whatever happens…

'And whatever happens, I shall always love you, my sweet-heart.'

Larry drove to Leigh. During the ride they were silent, content to hold hands when the road allowed them to. Larry flatly refused to let the 'whatever happens' take over his mind. Soon enough when he faced the music.

He pulled into the kerb beside the town's only hotel. The bar was full of fishermen. Some he knew well from working on their boats. Some he knew by sight. Some had met Mary. Some had met Suzie. That Larry had yet another woman with him didn't cause a lifted eyebrow; commercial fishermen are a broad-minded bunch of blokes as a rule. But curious. When they heard the heather in Moira's voice, they found excuses to cluster around. 'You're from Scotland, miss?'

'Aye, from Dundee.'

'Good-oh! My wife's father's from Glasgow. Tight old bastard, though,' to much laughter. 'No worse than his son-in-law,' from another, waving an empty glass.

'You on holiday, miss?'

'Aye, I am, and loving every wee moment of it. I'll no' want to go home.'

And finally, 'You met this young fellow in the war? He fixes our radios, you know.'

'Aye, he told me so. We met in Scotland, before he served in North Africa and Italy. He's a dear friend.'

'Hey, lad! You didn't tell me you were in Italy! My boy was there, you know,' from yet another.

Once the pleasantries were talked out, and after a couple of drinks, Larry quietly ordered dinner for two in the dining room, and a room as far as possible from the bar, for often in this remote town, where the fishermen worked shifts, the drinking continued late into the night. The champagne came compliments of the proprietor.

Whatever reservations Moira may have had about committing adultery, she abandoned them that night. The champagne may have had something to do with it, or the fierce needs of her young body, or the knowing that they'd have to face Suzie, in which case, if Suzie possessed the power of absolution, surely it made little difference the extent of their misdeed.

Sometime in the early morning hours, at the edge of his consciousness, Larry heard the rumble of traffic on the gravel road. The lorries meeting the returning fishing fleet, to take the fish to Auckland, he thought. The noise stirred Moira from a half sleep. She snuggled her head into his shoulder.

'Tell me again, my heart, that you love me,' she whispered. Larry kissed her forehead. 'I love you more than I know how to describe,' he responded. 'More than the ocean has waves. More than the sky has clouds. More than... He hunted for words, but then fell asleep.

Dear heart,
One day, one night. I live them over and over. I feel your hands. I feel your lips. I feel your heart beating against mine. I remember the rain, so cold, and me shivering, but oh! so invigorating. And you... you laughing and laughing. Let it rain! you say. Let it thunder! you say. And then it does both. As if you had arranged it! The sun again. We hold each other. Oh, Larry. I remember. I will never leave you again, you say. I love you, I say. The sun going down. The moon already high. America over there. Is Ian wondering what I am doing? I am still his wife. And you say, Suzie will be wondering what has happened to us. We drive down the hill. And then you drive on. My heart sings. What we are doing is dreadfully sinful, but I am beyond care. This night is our night. To remember. I remember. I'm crying.

Dear heart, in the morning, when we drove back to your cottage and Suzie had not come home last night, oh, how *my heart rejoiced. It's an omen, I thought. Let us take our happiness and run, I wanted to urge you. And when Suzie came home and she said, where were you two last night and said that she had tried to telephone you from Auckland, how desperately I wanted you to tell her about us! Poor, dear Suzie. But of course you couldn't tell her. As I cannot tell Ian. Since I have come home, Ian has tried so hard to please me, but his touch is ice on my skin. Sex without love is as harsh as Highland sleet against the cheek. My love, is there not an answer? Must our values be our prisons?*

Last week Ian was offered a permanent position here when his fellowship is up, but he says that he won't consider it...

Larry had torn the letter open in the post office and sat in the van to read it. But the round-faced little grocer stuck his head in the window. 'G'day, Larry. Nice day, eh?'

Shit...

'Yes. Not bad.'

Larry started the engine, let the clutch out. But where to? Not home. Oh, Moira...

THE DOG KURI WAS in deep tutae. His fall from grace had begun the evening before, when Larry had brought him back from being dosed for a hydatids check.

The laxative had had a sequential, double-barrelled effect. It had not only caused the dog Kuri to obediently produce the sample the veterinarian required, it caused him to produce later samples he dropped randomly about the bakery floor. Suzie accidentally transferred one to her sandal. That was the beginning.

This morning, Larry hacked at his beard with a blunt razor, blunt because Suzie had cut a corn off her toe with his last blade. While he scraped, he considered the reason for her mood. It had started not long after Moira had returned to America, and had more or less continued since. When she had asked where they had been the evening she had phoned, he had said at the pictures. Perhaps she had remembered later, as he had, that the pictures were shown on Mondays, Wednesdays and Fridays in Warkworth. The night he had taken Moira to Leigh had been a Saturday.

In the early hours the dog Kuri had found a pocket of mice. He extruded them on the kitchen floor as Suzie entered the kitchen to start breakfast. She broomed him out the door.

'Dogs have no bloody business in the house! You let that bloody mongrel do whatever he likes.'

Larry cleaned up the mess and dripped blood from his face on to the floor. She began a fresh onslaught.

'Enough!' he told her.

'He lets his bloody mongrel shit and spew all over the place and he argues with me when I say something about it. A dog shouldn't be in the house!'

There was no stopping her.

He took the .22 from its nails in the wall. He sighted about six inches behind the dog Kuri, who sat just outside the doorway, and pulled the trigger.

That didn't stop her either, but it surely caused a change in her direction.

'You've killed him!'

She ran outside.

'You bloody fool!' she screamed at Larry.

Larry sought to make amends; he put an arm around her shoulders, rubbed his bloody face against her.

She pulled away.

'It was a bloody stupid thing you did! If he'd moved, you could have killed him.'

'You couldn't kill him if you tried.'

'It was a stupid thing to do.'

'I thought you didn't like him?'

'I didn't say I wanted him shot!'

He turned away. Women! He started up the Velocette, seldom ridden since he'd bought the Thames. He put the dog Kuri in the apple box and rode out to Hepburn Creek Road. He climbed up the bank to the spot under the pongas where he and Moira had trysted. The ground was wet – it had rained in the night. The smell was the sweet bush smell of decaying leaves. He spoke to Moira.

My love. Suzie's as feisty as a wild she-cat with kittens. She knows about us, I'm sure of it. Why is it so sinful to love? Must we all be hurt – your husband because you are unable to love him, Suzie because I have fallen in love with you? Us because we can't have each other? I know that Suzie is a good person, a fine, honest person, smart and, I admit it, a better businesswoman than I am a businessman, but she cares nothing for dewdrops on a tulip, the smell of the mangroves. She sees nothing of the beauty from where I stand, only that it's too steep to build on! Or am I finding excuse for my perfidy?

My love, I cannot come to you in America. Although the Americans open their arms to the poor, the oppressed – most everyone it seems – they close them against New Zealanders, who fought shoulder to shoulder with them throughout the war – two wars in fact, for my father fought beside them in France in the first one. And I'm tired of trying and waiting. Should my visa come through tomorrow, if it were not that I would be closer to you, I would find it difficult to leave this country now – I've grown to love it so. But my problem, sweetheart, is that I can't live on beauty, unless I'm prepared to remain the shopkeeper I've become – answering the phone, taking orders, sending out bills, building radios only in the evenings. No doubt New Zealand will one day catch up with the rest of the world and there'll be opportunities for the likes of me, but what in the meantime? Help me, Moira.

THE SCHOOL BUS RETURNED from Matakana. The driver peered at the road through heavy rain and wiped at the fogged-up windshield. He didn't see Percy on the bridge until he was fifteen feet from him. He applied the brakes, causing the wheels to hydroplane on the wet concrete. Percy saw the bus coming. He lifted his crutch, held it horizontally. The radiator pushed it aside.

The driver explained it later to Larry:

'It was raining cats and dogs. He was right in the middle of the bloody bridge. I couldn't stop in time. I just couldn't! He was right in the middle of the bridge!'

Larry told Suzie what the driver had said.

'He should have been more careful,' she snapped.

'Suzie. It was pouring down! I was in second gear most of the way coming home; the visibility was terrible. He couldn't help it.'

'Of course he could. You're supposed to drive at a safe speed.'

'Poker…'

'You can talk all you like. You won't convince me. He was speeding!'

A small funeral. Suzie and Larry, and their friends; the bus driver and his wife – the two stood apart from the others – the butcher and Constable Weatherspoon. A Church of England minister conducted the service.

There was a wake of sorts in the private bar. The drinkers were solemn and mostly silent. They sipped at the drinks until John Arrf lifted his glass.

'God bless his soul,' he said.

'Percy!' they said in unison.

Suzie cried. Larry put his arm around her.

Joe Montini said, 'I'll miss the old fellow. I'd kinda got used to him – you know what I mean – part of the town. You don't miss them until they're gone.'

The proprietor said, 'He never was a customer of mine – though I'm told he could stow it away if he got hold of it – but, as you say, he was part of the town. We'll all miss the old coot.'

The lawyer in John said, 'I wonder who's handling his estate.'

Larry said, 'For God's sake, John, what could he have had?'

'You never know,' John replied.

As it turned out, Percy had quite a lot, and a sister in Christchurch who came to Warkworth to be sure that no one else got any of it – other than the modest fee John charged for handling the estate. Percy had had a sum of money left to him before his accident, which he'd put into two savings accounts. Each had compounded over the years. Meanwhile he had lived on a disability pension. No one knew if he remembered the savings accounts.

Larry asked the sister to contribute a little to a headstone.

'Why? I live in Christchurch.'

'I thought that you'd like to do it.'

'And who's going to look at it?' She turned to John. 'And I want that shack of his put on the market immediately. Goodness knows what kind of vandals you've got in this place.'

John said, 'Madam, I assure you, Warkworth's not that kind of place. You may…'

'Just get it on the market. And remember, I have a list of everything in it. I expect you to account for it all.'

'It shall be as you say, madam.'

The next day, at the bakery, Suzie held up the enamelled pannikin she had bought for Percy because she hadn't liked him drinking out of the cups they used. 'What'll I do with it?' she asked.

'It'll come in handy when we have visitors.'

'No! It's Percy's.'

She planted a pansy in the mug. She put it on the windowsill near the door where Percy had usually stood.

A RE YOU ASLEEP?'

'Yes!'

'Then wake up.' To encourage him, Suzie bit an ear, a number ten bite.

'Ouch! Why'd you do that?'

'To wake you up!'

'Oh, God! What time is it?'

'It's late. Nearly six.'

'Six! It's the middle of the bloody night!'

'All men want to do is sleep.'

'You're the one who's always at me to build up my strength. Sleep builds strength.'

'I'm not talking about that! I want you to listen. I've got an idea. Let's start a branch in Wellington.'

'A branch! Hey! We don't have a trunk grown here yet! And what are we going to use for money?'

'Where there's a way there's a will. It's knowing how to go about getting it that does it. My father...' Larry rolled his eyes up in disbelief.

'Poker! Now... please. Listen! It's not just money. Who do we get to run it? It's not easy to find the right person.'

'Phooey!'

'What about America? Last night you were giving me hell for not following through and now you're wanting me involved in another business.'

'A large business is insurance. Something for me if you leave.'

'You wouldn't come with me?'

'I wish you wouldn't keep talking about that!'

'Oh, Lord, give me the strength to deal with this crazy woman...'

'Damn it! Can't you see that I'd just be a drag on you! What the hell do you think those high-falutin Yanks would think of a bumpkin who doesn't know *poulet* from chook?'

'...who thinks she's not good enough. Tell her, oh Lord, that she can hold her own with anybody. Amen.'

'You're a snob, you know. You should marry Moira.'

Suzie put flowers on Percy's grave, watered the pansy. Yet not once did she mention Percy's name. She mentioned Percy's sister's name often enough – rather rudely.

Except that she avoided talking about America, Suzie was friendly again. Two months before Christmas she said, 'I've got to talk to you.'

'You've never stopped!' Adroitly avoiding her fist, he pinioned her arms and planted a sloppy kiss on her forehead. 'Let 'er rip, my princess!'

'It's about the Wellington branch of the business...'

'That's all! I thought that by now we'd have bought Hong Kong!' He was relieved that she'd brought the subject up – he'd known all along that she hadn't let it go.

'Stop being a smart-arse and listen! I was talking to Al Willard last Monday, and I told him about our plans to open a branch...'

'Our plans!'

'Shut up and let me finish! Al Willard has space available. The rent's cheap, he knows the man to run it, and he'll invest money in the business himself if you'll give up the idea of going to America. But if you do decide to go, I think I can talk him into still putting money in.'

'Suzie! Suzie!' Slowing Suzie was harder than trying to halt a rugby fullback the size and weight of Speed. Realising that he was defeated – no doubt she had it all worked out and under way already – he headed out the door, saying over his shoulder that he missed Percy because at least he talked sense. He climbed aboard the Velocette and drove around without any destination in mind, just happy to be by himself for a while, except for the dog Kuri who, fortunately, knew when to keep his mouth shut.

MAIL. THE AMERICAN CONSULATE. Would he supply them with a copy of his contract with *CQ Magazine* at his earliest convenience?

He'd been in Waipu. It was eight o'clock when he got the mail. He came looking for Suzie to tell her about it and groaned when he saw her in bed, because that meant she'd be up well before the pigeons started their alarm-clock racket from the old bakery rooftop in the morning. Taking a certain satisfaction in shaking her shoulder, he told her about the letter from the US Consulate.

'You woke me to tell me that!'

'Suzie, can't you see what it means? They're working on my application!'

'So?' She turned her back to him and buried her head in the pillow. He should pour cold water on her, he thought, marching back to the kitchen. He looked in the oven. Perchance Suzie had left him some dinner, but she hadn't, so he headed for the bakery, then remembered that he hadn't fed the dog. Back in the cottage, he put the dog tucker in the dish – meat on a shank bone and some scraps from the butcher's. Closing the refrigerator door, he saw the packet of sausages – Suzie couldn't exist without her morning sausages. The dog Kuri couldn't believe his good fortune; he put them away in short measure. Some of them reappeared upon the linoleum, but were soon taken back down. Larry took the empty packet to the old bakery and burned it in the number one oven.

He looked at his watch. A little after eight-thirty. He had a day to make up. The telephone rang.

'Hey, e hoa. That you?'

'Speed!' Why was Speed calling? He hadn't done that before.

'I'm calling about the boss. A spool of bloody cable buggered up his leg. They're going to chop it off. Thought you'd like to know.'

'My God!'

Speed gave him the details – a timber jack slipping, the spool of cable rolling – and Mac unable to get out of the way.

Speed's report about Mac somehow negated the news from the consulate – not that he was sure he wanted the consulate news anymore. His father had said that ambition erodes with age and it seemed that he might be right. Or, in Larry's case, had his ambition been too weak to begin with? He reached into the number two oven and pulled out a partially empty bottle of Mac's Black and White. Pouring it into a cup, he wrinkled his nose at the smell of the stuff. He topped it off with water, took a sip and shuddered, and drank to Mac's recovery.

He wondered was Suzie really indifferent about the letter from the consulate, or pretending to be? He finished the drink, felt better for the glow, but felt even less like work. He picked up the pen.

My precious one,

The bad news first. Old Mac has had an accident. Tomorrow they will take off a leg. I feel so bad about it. His job is his whole life and I wonder if he'll be able to continue at it. The thought of him getting around on crutches like poor old Percy appalls me. And how will he drive?

But now the good news! A few months ago, an American friend I met via amateur radio discovered the existence of a preference quota system that bypasses the normal immigration quota system. On his advice, I re-applied under that category. Now the American Consulate has requested that I supply it with further information. So surely this must mean that they are processing my application. But you will be returning to Scotland. My darling, does it have to end this way?

WITH LA SALLE ELECTRONICS (Wellington) Limited doing well, the tail started to wag the dog, so to speak. In five months the Wellington branch had doubled their total sales volume, and Suzie was inclined not to let Larry forget it. And the new manager had proved to be a competent circuit designer. Suzie preened.

John Arrf announced that he would marry Joan Anderson, née Joan Burchett. He built a new home for her because, he told Larry, he didn't want his new wife to be contaminated by the ghost of the old one.

Grunter and Speed were up from Wellington for the duration of Christmas and the New Year. They stayed at Orewa Beach. Grunter picked up where he had left off with one of the local girls, and Speed had in tow a robust woman he called Big Mama. Big Mama had a sixty-inch waistline and an equally large thirst for beer.

They came to Warkworth for John's stag party, which turned out not to be a stag party at all because Grunter brought his girl and Speed brought Big Mama. Rangi fetched Ngaire. And Suzie was there because she lived and worked there. When Suzie saw Big Mama, she ordered Speed, 'Don't you dare let that slob sleep on the air mattress!'

Big Mama had a pleasant voice – Speed instinctively chose women with good voices – and she became the focal point. They sang Maori songs and American songs and ribald army ballads.

John tapped his foot in time with the music, his bright little eyes glowing with happiness. Since he'd decided to remarry, in spite of his previous unhappy marriage, he was a new and excited man.

'Jolly good,' he congratulated, 'jolly good.'

Mac sat on a stool with his new aluminium leg stuck straight out – he didn't know what else to do with it. Grunter's girl backed into it. Mac found a use for it.

'Buster, you do that again and I'll clobber the shit out of you,' she screamed.

Ngaire apologised to John that she had to leave. 'Really, I shouldn't be here, but I do wish both of you the very best.'

John took her hand.

'That's all right, my dear. Under the circumstances I think it was most generous of you to come.' The circumstances were that in two weeks Ngaire was scheduled to have another baby.

Grunter's girl asked them to sing 'Sentimental Journey'.

At eleven, Big Mama toppled over. The party slowed. Mac half-heartedly told Grunter's girl about 'the wee Scots lass who asked Jock wha' he had under his kilt' but she wasn't listening. John danced a languid fox-trot with Suzie. Grunter sat on a box, his back against the wall, his eyes closed. The dog Kuri inspected his feet for opportunity. Larry sat morosely in a corner and wondered what Moira was doing at this minute. Her letter, arrived this morning, was in his pocket. He yearned for time alone to read it fully. She returned to Dundee in June, that much he had read. Would he ever see her again? A day, a night. Not enough.

He had known that his involvement with Suzie was an affectionate and physical convenience – which Suzie seemed to find enough, and which he had found sufficient. Until Moira.

The music petered to a stop. John thanked Suzie for the dance. He replenished his glass with gin.

Seeing Larry alone in the corner, he ambled over. 'My boy, you don't look happy. Is it America? You heard from them yet?'

'Nothing,' Larry said, suddenly further dejected. 'Not a bloody word.'

Speed strummed the uke again. John took a long pull at the glass. 'You know, my boy, perhaps now is the time to take stock of your immediate situation. You have a good thing going here, and that Australian outlet is a capital idea. Have you given thought to calling off the American pilgrimage?' Australian subsidiary. Suzie!

Haere mai! Ev'rything is ka pai...

'Yes, I've got to decide pretty soon. The uncertainty is killing me.'

'Yes, you need to get your priorities straightened out. Now, if there's anything I can do for you at any time...'

'Thank you, John. You've been a wonderful friend.'

'Now, my boy, a favour. Old Fritz is gone and his daughter's gone, but that bloody bull remains. Every time I come out of my office I see it. Before I begin my new life I've got to rid myself of the vexing remnant of the old. Do you happen to have a ladder and saw about the place?'

'John, you can't...'

'I can! I own the building.'

They climbed the ladder. Larry stood on the one side of the parapet and John the other. They sawed at Ferdinand's head. Before it was fully cut through, its weight splintered it from the body. It dropped to the veranda, rolled down the corrugated iron slope, and fell to the road.

John carried the pieces back to the bakery.

Mac said, 'Hey, that's the head from the bull on the butcher shop over yonder! What the hell you up to?'

Speed stopped strumming. Grunter opened his eyes.

'A small ceremony, McKenzie. Grunter, my good man, be so kind as to lift your arse off that box. I need it for kindling.' John broke up the box, laid the kindling on crumpled newspaper and reverently placed the splintered and bullet-scarred head on the kindling. 'And now, ladies and gentlemen, I ask you to charge your glasses.'

'Stone the bloody crows! What's going on?'

John lit the newspaper.

'A toast, ladies and gentlemen... to my dear departed father-in-law, Fritz Kler – God bless his soul.'

'Fritz Kler,' they toasted.

'To my departed wife...'

'Departed wife!'

'And finally, to our friend, Ferdinand, as Larry calls him, the last symbol of Kler repression.'

'Ferdinand,' they toasted.

'May they all roast in hell,' John said.

He gulped his drink down, threw his glass at the oven. Glass scattered about the room.

'Stone the bloody crows!'

'I knew he was off his rocker,' Grunter's girl said.

'Now, thank you, Larry. Thank you, Suzie, everyone. And a happy New Year to you all if I don't see you before then. Good night.'

My darling,

Our date of departure has been set – June 10. So keen is Ian to leave, he has already purchased the tickets. And he's talking about beginning a family when we return. My love, though I yearn to see my mother and Pam again, and to feel the spring of heather beneath my feet, my heart rebels and my body shrinks at what going home augurs. Oh my love… why can I not defy my upbringing? Is it not a greater sin than adultery to have children with someone you do not love? Help me, Larry, help me…

Larry thumped one hand into the other. She was going home while he sat like a bloody idiot twiddling his thumbs, knowing full well that if she returned to Scotland she was lost to him. He had to do something! He read her plea again. Wasn't she asking him to take her away? Didn't that mean that she would come to him in New Zealand if he were to ask? Suddenly he realised that Suzie's plan about an Australian branch could be his salvation. He could move to Australia, where there was more of his kind of work anyway, and let Suzie run the New Zealand end of the business. She was doing it anyhow.

The cable took twenty words. He knew that because they'd charged by the word. *MY DARLING STOP DON'T GO STOP I LOVE YOU STOP MARRY ME STOP I WILL COME FOR YOU STOP LARRY*

It was done! Now to tell Suzie. She stood at the sink preparing lunch – some kind of sandwiches. He pulled a chair out, turned it around, and sat with his arms across its back, facing her.

'Tell me about the Australian outlet,' he said, wanting to get that out of the way first.

Suzie slapped his plate on the table. He sensed that he could have chosen a better time, but no time seemed a good time with Suzie anymore.

'If I tell you, you'll only pour cold water on it.'

'Try me.'

'Not yet.'

'Am I not to know what's going on in my own business?'

'Without me, there wouldn't be a business.'

She was right, of course. But that was not good reason not to tell him.

'Suzie, I demand to know what's going on. This is my business – you seem to have forgotten that.'

She turned on him.

'You bloody turd! And next you'll want to sack me. Well, just you try and you'll pay me wages for all the time I've put in here. And I'll have your loan called in.'

Larry was totally bewildered by her intensity. What had brought this on?

'Poker, why would I sack you, for crissake? Can't I ask you what's going on in my own business without you thinking I'm going to sack you?'

He rose from the chair, put an arm around her. Held her until she calmed. It took a while to worm it out of her. She planned to ship radios from New Zealand when she'd found a suitable Australian distributor. She would go to Australia soon and seek one. John Arrf had connections. Later, perhaps, they could set up a manufacturing plant over there.

He took her by the shoulders.

'Now tell me, my little tycoon, where do we get the money to do this? I'm up to my neck in debt now – thanks to Wellington! If the Americans were to come through with a visa tomorrow, I couldn't go – I don't have any money.'

'I'm buying half the business,' she said.

'*You're what!*'

He pulled away from her.

'Where does Suzie Robinson get the money to buy half my business?'

'My father.'

A film formed over Larry's eyes. She'd worked all this out without a word to him. How soon before she gobbled up the other half? He called the dog Kuri. 'Fleabag, let's get to hell out of here before I go mad too,' he said.

T HE BULL REMAINED HEADLESS. Constable Weatherspoon asked questions, but when John Arrf refused to register a complaint, he let the matter drop. Privately, he dug away at it. Half the town knew about it and was amused. Gives him something to do, they said. One morning, he came into the old bakery.

'I'd like to take a look at your saws,' he said.

Larry brought out a hacksaw and a carpenter's handsaw.

'I've got a jeweller's saw too, somewhere,' he said, 'but I don't think they'd have used that to cut the head off.'

'No, I suppose not. But tell me, who are the "they" you're referring to? Those friends of yours?'

'Whoever it was who did it.'

'And of course you have no idea who "they" may be, eh? It's strange how nothing much happens around here until those friends of yours come to town.'

A twist Larry hadn't anticipated.

'I can assure you, they had nothing to do with it.'

'It didn't take them long to get out of town this time, I notice.'

'They're staying in Orewa. They came up for the party.'

'Ah, another party. There always seems to be a party. All right, thank you.'

Larry saw him pass the side window. A moment later he was back.

'That your ladder around the side?'

'Yes. I use it to fix the roof when it leaks, which is about every time it rains.'

'I see.' He left.

'Bloody drongo!' Suzie said.

'He's just curious.'

'He's *just curious*,' she mimicked, using a singsong voice. 'Oh la-de-da!'

Larry laughed. 'No sense in antagonising him,' he said.

'Oh la-de-da!' Two days later Larry drove to Auckland specifically to cancel his immigration visa application. He was ushered into the under secretary's office – why?

'Ah, Mr La Salle. We've been trying to phone you. Your secretary said that you were in Auckland today. Congratulations. You've been granted a visa under the preference quota system.' He proffered a hand.

Larry gaped in shock. His knees began little gyrations. 'But I came to tell you…' He swallowed. 'Thank you.'

'As soon as I receive the complete paperwork from Los Angeles, I'll have you come back in. You'll be needing a medical and there'll be a few formalities to complete before we can issue the visa. But three months and you should be on your way. Again, my congratulations.'

Larry stumbled down the stairs. He knew he should feel exhilarated but, strangely, he didn't. Suddenly he saw a host of problems he should have foreseen long ago. First, could Suzie run the business without him? Second, even with her buying into the business, because of the Australian deal she was so set on, there'd be no extra money; he'd be entering America penniless, with only his meagre writings to support him. How to manage without money in a land where nobody knew him? He climbed into the van. And what to tell Moira? That she'd have to support herself until he was established? Yi, yi.

'And you, what do I do with you, you stupid fleabag?' he called over his shoulder to the dog Kuri. The dog Kuri responded by squeezing between the seats and licking his master's cheek. Larry roughly pushed him away.

'It'll be my pleasure to leave you behind,' he said.

Then slowly, as he analysed the plus factors, his spirits rose. He'd come to Warkworth with nothing, yet he'd learned how to run a business; he'd improved his education so that he could design communication equipment on a par with anything available overseas; his most recent articles on single sideband suppressed carrier radio communication systems had been translated into half-a-dozen languages around the world and printed in prominent magazines, so he wasn't unknown, nor without experience. He should not find it hard to obtain a job in America. He burst into song.

> The Yankees down in Trinidad
> Say that they are very glad…

The dog Kuri lifted his head and howled. 'Who the hell asked you to sing?' Larry scolded.

> The young girls there all treat them nice
> And make Trinidad like paradise…

THE BUTCHER PUMPED HIS hand.

'I come to vish you cholly good luck in Yankeeland. By chorge, if I vas younger I go with you. You come over to the shop, I give you some lamb chops – you have a good meal before you go, eh?'

Larry found an excuse to go behind the ovens so that Suzie wouldn't see his tears. Going wasn't easy.

Constable Weatherspoon came to the door, to also wish him luck, Larry thought, but he asked to borrow the ladder. He offered his congratulations when he brought the ladder back, after reporting that he had matched the scratch marks on the butcher shop's veranda with the ladder.

'La-de-da,' Suzie said from the bench.

'Quite a coincidence,' Larry said.

The constable shook his hand. 'The Yanks are a lawless lot, lad. You should fit right in. But good luck anyhow.'

His mother called on the telephone. She blamed the war.

'You're not the same boy,' she said. His father wished him good luck. His mother came back on the line, crying now, asking him did he have to go. 'Don't forget us, son,' she sobbed, breaking up. His father took the receiver from her, 'Son…' but his heart was too full to speak the words.

Two days before the ship was to sail, Suzie said, 'Let's go to Leigh.' They took the Velocette. Larry put the dog Kuri in the apple box.

'I'll miss the miserable fleabag,' he said, 'and you, too, Poker.'

'So now he equates me with his dog,' she said.

She climbed on to the pillion seat, her arms tight around him. 'Like the old days,' she said into his ear.

He reached back, ran his hand up her leg, the first time he'd touched her in months.

'Bold as silver when he's leaving.'

'It's brass.'

'What's brass?'

He rode the bike under the pohutukawas. The dog Kuri quickly established area ownership.

'Full circle, Poker. I found you here; here's where I dump you. You bloody old…' He choked. They held each other. The dog climbed for his share.

'I'll look after him,' Suzie said.

'I know you will.'

'And I'll put a pansy in your mug.'

'I thought that the mug planting was for the dead.'

'I'll replant it in the garden if you come back.'

They sat on the grass.

'Poker, there's several things I have to tell you. First, I've left a paper with John. If I'm not back in two years, my half of the business is yours. On the house.'

'What are you talking about? You'll manage the American branch. I've already talked to John about it. And he says that it's time we formed ourselves into a limited company and started issuing shares…'

'Poker… please! Let me at least get to America first, eh? But I want you to know what I've done. And the other thing – it's about Moira and me…'

'Do they have bellbirds in America?'

'Poker, I don't know. I can't imagine them being in Los Angeles. It's a huge city, a dozen times the size of Auckland at least. Now…'

'Sounds like a bloody madhouse to me.'

'Poker, I have to tell you this before I leave, I…'

'Yak! yak! yak! When are you going to open one of those beers?'

Larry opened the beer, held his thumb over the top of the bottle and shook. Then he directed the contents at Suzie who soon grabbed a bottle and retaliated. So then they had to swim to clean off, and the subject of Moira didn't get brought up again, for which, in his heart, Larry was thankful. His deceit had been bothering him, and having to confess it even more so. He had tried. Suzie must have her reasons for not wanting to hear about it.

This last morning, Larry was up before Suzie. He drove out to Hepburn Creek Road and waited for the sun to come up. As it did, and painted a golden path up the river, he imagined it stretching all the way from America – not a one-way path, but two-way. When New Zealand caught up with the world electronically, he would come back, he told himself, for this was his country, this was his home. Then he cried. He cried with happiness. He cried with sorrow. And when he was cried out, he spoke to Moira.

'I'm coming, sweetheart.'

Back at the bakery, he rang his parents. His mother, having little conception of how far away America was, said, 'Well, don't leave it so long this time before you come to see us.' His father knew. His voice shook. But he said, 'Remember, son, there's no shame in returning if it doesn't work out. The shame's in not trying. God go with you.'

When he phoned his sister, Clarice, she was busy getting her children off to school. He could hear them squabbling in the background.

She said, 'At this moment I wouldn't mind dumping the whole blooming lot here and coming with you – Jimmy! Stop throwing food around! Yes, well don't forget to write. Ta ta, then.'

The friends met up at the Auckland Tourist Hotel: Grunter and Speed had come by train from Wellington; Rangi and Ngaire with John Arrf and his new wife; Mac, who had been staying with Lady Loomis again, with Larry and Suzie.

The Arrfs ordered wine. Mac ordered Black and White, neat. 'Neat!' the waiter queried.

'You hard o' hearing, laddie?'

Suzie told the waiter, '*Poulet* with *pomme de terre*. And none of that rotten cheese on it.' Grunter said, 'What's that you're ordering?'

'*Poulet* and *pomme de terre*. I don't like anything too fancy.'

'Gimme the same,' Speed said.

There were so many people on the wharf it was difficult to stay together. Those passengers already aboard tossed streamers. Their ends were quickly taken up by those on the pier. A Maori choir sang 'Hoki Mai Ki Au' – 'Return To Me'. Larry held Suzie. Suzie's eyes echoed the song's message. Grunter sternwheeled his way in.

'Haere ra, you bloody pakeha. You come back, eh?'

Then it was Speed, and Rangi, and Mac. And Ngaire and John, and John's new wife. Even the butcher and Joe the baker had driven down.

The ship's horn blasted a sad 'whoo-oo' and the loudspeaker system announced that all passengers should be aboard.

Larry held Suzie again. She gave him a letter. Through tears, she said, 'Open it when you can no longer see us.' She kissed him, turned to Ngaire and held her in a way that meant she couldn't see him leave.

'Good-bye. Good-bye. Kia ora. Good luck.'

The huge liner inched away from the wharf.

> Po Atarau,
> E moea iho nei...
> Now is the hour,
> For us to say good-bye...

They were gone. The ship gave a final, deep-throated 'whoo-oo, whoo-oo' and turned to course. Larry thought, how different this departure from when his ship had sneaked out of harbour in the dead of night, not a light showing, when he'd gone to war. Was it a century ago?

He found his cabin, a two-berth. The other passenger's luggage was stacked neatly on the lower bunk. Larry unpacked some of his clothing into one of the dresser drawers then climbed to the upper bunk to read Suzie's letter.

Larry. I have known from the first day Moira came to Warkworth that you two were made for each other, probably before you discovered it yourself. Go to her. You've left me a business. John says I'm a natural. And don't forget about the American division. I will never forget you. Kia ora. Suzie

She had left a light lipstick imprint. Inadvertently, he smeared it with a tear.